THE ARGYLE PATTERN
FOR MURDER

For weeks the newspapers carried the shocking details of the Argyle murder case, of Jack Argyle's trial and conviction for the brutal slaying of his mother, and finally of Jack's death.

Only two people knew that justice had not been done. One was the stranger who could have proved Jack's alibi—and the other was the real murderer.

Then suddenly the missing witness returned to clear Jack's name. And the killer—an "innocent" member of the Argyle house-hold—moved to strike once again.

Books by Agatha Christie

Published by POCKET BOOKS

Agatha Christie

Ordeal by Innocence

PUBLISHED BY POCKET BOOKS NEW YORK

**POCKET BOOKS, a Simon & Schuster division of
GULF & WESTERN CORPORATION**
1230 Avenue of the Americas, New York, N.Y. 10020

Copyright © 1958 by Agatha Christie Limited

Published by arrangement with Dodd, Mead & Company

ISBN: 0-671-82613-1

First Pocket Books printing February, 1960

19 18 17 16 15 14 13 12 11 10

Trademarks registered in the United States and other countries.

Printed in the U.S.A.

To BILLY COLLINS

with affection and gratitude

CAST OF CHARACTERS

Ordeal by Innocence

If I justify myself, mine own mouth shall condemn me.

I am afraid of all my sorrows. I know that Thou wilt not hold me innocent.

JOB

CHAPTER 1 . . .

IT WAS DUSK when he came to the ferry.

He could have been there much earlier. The truth was, he had put it off as long as he could.

First his luncheon with friends in Redquay; the light desultory conversation, the interchange of gossip about mutual friends—all that had meant only that he was inwardly shrinking from what he had to do. His friends had invited him to stay on for tea and he had accepted. But at last the time had come when he knew that he could put things off no longer.

The car he had hired was waiting. He said good-bye and left to drive the seven miles along the crowded coast road and then inland down the wooded lane that ended at the little stone quay on the river.

There was a large bell there which his driver rang vigorously to summon the ferry from the far side.

"Youn won't be wanting me to wait, sir?"

"No," said Arthur Calgary. "I've ordered a car to meet me over there in an hour's time—to take me to Drymouth."

The man received his fare and tip. He said, peering across the river in the gloom:

"Ferry's coming now, sir."

With a soft-spoken good night he reversed the car and drove away up the hill. Arthur Calgary was left alone waiting on the quayside. Alone with his thoughts and his apprehension of what was in front of him. How wild the scenery was here, he thought. One could fancy oneself on a Scottish loch, far from anywhere. And yet, only a few miles away, were the hotels, the shops, the cocktail bars and the crowds of Redquay. He reflected, not for the first time, on the extraordinary contrasts of the English landscape.

He heard the soft plash of the oars as the ferry boat drew in to the side of the little quay. Arthur Calgary walked down the sloping ramp and got into the boat as the ferryman steadied it with a boathook. He was an old man and gave

Calgary the fanciful impression that he and his boat belonged together, were one and indivisible.

A little cold wind came rustling up from the sea as they pushed off.

" 'Tis chilly this evening," said the ferryman.

Calgary replied suitably. He further agreed that it was colder than yesterday.

He was conscious, or thought he was conscious, of a veiled curiosity in the ferryman's eyes. Here was a stranger. And a stranger after the close of the tourist season proper. Moreover, this stranger was crossing at an unusual hour—too late for tea at the café by the pier. He had no luggage so he could not be coming to stay. (Why, Calgary wondered, *had* he come so late in the day? Was it really because, subconsciously, he had been putting this moment off? Leaving as late as possible, the thing that had to be done?) Crossing the Rubicon—the river . . . the river . . . his mind went back to that other river—the Thames.

He had stared at it unseeingly (was it only yesterday?) then turned to look again at the man facing him across the table. Those thoughtful eyes with something in them that he had not quite been able to understand. A reserve, something that was being thought but not expressed. . . .

"I suppose," he thought, "they learn never to show what they are thinking."

The whole thing was pretty frightful when one came right down to it. He must do what had to be done—and after that —*forget!*

He frowned as he remembered the conversation yesterday. That pleasant, quiet, noncommittal voice, saying:

"You're quite determined on your course of action, Dr. Calgary?"

He had answered, hotly:

"What else *can* I do? Surely you see that? You must agree? It's a thing I can't possibly shirk."

But he hadn't understood the look in those withdrawn grey eyes, and had been faintly perplexed by the answer.

"One has to look all around a subject—consider it from all aspects."

"Surely there can be only one aspect from the point of view of justice?"

He had spoken hotly, thinking for a moment that this was an ignoble suggestion of "hushing up" the matter.

2

"In a way, yes. But there's more to it than that, you know. More than—shall we say—justice?"

"I don't agree. There's the family to consider."

And the other had said quickly: "Quite—oh, yes—quite. I *was* thinking of them."

Which seemed to Calgary nonsense! Because if one were thinking of *them*—

But immediately the other man had said, his pleasant voice unchanged:

"It's entirely up to you, Dr. Calgary. You must, of course, do exactly as you feel you have to do."

The boat grounded on the beach. He had crossed the Rubicon.

The ferryman's soft West Country voice said:

"That will be fourpence, sir, or do you want a return?"

"No," Calgary said. "There will be no return." (How fateful the words sounded!)

He paid. Then he asked:

"Do you know a house called Sunny Point?"

Immediately the curiosity ceased to be veiled. The interest in the old man's eyes leaped up avidly.

"Why, surely. 'Tis there, up along to your right—you can just see it through them trees. You go up the hill and along the road to the right, and then take the new road through the building estate. 'Tis the last house—at the very end."

"Thank you."

"You did say Sunny Point, sir? Where Mrs. Argyle—"

"Yes, yes—" Calgary cut him short. He didn't want to discuss the matter. "Sunny Point."

A slow and rather peculiar smile twisted the ferryman's lips. He looked suddenly like an ancient sly faun.

"It was *her* called the house that—in the war. It were a new house, of course, only just been built—hadn't got a name. But the ground 'tis built on—that wooded spit—Viper's Point, that is! But Viper's Point wouldn't do for *her*—not for the name of her house. Called it Sunny Point, she did. But Viper's Point's what *we* allus call it."

Calgary thanked him brusquely, said good evening, and started up the hill. Everyone seemed to be inside their houses, but he had the fancy that unseen eyes were peering through the windows of the cottages; all watching him with the knowledge of where he was going. Saying to each other, "He's going to Viper's Point . . ."

3

Viper's Point. What a horribly apposite name that must have seemed. . . .

For sharper than a serpent's tooth . . .

He checked his thoughts brusquely. He must pull himself together and make up his mind exactly what he was going to say. . . .

ii.

Calgary came to the end of the nice new road with the nice new houses on either side of it, each with its eighth of an acre of garden; rock plants, chrysanthemums, roses, salvias, geraniums, each owner displaying his or her individual garden taste.

At the end of the road was a gate with SUNNY POINT in Gothic letters on it. He opened the gate, passed through, and went along a short drive. The house was there ahead of him, a well-built, characterless modern house, gabled and porched. It might have stood on any good-class suburban site, or a new development anywhere. It was unworthy, in Calgary's opinion, of its view. For the view was magnificent. The river here curved sharply round the point almost turning back on itself. Wooded hills rose opposite; upstream to the left was a further bend of the river with meadows and orchards in the distance.

Calgary looked for a moment up and down the river. One should have built a castle here, he thought, an impossible, ridiculous fairy tale, castle! The sort of castle that might be made of gingerbread or of frosted sugar. Instead there was good taste, restraint, moderation, plenty of money and absolutely no imagination.

For that, naturally, one did not blame the Argyles. They had only bought the house, not built it. Still, they, or one of them (Mrs. Argyle?) had chosen it. . . .

He said to himself: *"You can't put it off any longer . . ."* and pressed the electric bell beside the door.

He stood there, waiting. After a decent interval he pressed the bell again.

He heard no footsteps inside but, without warning, the door swung suddenly open.

He moved back a step, startled. To his already over-stimulated imagination, it seemed as though Tragedy herself stood there barring his way. It was a young face; indeed

4

it was in the poignancy of its youth that tragedy had its very essence. The Tragic Mask, he thought, should always be a mask of youth. . . . Helpless, foreordained, with a doom approaching . . . from the future. . . .

Rallying himself, he thought, rationalising: "Irish type." The deep blue of the eyes, the dark shadow round them, the up-springing black hair, the mournful beauty of the bones of the skull and cheekbones—

The girl stood there, young, watchful and hostile.

She said:

"Yes? What do you want?"

He replied conventionally.

"Is Mr. Argyle in?"

"Yes. But he doesn't see people. I mean, people he doesn't know. He doesn't know you, does he?"

"No. He doesn't know me, but—"

She began to close the door.

"Then you'd better write . . ."

"I'm sorry, but I particularly want to see him. Are you—Miss Argyle?"

She admitted it grudgingly.

"I'm Hester Argyle, yes. But my father doesn't see people —not without an appointment. You'd better write."

"I've come a long way . . ." She was unmoved.

"They all say that. But I thought this kind of thing had stopped at last." She went on accusingly, "You're a reporter, I suppose?"

"No, no, nothing of the sort."

She eyed him suspiciously as though she did not believe him.

"Well, what do you want then?"

Behind her, some way back in the hall, he saw another face. A flat homely face. Describing it, he would have called it a face like a pancake, the face of a middle-aged woman, with frizzy yellowish grey hair plastered on top of her head. She seemed to hover, waiting, like a watchful dragon.

"It concerns your brother, Miss Argyle."

Hester Argyle drew in her breath sharply. She said, without belief, "Michael?"

"No, your brother Jack."

She burst out: "I knew it! I *knew* you'd come about Jacko! Why can't you leave us in peace? It's all over and finished with. Why go on about it?"

"You can never really say that anything is finished."

"But this *is* finished! Jacko is dead. Why can't you let him be? All that's *over*. If you're not a journalist, I suppose you're a doctor, or a psychologist, or something. Please go away. My father can't be disturbed. He's busy."

She began to close the door. In a hurry, Calgary did what he ought to have done at first, pulled out the letter from his pocket and thrust it towards her.

"I have a letter here—from Mr. Marshall."

She was taken aback. Her fingers closed doubtfully on the envelope. She said uncertainly:

"From Mr. Marshall—in London?"

She was joined now suddenly by the middle-aged woman who had been lurking in the recesses of the hall. She peered at Calgary suspiciously and he was reminded of foreign convents. Of course, this should have been a nun's face! It demanded the crisp white. coif or whatever you called it, framed tightly round the face, and the black habit and veil. It was the face, not of a contemplative, but of the lay sister who peers at you suspiciously through the little opening in the thick door, before grudgingly admitting you and taking you to the visiting parlour, or to Reverend Mother.

She said: "You come from Mr. Marshall?"

She made it almost an accusation.

Hester was staring down at the envelope in her hand. Then, without a word, she turned and ran up the stairs.

Calgary remained on the doorstep, sustaining the accusing and suspicious glance of the dragon-cum-lay-sister.

He cast about for something to say, but he could not think of anything. Prudently, therefore, he remained silent.

Presently Hester's voice, cool and aloof, floated down to them.

"Father says he's to come up."

Somewhat unwillingly, his watchdog moved aside. Her expression of suspicion did not alter. He passed her, laid his hat on a chair, and mounted the stairs to where Hester stood waiting for him.

The inside of the house struck him as vaguely hygienic. It could almost, he thought, have been an expensive nursing home.

Hester led him along a passage and down three steps. Then she threw open a door and gestured to him to pass through it. She came in behind him, closing the door after her.

The room was a library, and Calgary raised his head with a sense of pleasure. The atmosphere of this room was quite different from the rest of the house. This was a room where a man *lived*, where he both worked and took his ease. The walls were lined with books, the chairs were large, rather shabby, but easeful. There was a pleasant disorder of papers on the desk, of books lying about on tables. He had a momentary glimpse of a young woman who was leaving the room by a door at the far end, rather an attractive young woman. Then his attention was taken by the man who rose and came to greet him, the open letter in his hand.

Calgary's first impression of Leo Argyle was that he was so attenuated, so transparent, as hardly to be there at all. A wraith of a man! His voice when he spoke was pleasant, though lacking in resonance.

"Dr. Calgary?" he said. "Do sit down."

Calgary sat. He accepted a cigarette. His host sat down opposite him. All was done without hurry, as though in a world where time meant very little. There was a faint gentle smile on Leo Argyle's face as he spoke, tapping the letter gently with a bloodless finger as he did so.

"Mr. Marshall writes that you have an important communication to make to us, though he doesn't specify its nature." His smile deepened as he added: "Lawyers are always so careful not to commit themselves, aren't they?"

It occurred to Calgary with a faint shock of surprise, that this man confronting him was a happy man. Not buoyantly or zestfully happy, as is the normal way of happiness—but happy in some shadowy but satisfactory retreat of his own. This was a man on whom the outer world did not impinge and who was contented that this should be so. He did not know why he should be surprised by this—but he was.

Calgary said:

"It is very kind of you to see me." The words were a mere mechanical introduction. "I thought it better to come in person than to write." He paused—then said in a sudden rush of agitation, "It is difficult—very difficult . . ."

"Do take your time."

Leo Argyle was still polite and remote.

He leaned forward; in his gentle way he was obviously trying to help.

7

"Since you bring this letter from Marshall, I presume that your visit has to do with my unfortunate son Jacko—Jack, I mean—Jacko was our own name for him."

All Calgary's carefully prepared words and phrases had deserted him. He sat here, faced with the appalling reality of what he had to tell. He stammered again.

"It's so terribly difficult . . ."

There was a moment's silence, and then Leo said cautiously:

"If it helps you—we're quite aware that Jacko was—hardly a normal personality. Nothing that you have to tell us will be likely to surprise us. Terrible as the tragedy was, I have been fully convinced all along that Jack was not really responsible for his actions."

"Of course he wasn't." It was Hester, and Calgary started at the sound of her voice. He had momentarily forgotten about her. She had sat down on the arm of a chair just behind his left shoulder. As he turned his head, she leaned forward eagerly towards him.

"Jacko was always awful," she said confidentially. "He was just the same as a little boy—when he lost his temper, I mean. Just caught up anything he could find and—and went for you . . ."

"Hester—Hester—my dear." Argyle's voice was distressed.

Startled, the girl's hand flew to her lips. She flushed and spoke with the sudden awkwardness of youth.

"I'm sorry," she said. "I didn't mean—I forgot—I—I oughtn't to have said a thing like that—not now that he's—I mean, now that it's all over and . . . and . . ."

"Over and done with," said Argyle. "All of this is in the past. I try—we all try—to feel that the boy must be regarded as an invalid. One of Nature's misfits. That, I think, expresses it best." He looked at Calgary. "You agree?"

"No," said Calgary.

There was a moment's silence. The sharp negative had taken both his listeners aback. It had come out with almost explosive force. Trying to mitigate its effect, he said awkwardly:

"I—I'm sorry. You see, you don't understand yet."

"Oh!" Argyle seemed to consider. Then he turned his head towards his daughter. "Hester, I think perhaps you'd better leave us—"

"I'm not going away! I've got to hear—to know what it's all about."

"It may be unpleasant—"

Hester cried out impatiently:

"What does it matter what other awful things Jacko may have done? That's all *over*."

Calgary spoke quickly.

"Please believe me—there is no question of anything that your brother has done—quite the opposite."

"I don't see—"

The door at the far end of the room opened and the young woman whom Calgary had just glimpsed earlier came back into the room. She wore an outdoor coat now, and carried a small attaché-case.

She spoke to Argyle.

"I'm going now. Is there anything else—?"

There was a momentary hesitation on Argyle's part (he would always hesitate. Calgary thought) and then he laid a hand on her arm and drew her forward.

"Sit down, Gwenda," he said. "This is—er—Dr. Calgary. This is Miss Vaughan, who is—who is—" Again he paused as though in doubt. "Who has been my secretary for some years now." He added: "Dr. Calgary has come to tell us something—or—ask us something—about Jacko—"

"To tell you something," Calgary interrupted. "And although you don't realise it, every moment you are making it more difficult for me."

They all looked at him in some surprise, but in Gwenda Vaughan's eyes he saw a flicker of something that looked like comprehension. It was as though he and she were momentarily in alliance, as though she had said: "Yes—I know how difficult the Argyles can be."

She *was* an attractive young woman, he thought, though not so very young—perhaps thirty-seven or eight. A well-rounded figure, dark hair and eyes, a general air of vitality and good health. She gave the impression of being both competent and intelligent.

Argyle said with a frosty touch in his manner: "I am not at all aware of making things difficult for you, Dr. Calgary. Such was certainly not my intention. If you will come to the point—"

"Yes, I know. Forgive me for saying what I did. But it is the persistence with which you—and your daughter—are continually underlining that things are *over—done with—finished*. They are *not* over. Who is it who said: '*Nothing is ever settled until—*'"

"'*Until it is settled right,*'" Miss Vaughan finished for him. "Kipling."

She nodded at him encouragingly. He felt grateful to her.

"But I'll come to the point." Calgary went on. "When you've heard what I have to say, you'll understand my—my reluctance. More my distress. To begin with, I must mention a few things about myself. I am a geophysicist, and have recently formed part of an Antarctic expedition. I only returned to England a few weeks ago."

"The Hayes Bentley Expedition?" asked Gwenda.

He turned towards her gratefully.

"Yes. It was the Hayes Bentley Expedition. I tell you this to explain my background, and also to explain that I have been out of touch for about two years with—with current events."

She went on helping him:

"You mean—with such things as murder trials?"

"Yes, Miss Vaughan, that is exactly what I mean."

He turned to Argyle.

"Please forgive me if this is painful, but I must just check over with you certain times and dates. On November 9th, the year before last, at about six o'clock in the evening, your son, Jack Argyle (Jacko to you), called here and had an interview with his mother, Mrs. Argyle."

"My wife, yes."

"He told her that he was in trouble and demanded money. This had happened before—"

"Many times," said Leo with a sigh.

"Mrs. Argyle refused. He became abusive, threatening. Finally he flung away and left, shouting out that he was coming back and that she had 'jolly well *got* to stump up.' He said. 'You don't want me to go to prison, do you?' and she replied, 'I am beginning to believe that it may be the best thing for you.'"

Leo Argyle moved uneasily.

"My wife and I had talked it over together. We were —very unhappy about the boy. Again and again we had come to his rescue, tried to give him a fresh start. It had seemed to us that perhaps the shock of a prison sentence— the training—" His voice died away. "But please go on."

10

Calgary went on:

"Later that evening, your wife was killed. Attacked with a poker and struck down. Your son's fingerprints were on the poker, and a large sum of money was gone from the bureau drawer where your wife had placed it earlier. The police picked up your son in Drymouth. The money was found on him, most of it was in five-pound notes, one of which had a name and address written on it which enabled it to be identified by the bank as one that had been paid out to Mrs. Argyle that morning. He was charged and stood his trial." Calgary paused. "The verdict was wilful murder."

It was out—the fateful word. *Murder* . . . Not an echoing word; a stifled word, a word that got absorbed into the hangings, the books, the pile carpet. . . . The word could be stifled—but not the act. . . .

"I have been given to understand by Mr. Marshall, the solicitor for the defence, that your son protested his innocence when arrested, in a cheery, not to say cocksure manner. He insisted that he had a perfect alibi for the time of the murder which was placed by the police at between seven and seven-thirty. At that time, Jack Argyle said, he was hitchhiking into Drymouth, having been picked up by a car on the main road from Redmyn to Drymouth about a mile from here just before seven. He didn't know the make of the car (it was dark by then) but it was a black or dark blue saloon driven by a middle-aged man. Every effort was made to trace this car and the man who drove it, but no confirmation of his statement could be obtained, and the lawyers themselves were quite convinced that it was a story hastily fabricated by the boy and not very cleverly fabricated at that. . . .

"At the trial the main line of defence was the evidence of psychologists who sought to prove that Jack Argyle had always been mentally unstable. The judge was somewhat scathing in his comments on this evidence and summed up dead against the prisoner. Jack Argyle was sentenced to imprisonment for life. He died of pneumonia in prison six months after he began to serve his sentence."

Calgary stopped. Three pairs of eyes were fastened on him. Interest and close attention in Gwenda Vaughan's, suspicion still in Hester's. Leo Argyle's seemed blank.

Calgary said, "You will confirm that I have stated the facts correctly?"

"You are perfectly correct," said Leo, "though I do not yet see why it has been necessary to go over painful facts which we are all trying to forget."

"Forgive me. I had to do so. You do not, I gather dissent from the verdict?"

"I admit that the *facts* were as stated—that is, if you do not go behind the facts, it was, crudely, murder. But if you *do* go behind the facts, there is much to be said in mitigation. The boy was mentally unstable, though unfortunately not in the legal sense of the term. The McNaughton rules are narrow and unsatisfactory. I assure you, Dr. Calgary, that Rachel herself—my late wife, I mean—would have been the first to forgive and excuse that unfortunate boy for his rash act. She was a most advanced and humane thinker and had a profound knowledge of psychological factors. *She* would not have condemned."

"She knew just how awful Jacko could be," said Hester. "He always was—he just didn't seem able to help it."

"So you all," said Calgary slowly, "had no doubts? No doubts of his guilt, I mean."

Hester stared.

"How could we? Of course he was guilty."

"Not really *guilty*," Leo dissented. "I don't like that word."

"It isn't a true word, either." Calgary took a deep breath. "Jack Argyle was—innocent!"

CHAPTER 2

IT SHOULD have been a sensational announcement. Instead, it fell flat. Calgary had expected bewilderment, incredulous gladness struggling with incomprehension, eager questions. . . . There was none of that. There seemed only wariness and suspicion. Gwenda Vaughan was frowning. Hester stared at him with dilated eyes. Well, perhaps it was natural—such an announcement was hard to take in all at once.

Leo Argyle said hesitantly:

"You mean, Dr. Calgary, that you agree with my attitude? You don't feel he was responsible for his actions?"

"I mean he *didn't do it!* Can't you take it in, man? *He didn't do it.* He *couldn't* have done it. But for the most extraordinary and unfortunate combination of circumstances he could have *proved* that he was innocent. *I* could have proved that he was innocent."

"You?"

"I was the man in the car."

He said it so simply that for the moment they did not take it in. Before they could recover themselves, there was an interruption. The door opened and the woman with the homely face marched in. She spoke directly and to the point.

"I hear as I am passing the door outside. This man is saying that Jacko did not kill Mrs. Argyle. Why does he say this? How does he know?"

Her face, which had been militant and fierce, suddenly seemed to pucker.

"I must hear too," she said piteously. "I cannot stay outside and not know."

"Of course not, Kirsty. You're one of the family." Leo Argyle introduced her. "Miss Lindstrom, Dr. Calgary. Dr. Calgary is saying the most incredible things."

Calgary was puzzled by the Scottish name of Kirsty. Her English was excellent but a faint foreign intonation remained.

She spoke accusingly to him.

13

"You should not come here and say things like that—upsetting people. They have accepted tribulation. Now you upset them by what you tell. What happened was the will of God."

He was repelled by the glib complacence of her statement. Possibly, he thought, she was one of those ghoulish people who positively welcome disaster. Well, she was going to be deprived of all that.

He spoke in a quick, dry voice.

"At five minutes to seven on that evening, I picked up a young man on the main Redmyn to Drymouth road who was thumbing for a lift. I drove him into Drymouth. We talked. He was, I thought, an engaging and likeable young man."

"Jacko had great charm," said Gwenda. "Everyone found him attractive. It was his temper let him down. And he was crooked, of course," she added thoughtfully. "But people didn't find that out for some time."

Miss Lindstrom turned on her.

"You should not speak so when he is dead."

Leo Argyle said with a faint asperity:

"Please go on, Dr. Calgary. Why didn't you come forward at the time?"

"Yes." Hester's voice sounded breathless. "Why did you skulk away from it all? There were appeals in the paper—advertisements. How could you be so selfish, so wicked—"

"Hester—Hester—" her father checked her. "Dr. Calgary is still telling us his story."

Calgary addressed the girl direct.

"I know only too well how you feel. I know what I feel myself—what I shall always feel. . . ." He pulled himself together and went on:

"To continue with my story: There was a lot of traffic on the roads that evening. It was well after half past seven when I dropped the young man, whose name I did not know, in the middle of Drymouth. That, I understand, clears him completely, since the police are quite definite that the crime was committed between seven and half past."

"Yes," said Hester. "But you—"

"Please be patient. To make you understand, I must go back a little. I had been staying in Drymouth for a couple of days in a friend's flat. This friend, a naval man, was at sea. He had also lent me his car which he kept in a private lock-up. On this particular day, November the 9th, I was due to

14

return to London. I decided to go up by the evening train and to spend the afternoon seeing an old nurse of whom our family were very fond and who lived in a little cottage at Polgarth about forty miles west of Drymouth. I carried out my programme. Though very old and inclined to wander in her mind, she recognised me and was very pleased to see me, and quite excited because she had read in the papers about my 'going to the Pole,' as she put it. I stayed only a short time, so as not to tire her, and on leaving decided not to return direct to Drymouth along the coast road as I had come, but instead to go north to Redmyn and see old Canon Peasmarsh, who has some very rare books in his library, including an early treatise on navigation from which I was anxious to copy a passage. The old gentleman refuses to have the telephone which he regards as a device of the devil, and on a par with radio, television, cinema organs and jet planes, so I had to take a chance of finding him at home. I was unlucky. His house was shuttered and he was evidently away. I spent a little time in the Cathedral, and then started back to Drymouth by the main road, thus completing the third side of a triangle. I had left myself comfortable time to pick up my bag from the flat, return the car to its lock-up, and catch my train.

"On the way, as I have told you, I picked up an unknown hitchhiker, and after dropping him in the town, I carried out my own programme. After arrival at the station, I still had time in hand, and I went outside the station into the main street to get some cigarettes. As I crossed the road a lorry came round a corner at high speed and knocked me down.

"According to the accounts of passers-by, I got up, apparently uninjured and behaving quite normally. I said I was quite all right and that I had a train to catch and hurried back to the station. When the train arrived at Paddington I was unconscious and taken by ambulance to hospital, where I was found to be suffering from concussion—apparently this delayed effect is not uncommon.

"When I regained consciousness, some days later, I remembered nothing of the accident, or of coming to London. The last thing I could remember was starting out to visit my old nurse at Polgarth. After that, a complete blank. I was reassured by being told that such an occurrence is quite common. There seemed no reason to believe that the missing hours in my life were of any importance. Neither I myself, nor anyone else had the faintest idea that I had driven along the Redmyn-Drymouth road that evening.

"There was only a very narrow margin of time before I was due to leave England. I was kept in hospital, in absolute quiet, with no newspapers. On leaving I drove straight to the airport to fly to Australia and to join up with the Expedition. There was some doubt as to whether I was fit to go, but this I overruled. I was far too busy with my preparations and anxieties to take any interest in reports of murders, and in any case excitement died down after the arrest, and by the time the case came to trial and was fully reported, I was on my way to the Antarctic."

He paused They were listening to him with close attention.

"It was about a month ago, just after my return to England, that I made the discovery. I wanted some old newspapers for packing specimens. My landlady brought me up a pile of old papers out of her stokehold. Spreading one out on the table I saw the reproduced photograph of a young man whose face seemed very familar to me. I tried to remember where I had met him and who he was. I could not do so and yet, very strangely, I remembered holding a conversation with him—it had been about eels. He had been intrigued and fascinated by hearing the saga of an eel's life. But when? Where? I read the paragraph, read that this young man was Jack Argyle, accused of murder, read that he had told the police that he had been given a lift by a man in a black saloon car.

"And then, quite suddenly, that lost bit of my life came back. I had picked up this selfsame young man, and driven him into Drymouth, parting from him there, going back to the flat—crossing the street on foot to buy my cigarettes. I remembered just a glimpse of the lorry as it hit me—after that, nothing until hospital. I still had no memory of going to the station and taking the train to London. I read and re-read the paragraph. The trial was over a year ago, the case almost forgotten. 'A young fellow what did his mother in,' my landlady remembered vaguely. 'Don't know what happened—think they hanged him.' I read up the files of the newspapers for the appropriate dates, then I went to Marshall, Marshall & Marshall, who had been the lawyers for the defence. I learned that I was too late to free the unfortunate boy. He had died of pneumonia in prison. Though justice could no longer be done to him, justice *could* be done to his memory. I went with Mr. Marshall to the police. The case is being laid before the Public Prosecutor. Marshall has little doubt that he will refer it to the Home Secretary.

"You will, of course, receive a full report from him. He has only delayed it because I was anxious to be the one who first acquainted you with the truth. I felt that that was an ordeal it was my duty to go through. You understand, I am sure, that I shall always feel a deep load of guilt. If I had been more careful crossing the street——" He broke off. "I understand your feelings towards me can never be kindly —though I am, technically, blameless—you, all of you, *must* blame me."

Gwenda Vaughan said quickly, her voice warm and kindly:

"Of course we don't blame you. It's just—one of those things. Tragic—incredible—but there it is."

Hester said:

"Did they believe you?"

He looked at her in surprise.

"The police—did they believe you? Why shouldn't you be making it all up?"

He smiled a little in spite of himself.

"I'm a very reputable witness," he said gently. "I have no axe to grind, and they have gone into my story very closely; medical evidence, various corroborating details from Drymouth. Oh yes. Marshall was cautious, of course, like all lawyers. He didn't want to raise your hopes until he was pretty certain of success."

Leo Argyle stirred in his chair and spoke for the first time.

"What exactly do you mean by *success?*"

"I apologise," said Calgary quickly. "That is not a word that can rightly be used. Your son was accused of a crime he did not commit, was tried for it, condemned—and died in prison. Justice has come too late for him. But such justice as can be done, almost certainly will be done, and will be seen to be done. The Home Secretary will probably advise the Queen that a free pardon should be granted."

Hester laughed.

"A free pardon—for something he didn't do?"

"I know. The terminology always seems unrealistic. But I understand that the custom is for a question to be asked in the House, the reply to which will make it clear that Jack

Argyle did not commit the crime for which he was sentenced, and the newspapers will report that fact freely."

He stopped. Nobody spoke. It had been, he supposed, a great shock to them. But after all, a happy one.

He rose to his feet.

"I'm afraid," he said uncertainly, "that there is nothing more that I can say. . . . To repeat how sorry I am, how unhappy about it all, to ask your forgiveness—all that you must already know only too well. The tragedy that ended his life has darkened my own. But at least"—he spoke with pleading—"surely it means *something*—to know that he didn't do this awful thing—that his name—your name—will be cleared in the eyes of the world . . . ?"

If he hoped for a reply he did not get one.

Leo Argyle sat slumped in his chair. Gwenda's eyes were on Leo's face. Hester sat staring ahead of her, her eyes wide and tragic. Miss Lindstrom grunted something under her breath and shook her head.

Calgary stood helplessly by the door, looking back at them.

It was Gwenda Vaughan who took charge of the situation. She came up to him and laid a hand on his arm, saying in a low voice:

"You'd better go now, Dr. Calgary. It's been too much of a shock. They must have time to take it in."

He nodded and went out. On the landing Miss Lindstrom joined him.

"I will let you out," she said.

He was conscious, looking back before the door closed behind him, of Gwenda Vaughan slipping to her knees by Leo Argyle's chair. It surprised him a little.

Facing him, on the landing, Miss Lindstrom stood like a Guardsman and spoke harshly.

"You cannot bring him back to life. So why bring it all back into their minds? Till now, they were resigned. Now they will suffer. It is better, always, to leave well alone."

She spoke with displeasure.

"His memory must be cleared," said Arthur Calgary.

"Fine sentiments! They are all very well. But you do not really think of what it all means. Men, they never think." She stamped her foot. "I love them all. I came here, to help Mrs. Argyle, in 1940—when she started here a war nursery —for children whose homes had been bombed. Nothing was too good for those children. Everything was done for them. That is nearly eighteen years ago. And still, even after she is dead, I stay here—to look after them—to keep the house clean and comfortable, to see they get good food. I love them all—yes, I love them . . . and Jacko—he was no good! Oh yes, I loved him too. But—he was no good!"

She turned abruptly away. It seemed she had forgotten her offer to show him out. Calgary descended the stairs slowly. As he was fumbling with the front door which had a safety lock he did not understand, he heard light footsteps on the stairs. Hester came flying down them.

She unlatched the door and opened it. They stood looking at each other. He understood less than ever why she faced him with that tragic reproachful stare.

She said, only just breathing the words:

"Why did you come? Oh, why ever did you come?"

He looked at her helplessly.

"I don't understand you. Don't you want your brother's name cleared? Don't you want him to have justice?"

"Oh, justice!" She threw the word at him.

He repeated: "I don't understand . . ."

"Going on so about justice! What does it matter to Jacko now? He's dead. It's not Jacko who matters. It's *us!*"

"What do you mean?"

"It's not the guilty who matter. It's the innocent."

She caught his arm, digging her fingers into it.

"It's *we* who matter. Don't you see what you've done to us all?"

He stared at her.

Out of the darkness outside, a man's figure loomed up.

"Dr. Calgary?" he said. "Your taxi's here, sir. To drive you to Drymouth."

"Oh—er—thank you."

Calgary turned once more to Hester, but she had withdrawn into the house.

The front door banged.

CHAPTER 3 ...

HESTER WENT slowly up the stairs pushing back the dark hair from her high forehead. Kirsten Lindstrom met her at the top of the stairs.

"Has he gone?"

"Yes, he's gone."

"You have had a shock, Hester." Kirsten Lindstrom laid a gentle hand on her shoulder. "Come with me. I will give you a little brandy. All this, it has been too much."

"I don't think I want any brandy, Kirsty."

"Perhaps you do not want it, but it will be good for you."

Unresisting, the young girl allowed herself to be steered along the passage and into Kirsten Lindstrom's own small sitting room. She took the brandy that was offered her and sipped it slowly. Kirsten Lindstrom said in an exasperated voice:

"It has all been too sudden. There should have been warning. Why did not Mr. Marshall write first?"

"I suppose Dr. Calgary wouldn't let him. He wanted to come and tell us himself."

"Come and tell us himself, indeed! What does he think the news will do to us?"

"I suppose," said Hester, in an odd, toneless voice, "he thought we should be pleased."

"Pleased or not pleased, it was bound to be a shock. He should not have done it."

"But it was brave of him, in a way," said Hester. The colour came up in her face. "I mean, it can't have been an *easy* thing to do. To come and tell a family of people that a member of it who was condemned for murder and died in prison was really innocent. Yes, I think it was brave of him—but I wish he hadn't all the same," she added.

"That—we all wish that," said Miss Lindstrom briskly.

Hester looked at her with her interest suddenly aroused from her own preoccupation.

"So you feel that too, Kirsty? I thought perhaps it was only me."

"I am not a fool," said Miss Lindstrom sharply. "I can envisage certain possibilities that your Dr. Calgary does not seem to have thought about."

Hester rose. "I must go to Father," she said.

Kirsten Lindstrom agreed.

"Yes. He will have had time now to think what is best to be done."

As Hester went into the library Gwenda Vaughan was busy with the telephone. Her father beckoned to her and Hester went over and sat on the arm of his chair.

"We're trying to get through to Mary and to Micky," he said. "They ought to be told at once of this."

"Hallo," said Gwenda Vaughan. "Is that Mrs. Durrant? Mary? Gwenda Vaughan here. Your father wants to speak to you."

Leo went over and took up the receiver.

"Mary? How are you? How is Philip? . . . Good. Something rather extraordinary has happened . . . I thought you ought to be told of it at once. A Dr. Calgary has just been to see us. He brought a letter from Andrew Marshall with him. It's about Jacko. It seems—really a very extraordinary thing altogether—it seems that that story Jacko told at the trial, of having been given a lift into Drymouth in somebody's car, is perfectly true. This Dr. Calgary was the man who gave him the lift . . ." He broke off, as he listened to what his daughter was saying at the other end. "Yes, well, Mary, I won't go into all the details now as to why he didn't come forward at the time. He had an accident—concussion. The whole thing seems to be perfectly well authenticated. I rang up to say that I think we should all have a meeting here together as soon as possible. Perhaps we could get Marshall to come down and talk the matter over with us. We ought, I think, to have the best legal advice. Could you and Philip? . . . Yes . . . Yes, I know. But I really think, my dear, that it's *important*. . . . Yes . . . well ring me up later, if you like. I must try and get hold of Micky." He replaced the receiver.

Gwenda Vaughan came towards the telephone.

"Shall I try and get Micky now?"

Hester said:

"If this is going to take a little time, could I ring up first, please, Gwenda? I want to ring up Donald."

"Of course," said Leo. "You are going out with him this evening, aren't you?"

"I *was*," said Hester.

Her father gave her a sharp glance.

"Has this upset you very much, darling?"

"I don't know," said Hester. "I don't know quite what I feel."

Gwenda made way for her at the telephone and Hester dialled a number.

"Could I speak to Dr. Craig, please. Yes. Yes. Hester Argyle speaking."

There was a moment or two of delay and then she said:

"Is that you, Donald? . . . I rang up to say that I don't think I can come with you to the lecture tonight. . . . No, I'm not ill—it's not that, it's just—well, just that we've—we've had some rather queer news."

Again Dr. Craig spoke.

Hester turned her head towards her father. She laid her hand over the receiver and said to him:

"It isn't a secret, is it?"

"No," said Leo slowly. "No, it isn't exactly a secret but —well, I should just ask Donald to keep it to himself for the present, perhaps. You know how rumours get around, get magnified."

"Yes, I know." She spoke again into the receiver. "In a way I suppose it's what you'd call good news, Donald, but —it's rather upsetting. I'd rather not talk about it over the telephone. . . . No, no, *don't* come here. . . . Please—*not*. Not this evening. Tomorrow some time. It's about—Jacko. Yes—yes—my brother—it's just that we've found out that he didn't kill my mother after all. . . . But please don't say anything, Donald, or talk to *anyone*. I'll tell you all about it tomorrow. . . . No, Donald, *no*. . . . I just can't see *anyone* this evening—not even you. Please. And don't say anything." She put down the receiver, and motioned to Gwenda to take over.

Gwenda asked for a Drymouth number. Leo said gently:

"Why don't you go to the lecture with Donald, Hester? It will take your mind off things."

"I don't want to, Father. I couldn't."

Leo said:

"You spoke—you gave him the impression that it wasn't good news. But you know, Hester, that's not so. We were startled. But we're all very happy about it—very glad. . . . What else could we be?"

"That's what we're going to say, is it?" said Hester.

Leo said warningly:

"My dear child—"

"But it's not true, is it?" said Hester. "It's not good news. It's just terribly upsetting."

Gwenda said:

"Micky's on the line."

Again Leo came and took the receiver from her. He spoke to his son very much as he had spoken to his daughter. But his news was received rather differently from the way it had been received by Mary Durrant. Here there was no protest, surprise or disbelief. Instead there was quick acceptance.

"What the hell!" said Micky's voice. "After all this time? The missing witness! Well, well, Jacko's luck was out that night."

Leo spoke again. Micky listened.

"Yes," he said, "I agree with you. We'd better get together as quickly as possible, and get Marshall to advise us, too." He gave a sudden quick laugh, the laugh that Leo remembered so well from the small boy who had played in the garden outside the window. "What's the betting?" he said. *Which of us did it?*"

Leo dropped the receiver down and left the telephone abruptly.

"What did he say?" Gwenda said.

Leo told her.

"It seems to me a silly sort of joke to make," said Gwenda.

Leo shot a quick glance at her. "Perhaps," he said gently, "it wasn't altogether a joke."

ii.

Mary Durrant crossed the room and picked up some fallen petals from a vase of chrysanthemums. She put them carefully into the wastepaper basket. She was a tall, serene-looking young woman of twenty-seven who, although her face was unlined, yet looked older than her years, probably from a sedate maturity that seemed part of her make-up.

She had good looks, without a trace of glamour. Regular features, a good skin, eyes of a vivid blue, and fair hair combed off her face and arranged in a large bun at the back of her neck; a style which at the moment happened to be fashionable although that was not her reason for wearing it so. She was a woman who always kept to her own style. Her appearance was like her house; neat, well kept. Any kind of dust or disorder worried her.

The man in the invalid chair watching her as she put the fallen petals carefully away, smiled a slightly twisted smile.

"Same tidy creature," he said. "A place for everything and everything in its place." He laughed, with a faint malicious note in the laugh. But Mary Durrant was quite undisturbed.

"I do like things to be tidy," she agreed. "You know, Phil, you wouldn't like it yourself if the house was like a shambles."

Her husband said with a faint trace of bitterness:

"Well, at any rate *I* haven't got the chance of making it into one."

Soon after their marriage, Philip Durrant had fallen a victim to polio of the paralytic type. To Mary, who adored him, he had become her child as well as her husband. He himself felt at times slightly embarrassed by her possessive love. His wife had not got the imagination to understand that her pleasure in his dependence upon her sometimes irked him.

He went on now rather quickly, as though fearing some word of commiseration or sympathy from her.

"I must say your father's news beggars description! After all this time! How can you be so calm about it?"

"I suppose I can hardly take it in. . . . It's so extraordinary. At first I simply couldn't believe what father was saying. If it had been Hester, now, I should have thought she'd imagined the whole thing. You know what Hester's like."

Philip Durrant's face lost a little of its bitterness. He said softly:

"A vehement passionate creature, setting out in life to look for trouble and certain to find it."

Mary waved away the analysis. Other people's characters did not interest her.

She said doubtfully: "I suppose it's *true?* You don't think this man may have imagined it all?"

"The absent-minded scientist? It would be nice to think

so," said Philip, "but it seems that Andrew Marshall has taken the matter seriously. And Marshall, Marshall & Marshall are a very hard-headed legal proposition, let me tell you."

Mary Durrant said, frowning: "What will it actually *mean*, Phil?"

Philip said: "It means that Jacko will be completely exonerated. That is, if the authorities are satisfied—and I gather that there is going to be no question of anything else."

"Oh, well," said Mary, with a slight sigh, "I suppose it's all very *nice*."

Philip Durrant laughed again, the same twisted, rather bitter laughter.

"Polly!" he said, "you'll be the death of me."

Only her husband had ever called Mary Durrant Polly. It was a name ludicrously inappropriate to her statuesque appearance. She looked at Philip in faint surprise.

"I don't see what I've said to amuse you so much."

"You were so gracious about it!" said Philip. "Like Lady Somebody of the Sale of Work praising the Village Institute's handiwork."

Mary said, puzzled: "But it *is* very nice! You can't pretend it's been satisfactory to have had a murderer in the family."

"Not really *in* the family."

"Well, it's practically the same thing. I mean, it was all very worrying, and made one most uncomfortable. Everybody was so agog and curious. I hated it all."

"You took it very well," said Philip. "Froze them with that icy blue gaze of yours. Made them pipe down and look ashamed of themselves. It's wonderful the way you manage never to show emotion."

"I disliked it all very much. It was all most unpleasant," said Mary Durrant, "but at any rate he died and it was over. And now—now, I suppose, it will all be raked up again. So tiresome."

"Yes," said Philip Durrant thoughtfully. He shifted his shoulders slightly, a faint expression of pain on his face. His wife came to him quickly.

"Are you cramped? Wait. Let me just move this cushion. There. That better?"

"You ought to have been a hospital nurse," said Philip.

"I've not the least wish to nurse a lot of people. Only you."

25

It was said very simply but there was a depth of feeling behind the bare words.

The telephone rang and Mary went to it.

"Hallo . . . yes . . . speaking. . . . Oh, it's you . . ."

She said aside to Philip: "It's Micky."

"Yes . . . yes, we have heard. Father telephoned. . . . Well, of course. . . . Yes . . . Yes . . . Philip says if the lawyers are satisfied it must be all right. . . . Really, Micky, I don't see why you're so upset. . . . I'm not aware of being particularly dense. . . . Really, Micky, I do think you— Hallo? . . . Hallo? . . ." She frowned angrily. "He's rung off." She replaced the receiver. "Really, Philip, I can't understand Micky."

"What did he say exactly?"

"Well, he seems in such a state. He said that I was dense, that I didn't realise the—the repercussions. Hell to pay! That's the way he put it. But why? I don't understand."

"Got the wind up, has he?" said Philip thoughtfully.

"But why?"

"Well, he's right, you know. There will be repercussions." Mary looked a little bewildered.

"You mean that there will be a revival of interest in the case? Of course I'm glad Jacko is cleared, but it will be rather unpleasant if people begin talking about it again."

"It's not just what the neighbours say. There's more to it than that."

She looked at him enquiringly.

"The police are going to be interested, too!"

"The *police?*" Mary spoke sharply. "What's it got to do with them?"

"My dear girl," said Philip. *"Think."*

Mary came back slowly to sit by him.

"It's an unsolved crime again now, you see," said Philip.

"But surely · they won't bother—after all this time?"

"A very nice bit of wishful thinking," said Philip, "but fundamentally unsound, I fear."

"Surely," said Mary, "after they've been so stupid—making such a bad mistake over Jacko—they won't want to rake it all up again?"

"They mayn't want to—but they'll probably have to! Duty is duty."

"Oh, Philip, I'm sure you're wrong. There will just be a bit of talk and then it will all die down."

26

"And then our lives will go on happily ever afterwards," said Philip in his mocking voice.

"Why not?"

He shook his head. "It's not as simple as that. . . . Your father's right. We must all get together and have a consultation. Get Marshall down as he said."

"You mean—go over to Sunny Point?"

"Yes."

"Oh, we can't do that."

"Why not?"

"It's not practicable. You're an invalid and—"

"I'm not an invalid." Philip spoke with irritation. "I'm quite strong and well. I just happen to have lost the use of my legs. I could go to Timbuctoo with the proper transport laid on."

"I'm sure it would be very bad for you to go to Sunny Point. Having all this unpleasant business raked up—"

"It's not my mind that's affected."

"—And I don't see how we can leave the house. There have been so many burglaries lately."

"Get someone to sleep in."

"It's all very well to say that—as though it was the easiest thing in the world."

"Old Mrs. Whatshername can come in every day. Do stop making housewifely objections, Polly. It's you, really, who doesn't want to go."

"No, I don't."

"We won't be there long," said Philip reassuringly. "But I think we've got to go. This is a time when the family's got to present a united front to the world. We've got to find out exactly how we stand."

iii.

At the Hotel in Drymouth, Calgary dined early and went up to his room. He felt profoundly affected by what he had passed through at Sunny Point. He had expected to find his mission painful and it had taken him all his resolution to go through with it. But the whole thing had been painful and upsetting in an entirely different way from the one he had expected. He flung himself down on his bed and lit a cigarette as he went over and over it in his mind.

The clearest picture that came to him was of Hester's

face at that parting moment. Her scornful rejection of his plea for justice! What was it that she had said? "It's not the guilty who matter, it's the innocent." And then: "Don't you see what you've done to us all?" But what had he done? He didn't understand.

And the others. The woman they called Kirsty (why Kirsty? That was a Scottish name. She wasn't Scottish— Danish, perhaps, or Norwegian?). Why had she spoken so sternly—so accusingly?

There had been something odd, too, about Leo Argyle—a withdrawal, a watchfulness. No suggestion of the "Thank God my son was innocent!" which surely would have been the natural reaction!

And the girl—the girl who was Leo's secretary. She had been helpful to him, kindly. But she, too, had reacted in an odd way. He remembered the way she had knelt there by Argyle's chair. As though—as though—she were sympathising with him, consoling him. Consoling him for what? That his son was not guilty of murder? And surely—yes, surely— there was more there than a secretary's feelings—even a secretary of some years' standing. . . . What was it all *about?* Why did they—

The telephone on the table by the bed rang. He picked up the receiver.

"Hallo?"

"Dr. Calgary? There is someone asking for you."

"For me?"

He was surprised. As far as he was aware, nobody knew that he was spending the night in Drymouth.

"Who is it?"

There was a pause. Then the clerk said:

"It's a Mr. Argyle."

"Oh. Tell him—" Arthur Calgary checked himself on the point of saying that he would come down. If for some reason Leo Argyle had followed him to Drymouth and managed to find out where he was staying, then presumably the matter would be embarrassing to discuss in the crowded lounge downstairs.

He said instead:

"Ask him to come up to my room, will you?"

He rose from where he had been lying and paced up and down until the knock came on the door.

He went across and opened it.

"Come in, Mr. Argyle, I—"

He stopped, taken aback. It was not Leo Argyle. It was a young man whose dark, handsome face was marred by its expression of bitterness. A reckless, angry, unhappy face.

"Didn't expect me," said the young man. "Expected my—father. I'm Michael Argyle."

"Come in." Calgary closed the door after his visitor had entered. "How did you find out I was here?" he asked as he offered the boy his cigarette case.

Michael Argyle took one and gave a short unpleasant laugh.

"That one's easy! Rang up the principal hotels on the chance you might be staying the night. Hit it the second try."

"And why did you want to see me?"

Michael Argyle said slowly:

"Wanted to see what sort of a chap you were. . . ." His eyes ran appraisingly over Calgary, noting the slightly stooped shoulders, the greying hair, the thin sensitive face. "So you're one of the chaps who went on the 'Hayes Bentley' to the Pole. You don't look very tough."

Arthur Calgary smiled faintly.

"Appearances are sometimes deceptive," he said: "I was tough enough. It's not entirely muscular force that's needed. There are other important qualifications; endurance, patience, technical knowledge."

"How old are you, forty-five?"

"Thirty-eight."

"You look more."

"Yes—yes, I suppose I do." For a moment a feeling of poignant sadness came over him as he confronted the virile youth of the boy facing him.

He asked rather abruptly:

"Why did you want to see me?"

The other scowled.

"It's natural, isn't it? When I heard about the news you'd brought. The news about my dear brother."

Calgary did not answer.

Michael Argyle went on:

"It's come a bit late for him, hasn't it?"

"Yes," said Calgary in a low voice. "It is too late for him."

"What did you bottle it up for? What's all this about concussion?"

Patiently Calgary told him. Strangely enough, he felt heartened by the boy's roughness and rudeness. Here, at any rate, was someone who felt strongly on his brother's behalf.

"Gives Jacko an alibi, that's the point, is it? How do you know the times were as you say they were?"

"I am quite sure about the times." Calgary spoke with firmness.

"You may have made a mistake. You scientific blokes are apt to be absent-minded sometimes about little things like times and places."

Calgary showed slight amusement.

"You have made a picture for yourself of the absent-minded professor of fiction—wearing odd socks, not quite sure what day it is or where he happens to be? My dear young man, technical work needs great precision; exact amounts, times, calculations. I assure you there is no possibility of my having made a mistake. I picked up your brother just before seven and put him down in Drymouth at five minutes after the half hour."

"Your watch could have been wrong. Or you went by the clock in your car."

"My watch and the clock in the car were exactly synchronised."

"Jacko could have led you up the garden path some way. He was full of tricks."

"There were no tricks. Why are you so anxious to prove me wrong?" With some heat, Calgary went on: "I expected it might be difficult to convince the authorities that they had convicted a man unjustly. I did not expect to find his own family so hard to convince!"

"So you've found all of us a little difficult to convince?"

"The reaction seemed a little—unusual."

Micky eyed him keenly.

"They didn't want to believe you?"

"It—almost seemed like that . . ."

"Not only seemed like it. It was. Natural enough, too, if you only think about it."

"But why? Why should it be natural? Your mother is killed. Your brother is accused and convicted of the crime. Now it turns out that he was innocent. You should be pleased —thankful. Your own brother."

"He wasn't my brother. And she wasn't my mother."

"What?"

"Hasn't anyone told you? We were all adopted. The lot of us. Mary, my eldest 'sister,' in New York. The rest of us during the war. My 'mother,' as you call her, couldn't have any children of her own. So she got herself a nice little family by adoption. Mary, myself, Tina, Hester, Jacko. Comfortable, luxurious home and plenty of mother love thrown in! I'd say she forgot we weren't her own children in the end. But she was out of luck when she picked Jacko to be one of her darling little boys."

"I had no idea," said Calgary.

"So don't pull out the 'own mother, own brother' stop on me! Jacko was a louse!".

"But not a murderer," said Calgary.

His voice was emphatic. Micky looked at him and nodded.

"All right. It's your say so—and you're sticking to it. Jacko didn't kill her. Very well then—*who did kill her?* You haven't thought about that one, have you? Think about it now. Think about it—and then you'll begin to see what you're doing to us all. . . ."

He wheeled round and went abruptly out of the room.

CHAPTER 4 . . .

Calgary said apologetically, "It's very good of you to see me again, Mr. Marshall."

"Not at all," said the lawyer.

"As you know, I went down to Sunny Point and saw Jack Argyle's family."

"Quite so."

"You will have heard by now, I expect, about my visit?"

"Yes, Dr. Calgary, that is correct."

"What you may find it difficult to understand is why I have come back here to you again. . . . You see, things didn't turn out exactly as I thought they would."

"No," said the lawyer, "no, perhaps not." His voice was as usual dry and unemotional, yet something in it encouraged Arthur Calgary to continue.

"I thought, you see," went on Calgary, "that that would be the end of it. I was prepared for a certain amount of—what shall I say—natural resentment on their part. Although concussion may be termed, I suppose, an Act of God, yet from their viewpoint they could be forgiven for harbouring resentment against me. I was prepared for that, as I say. But at the same time I hoped it would be offset by the thankfulness they would feel over the fact that Jack Argyle's name was cleared. But things didn't turn out as I anticipated. Not at all."

"I see."

"Perhaps, Mr. Marshall, you anticipated something of what would happen? Your manner, I remember, puzzled me when I was here before. *Did* you foresee the attitude of mind that I was going to encounter?"

"You haven't told me yet, Dr. Calgary, what that attitude was."

Arthur Calgary drew his chair forward. "I thought that I was *end*ing something, giving—shall we say—a different end to a chapter already written. But I was made to feel, I was made to *see*, that instead of *end*ing something I was

32

*start*ing something. Something altogether new. Is that a true statement, do you think, of the position?"

Mr. Marshall nodded his head slowly. "Yes," he said, "it could be put that way. I did think—I admit it—that you were not realising all the implications. You could not be expected to do so because, naturally, you knew nothing of the background or of the facts except as they were given in the law reports."

"No. No, I see that now. Only too clearly." His voice rose as he went on excitedly, "It wasn't really relief they felt, it wasn't thankfulness. It was apprehension. A dread of what might be coming next. Am I right?"

Marshall said cautiously: "I should think probably that you are quite right. Mind you, I do not speak of my own knowledge."

"And if so," went on Calgary, "then I no longer feel that I can go back to my work satisfied with having made the only amends that I can make. I'm still involved. I'm responsible for bringing a new factor into various people's lives. I *can't* just wash my hands of it."

The lawyer cleared his throat. "That perhaps, is a rather fanciful point of view, Dr. Calgary."

"I don't think it is—not really. One must take responsibility for one's actions and not only one's *actions* but for the *result* of one's actions. Just on two years ago I gave a lift to a young hitch-hiker on the road. When I did that I set in train a certain course of events. I don't feel that I can disassociate myself from them."

The lawyer still shook his head.

"Very well, then," said Arthur Calgary impatiently. "Call it fanciful if you like. But my feelings, my conscience, are still involved. My only wish was to make amends for something it had been outside my power to prevent. I have not made amends. In some curious way I have made things worse for people who have already suffered. But I still don't understand clearly *why*."

"No," said Marshall slowly, "no, you would not see why. For the past eighteen months or so you've been out of touch with civilisation. You did not read the daily papers, the account of the criminal proceedings and the background account of this family that was given in the newspapers. Possibly you would not have read them anyway, but you could could not have escaped, I think, *hearing* about them. The facts are very simple, Dr. Calgary. They are not confidential. They were made public at the time. It resolves itself very simply into this. If Jack Argyle did not (and by your account he cannot have committed the crime), *then who did?* That brings us back to the circumstances in which the crime was committed. It was committed between the hours of seven and seventy-thirty on a November evening in a house where the deceased woman was surrounded by the members of her own family and household. The house was securely locked and shuttered and if anyone entered from outside, then the outsider must have been admitted by Mrs. Argyle herself or have entered with their own key. In other words, it must have been someone she knew. It resembles in some ways the conditions of the Borden case in America where Mr. Borden and his wife were struck down by blows of an axe on a Sunday morning. Nobody in the house heard anything, nobody was known or seen to approach the house. You can see, Dr. Calgary, why the members of the family were, as you put it, disturbed rather than relieved by the news you brought them?"

Calgary said slowly: "They'd rather, you mean, that Jack Argyle was guilty?"

"Oh yes," said Marshall. "Oh yes, very decidedly so. If I may put it in a somewhat cynical way, Jack Argyle was the perfect answer to the unpleasant fact of murder in the family. He had been a problem child, a delinquent boy, a man of violent temper. Excuses could be and were made for him within the family circle. They could mourn for him, have sympathy with him, declare to themselves, to each other, and to the world that it was not *really* his fault, that psychologists could explain it all! Yes, very, very convenient."

"And now—" Calgary stopped.

"And now," said Mr. Marshall, "it is different, of course. Quite different. Almost alarming perhaps."

Calgary said shrewdly, "The news I brought was unwelcome to you, too, wasn't it?"

"I must admit that. Yes. Yes, I must admit that I was—upset. A case which was closed satisfactorily—yes, I shall continue to use the word satisfactorily—is now reopened."

"Is that official?" Calgary asked. "I mean—from the police point of view, will the case be reopened?"

"Oh, undoubtedly," said Marshall. "When Jack Argyle was found guilty on everwhelming evidence—(the jury was only out a quarter of an hour)—that was an end of the matter as far as the police were concerned. But now, with the grant of a free pardon posthumously awarded, the case is opened again."

"And the police will make fresh investigations?"

"Almost certainly I should say. Of course," added Marshall, rubbing his chin thoughtfully, "it is doubtful after this lapse of time, owing to the peculiar features of the case, whether they will be able to achieve any result. . . . For myself, I should doubt it. They may know that someone in the house is guilty. They may get so far as to have a very shrewd idea of who that someone is. But to get definite evidence will not be easy."

"I see," said Calgary. "I see. . . . Yes, that's what she meant."

The lawyer said sharply: "Of whom are you speaking?"

"The girl," said Calgary. "Hester Argyle."

"Ah, yes. Young Hester." He asked curiously: "What did she say to you?"

"She spoke of the innocent," said Calgary. "She said it wasn't the guilty who mattered but the innocent. I understand now what she meant. . . ."

Marshall cast a sharp glance at him. "I think possibly you do."

"She meant just what you are saying," said Arthur Calgary. "She meant that once more the family would be under suspicion—"

Marshall interrupted. "Hardly once more," he said. "There was never *time* for the family to come under suspicion before. Jack Argyle was clearly indicated from the first."

Calgary waved the interruption aside.

"The family would come under suspicion," he said, "and it might remain under suspicion for a long time—perhaps for ever. If one of the family was guilty it is possible that they themselves would not know which one. They would look at each other and—wonder. . . . Yes, that's what would be the worst of all. They themselves would not know *which . . ."

There was silence. Marshall watched Calgary with a quiet, appraising glance, but he said nothing.

"That's terrible, you know . . ." said Calgary.

His thin, sensitive face showed the play of emotion on it.

"Yes, that's terrible. . . . To go on year after year not knowing, looking at one another, perhaps the suspicion affecting one's relationships with people. Destroying love, destroying trust . . ."

Marshall cleared his throat.

"Aren't you—er—putting it rather too vividly?"

"No," said Calgary, "I don't think I am. I think, perhaps, if you'll excuse me, Mr. Marshall, I see this more clearly than you do. I can imagine, you see, what it might mean."

Again there was silence.

"It means," said Calgary, "that it is the innocent who are going to suffer. . . . And the innocent should not suffer. Only the guilty. That's why—that's why I can't wash my hands of it. I *can't* go away and say 'I've done the right thing, I've made what amends I can—I've served the cause of justice.' Because you see what I have done has *not* served the cause of justice. It has not brought conviction to the guilty, it has not delivered the innocent from the shadow of guilt."

"I think you're working yourself up a little, Dr. Calgary. What you say has some foundation of truth, no doubt, but I don't see exactly what—well, what you can do about it."

"No. Nor do I," said Calgary frankly. "But it means that I've got to try. That's really why I've come to you, Mr. Marshall. I want—I think I've a right to know—the background."

"Oh, well," said Mr. Marshall, his tone slightly brisker. "There's no secret about all *that*. I can give you any *facts* you want to know. More than facts I am not in a position to give you. I've never been on intimate terms with the household. Our firm has acted for Mrs. Argyle over a number of years. We have co-operated with her over establishing various trusts and seeing to legal business. Mrs. Argyle herself I knew reasonably well and I also knew her husband. Of the atmosphere at Sunny Point, of the temperaments and characters of the various people living there, I only know as you might say, at second-hand through Mrs. Argyle herself."

"I quite understand all that," said Calgary, "but I've got to make a start somewhere. I understand that the children were not her own. That they were adopted?"

"That is so. Mrs. Argyle was born Rachel Konstam, the only daughter of Rudolph Konstam, a very rich man. Her mother was American and also a very rich woman in her own right. Rudolph Konstam had many philanthropic interests and brought his daughter up to take an interest in these benevolent schemes. He and his wife died in an aeroplane crash and Rachel then devoted the large fortune she inherited from her father and mother to what we may term, loosely, philanthropical enterprises. She took a personal interest in these benefactions and did a certain amount of settlement work herself. It was in doing the latter that she met Leo Argyle, who was an Oxford don, with a great interest in economics and social reform. To understand Mrs. Argyle you have to realise that the great tragedy of her life was that she was unable to have children. As is the case with many women, this disability gradually overshadowed the whole of her life. When after visits to all kinds of specialists, it seemed clear that she could never hope to be a mother, she had to find what alleviation she could. She adopted first a child from a slum tenement in New York—that is the present Mrs. Durrant. Mrs. Argyle devoted herself almost entirely to charities connected with children. On the outbreak of war in 1939 she established under the auspices of the Ministry of Health a kind of war nursery for children, purchasing the house you visited, Sunny Point."

"Then called Viper's Point," said Calgary.

"Yes, Yes. I believe that was the original name. Ah, yes, perhaps in the end a more suitable name than the name she chose for it—Sunny Point. In 1940 she had about twelve to sixteen children, mostly those who had unsatisfactory guardians or who could not be evacuated with their own families. Everything was done for these children. They were given a luxurious home. I remonstrated with her, pointing out to her it was going to be difficult for the children, after several years of war, to return from these luxurious surroundings to their own homes. She paid no attention to me. She was deeply attached to the children and finally she formed the project of adding some of them, those from particularly unsatisfactory homes or who were orphans, to her own family. This resulted in a family of five. Mary—now married to Philip Durrant—Michael, who works in Drymouth, Tina, a half-caste child, Hester, and of course, Jacko. They grew up regarding the Argyles as their father and mother. They were given the best education money could buy. If environment counts for anything they should have gone far. They certainly had every advantage. Jack—or Jacko, as they called

37

him—was always unsatisfactory. He stole money at school and had to be taken away. He got into trouble in his first year at the university. Twice he only avoided a jail sentence by a very narrow margin. He always had an ungovernable temper. All this, however, you probably have already gathered. Twice embezzlement on his part was made good by the Argyles. Twice money was spent in setting him up in business. Twice these business enterprises failed. After his death an allowance was paid, and indeed is still paid, to his widow."

"His *widow?* Nobody has ever told me that he was married."

"Dear, dear." The lawyer clicked his thumb irritably. "I have been remiss. I had forgotten, of course, that you had not read the newspaper reports. I may say that none of the Argyle family had any idea that he was married. Immediately after his arrest his wife appeared at Sunny Point in great distress. Mr. Argyle was very good to her. She was a young woman who had worked as a dance hostess in the Drymouth Palais de Danse. I probably forgot to tell you about her because she remarried a few weeks after Jack's death. Her present husband is an electrician, I believe, in Drymouth."

"I must go and see her," said Calgary. He added, reproachfully, "She is the first person I should have gone to see."

"Certainly, certainly. I will give you the address. I really cannot think *why* I did not mention it to you when you first came to me."

Calgary was silent.

"She was such a—well—negligible factor," said the lawyer apologetically. "Even the newspapers did not play her up much—she never visited her husband in prison—or took any further interest in him—"

Calgary had been deep in thought. He said now:

"Can you tell me exactly who was in that house on the night Mrs. Argyle was killed?"

Marshall gave him a sharp glance.

"Leo Argyle, of course, and the youngest daughter, Hester. Mary Durrant and her invalid husband were there on a visit. He had just come out of hospital. Then there was Kirsten Lindstrom—whom you probably met—she is a Swedish trained nurse and masseuse who originally came to help

38

Mrs. Argyle with her war nursery and has remained on ever since. Michael and Tina were not there—Michael works as a car salesman in Drymouth and Tina has a job in the County Library at Redmyn and lives in a flat there."

Marshall paused before going on.

"There was also Miss Vaughan, Mr. Argyle's secretary. She had left the house before the body was discovered."

"I met her also," said Calgary. "She seems very—attached to Mr. Argyle."

"Yes—yes. I believe there may shortly be an engagement announced."

"Ah!"

"He has been very lonely since his wife died," said the lawyer, with a faint note of reproof in his voice.

"Quite so," said Calgary.

Then he said:

"What about motive, Mr. Marshall?"

"My dear Dr. Calgary, I really cannot speculate as to that!"

"I think you can. As you have said yourself the facts are ascertainable."

"There was no direct monetary benefit to *anyone*. Mrs. Argyle had entered into a series of discretionary Trusts, a formula which as you know is much adopted nowadays. These Trusts were in favour of all the children. They are administered by three Trustees, of whom I am one, Leo Argyle is one and the third is an American lawyer, a distant cousin of Mrs. Argyle's. The very large sum of money involved is administered by these three Trustees and can be adjusted so as to benefit those beneficiaries of the Trust who need it most."

"What about Mr. Argyle? Did he profit in a monetary sense by his wife's death?"

"Not to any great extent. Most of her fortune, as I have told you, had gone into Trusts. She left him the residue of her estate, but that did not amount to a large sum."

"And Miss Lindstrom?"

"Mrs. Argyle had bought a very handsome annuity for Miss Lindstrom some years previously." Marshall added irritably, "Motive? There doesn't seem to me a ha'porth of motive about. Certainly not financial motive."

"And in the emotional field? Was there any special—friction?"

"There, I'm afraid, I can't help you." Marshall spoke with finality. "I wasn't an observer of the family life."

"Is there anyone who could?"

Marshall considered for a moment or two. Then he said, almost reluctantly:

"You might go and see the local doctor. Dr.—er—Mac-Master, I think his name is. He's retired now, but still lives in the neighbourhood. He was medical attendant to the war nursery. He must have known and seen a good deal of the life at Sunny Point. Whether you can persuade him to tell you anything is up to you. But I think that if he chose, he might be helpful, though—pardon me for saying this—do you think it likely that you can accomplish anything that the police cannot accomplish much more easily?"

"I don't know," said Calgary. "Probably not. But I do know this. I've got to try. Yes, I've got to try."

CHAPTER 5 . . .

THE CHIEF CONSTABLE's eyebrows climbed slowly up his forehead in a vain attempt to reach the receding line of his grey hair. He cast his eyes up to the ceiling and then down again to the papers on his desk.

"It beggars description!" he said.

The young man whose business it was to make the right responses to the Chief Constable, said:

"Yes, sir."

"A pretty kettle of fish," muttered Major Finney. He tapped with his fingers on the table. "Is Huish here?" he asked.

"Yes, sir. Superintendent Huish came about five minutes ago."

"Right," said the Chief Constable. "Send him in, will you?"

Superintendent Huish was a tall, sad-looking man. His air of melancholy was so profound that no one would have believed that he could be the life and soul of a children's party, cracking jokes and bringing pennies out of little boys' ears, much to their delight. The Chief Constable said:

"Morning, Huish, this is pretty kettle of fish we've got here. What d'you think of it?"

Superintendent Huish breathed heavily and sat down in the chair indicated.

"It seems as though we made a mistake two years ago," he said. "This fellow—what's-his-name—"

The Chief Constable rustled his papers. "Calory—no, Calgary. Some sort of a professor. Absent-minded bloke, maybe? People like that often vague about times and all that sort of thing?" There was perhaps a hint of appeal in his voice, but Huish did not respond. He said:

"He's a kind of scientist, I understand."

"So that you think we've got to accept what he says?"

"Well," said Huish, "Sir Reginald seems to have accepted it, and I don't suppose there's anything would get past *him*." This was a tribute to the Director of Public Prosecutions.

"No," said Major Finney, rather unwillingly. "If the D.P.P.'s convinced, well I suppose we've just got to take it. That means opening up the case again. You've brought the relevant data with you, have you, as I asked?"

"Yes, sir, I've got it here."

The superintendent spread out various documents on the table.

"Been over it?" the Chief Constable asked.

"Yes, sir. I went all over it last night. My memory of it was fairly fresh. After all, it's not so long ago."

"Well, let's have it, Huish. Where are we?"

"Back at the beginning sir," said Superintendent Huish. "The trouble is, you see, there really wasn't any doubt *at the time.*"

"No," said the Chief Constable. "It seemed a perfectly clear case. Don't think I'm blaming you, Huish. I was behind you a hundred per cent."

"There wasn't anything else really that we could think," said Huish thoughtfully. "A call came in that she'd been killed. The information that the boy had been there threatening her. the fingerprint evidence—his fingerprints on the poker, and the money. We picked him up almost at once and there the money was, in his possession."

"What sort of impression did he make on you at the time?"

Huish considered. "Bad," he said. "Far too cocky and plausible. Came reeling out with his times and his alibis. Cocky. You know the type. Murderers are usually cocky. Think they're so clever. Think whatever *they've* done is sure to be all right, no matter how things go for other people. He was a wrong 'un all right."

"Yes," Finney agreed, "he was a wrong 'un. All his record goes to prove that. But were you convinced at once that he was a killer?"

The superintendent considered. "It's not a thing you can be sure about. He was the type, I'd say, that very often ends up as a killer. Like Harmon in 1938. Long records behind *him* of pinched bicycles, swindled money, frauds on elderly women, and finally he does one woman in, pickles her in acid, gets pleased with himself and starts making a habit of it. I'd have taken Jacko Argyle for one of that type."

"But it seems," said the Chief Constable slowly, "that we were wrong."

42

"Yes," said Huish, "yes, we were wrong. And the chap's dead. It's a bad business. Mind you," he added, with sudden animation, "he was a wrong 'un all right. He may not have been a murderer—in fact he wasn't a murderer, so we find now—but he was a wrong 'un."

"Well, come on, man," Finney snapped at him, "who *did* kill her? You've been over the case, you say, last night. Somebody killed her. The woman didn't hit herself on the back of her head with the poker. Somebody else did. Who was it?"

Superintendent Huish sighed and leaned back in his chair.

"I'm wondering if we'll ever know," he said.

"Difficult as all that, eh?"

"Yes, because the scent's cold and because there'll be very little evidence to find and I should rather imagine that there never was very much evidence."

"The point being that it was someone in the house, someone close to her?"

"Don't see who else it could have been," said the superintendent. "It was someone there in the house or it was someone that she herself opened the door to and let in. The Argyles were the locking-up type. Burglar bolts on the windows, chains, extra locks on the front door. They'd had one burglary a couple of years before and it had made them burglar conscious." He paused and went on, "The trouble is, sir that we didn't look elsewhere at the time. The case against Jacko Argyle was complete. Of course, one can see now, the murderer took advantage of that."

"Took advantage of the fact that the boy had been there, that he'd quarrelled with her and that he'd threatened her?"

"Yes. All that person had to do was to step in the room, pick up the poker in a gloved hand, from where Jacko had thrown it down, walk up to the table where Mrs. Argyle was writing and biff her one on the head."

Major Fenney said one simple word:

"Why?"

Superintendent Huish nodded slowly.

"Yes, sir, that's what we've got to find out. It's going to be one of the difficulties. Absence of motive."

"There didn't seem at the time," said the Chief Constable, "to be any obvious motive knocking about, as you might say. Like most other women who have property and a considerable fortune of their own, she'd entered into such various

43

schemes as are legally permitted to avoid death duties. A beneficiary trust was already in existence, the children were all provided for in advance of her death. They'd get nothing further when she did die. And it wasn't as though she was an unpleasant woman, nagging or bullying or mean. She'd lavished money on them all their lives. Good education, capital sums to start them in jobs, handsome allowances to them all. Affection, kindness, benevolence."

"That's so, sir," agreed Superintendent Huish. "On the face of it there's no reason for anyone to want her out of the way. Of course—" He paused.

"Yes, Huish?"

"Mr. Argyle, I understand, is thinking of remarrying. He's marrying Miss Gwenda Vaughan, who's acted as his secretary over a good number of years."

"Yes," said Major Finney thoughtfully. "I suppose there's a motive there. One that we didn't know about at the time. She's been working for him for some years, you say. Think there was anything between them at the time of the murder?"

"I should rather doubt it, sir," said Superintendent Huish. "That sort of thing soon gets talked about in a village. I mean, I don't think there were any goings-on, as you might say. Nothing for Mrs. Argyle to find out about or cut up rough about."

"No," said the Chief Constable, "but he might have wanted to marry Gwenda Vaughan quite badly."

"She's an attractive young woman," said Superintendent Huish. "Not glamorous, I wouldn't say that, but good-looking and attractive in a nice kind of way."

"Probably been devoted to him for years," said Major Finney. "These women secretaries always seem to be in love with their boss."

"Well, we've got a motive of a kind for those two," said Huish. "Then there's the lady help, the Swedish woman. She mightn't really have been as fond of Mrs. Argyle as she appeared to be. There might have been slights or imagined slights; things she resented. She didn't benefit financially by the death because Mrs. Argyle had already bought her a very handsome annuity. She *seems* a nice, sensible kind of woman and not the sort you can imagine hitting anyone on the head with a poker! But you never know, do you? Look at the Lizzie Borden case."

"No," said the Chief Constable, "you never know. There's no question of an outsider of any kind?"

"No trace of one," said the superintendent. "The drawer where the money was was pulled out. A sort of attempt had been made to make the room look as though a burglar had been there, but it was a very amateurish effort. Sort of thing that fitted in perfectly with young Jacko having tried to create that particular effect."

"The ood thing to me," said the Chief Constable, "is the money."

"Yes," said Huish. "That's very difficult to understand. One of the fivers Jack Argyle had on him was definitely one that had been given to Mrs. Argyle at the bank that morning. Mrs. Bottleberry was the name written on the back of it. *He* said his mother had given the money to him, but both Mr. Argyle and Gwenda Vaughan are quite definite that Mrs. Argyle came into the library at a quarter to seven and told them about Jacko's demand for money and categorically said she'd refused to give him any."

"It's possible, of course," the Chief Constable pointed out, "with what we know now, that Argyle and the Vaughan girl might have been lying."

"Yes, that's a possibility—or perhaps—" the superintendent broke off.

"Yes, Huish?" Finney encouraged him.

"Say someone—we'll call him or her X for the moment —overheard the quarrel and the threats that Jacko was making. Suppose someone saw an opportunity there. Got the money, ran after the boy, said that his mother after all wanted him to have it, thus paving the way to one of the prettiest little frame-ups ever. Careful to use the poker that he'd picked up to threaten her with, without smearing his fingerprints."

"Dammit all," said the Chief Constable angrily. "None of it seems to fit with what I know of the family. Who else was in the house that evening besides Argyle and Gwenda Vaughan, Hester Argyle and this Lindstrom woman?"

"The eldest married daughter, Mary Durrant, and her husband were staying there."

"He's a cripple, isn't he? That lets him out. What about Mary Durrant?"

"She's a very calm piece of goods, sir. You can't imagine her getting excited or—well, or killing anyone."

"The servants?" demanded the Chief Constable.

"All dailies, sir, and they'd gone home by six o'clock."

"Let me have a look at the *Times*."

The Superintendent passed the paper to him.

"H'm . . . yes, I see. Quarter to seven Mrs. Argyle was in the library talking to her husband about Jacko's threats. Gwenda Vaughan was present during part of the conversation. Gwenda Vaughan went home just after seven. Hester Argyle saw her mother alive at about two or three minutes to seven. After that, Mrs. Argyle was not seen till half past seven, when her dead body was discovered by Miss Lindstrom. Between seven and half past there was plenty of opportunity. Hester could have killed her. Gwenda Vaughan could have killed her after she left the library and before she left the house. Miss Lindstrom could have killed her when she 'discovered the body,' Leo Argyle was alone in his library from ten past seven until Miss Lindstrom sounded the alarm. He could have gone to his wife's sitting room and killed her any time during that twenty minutes. Mary Durrant, who was upstairs, could have come down during the half hour and killed her mother. And"—said Finney thoughtfully—"Mrs. Argyle herself could have let anyone in by the front door as we thought she let Jack Argyle in. Leo Argyle said, if you remember, that he *thought* he did hear a ring at the bell, and the sound of the front door opening and closing, but he was very vague about the time. We assumed that that was when Jacko returned and killed her."

"He needn't have rung the bell," said Huish. "He had a key of his own. They all had."

"There's another brother, isn't there?"

"Yes, Michael. Works as a car salesman in Drymouth."

"You'd better find out, I suppose," said the Chief Constable, "what he was doing that evening."

"After two years?" said Superintendent Huish. "Not likely anyone will remember, is it?"

"Was he asked at the time?"

"Out testing a customer's car, I understand. No reason for suspecting him then, but he had a key and he *could* have come over and killed her."

The Chief Constable sighed.

"I don't know how you're going to get about it, Huish. I don't know whether we're ever going to get anywhere."

"I'd like to know myself who killed her," said Huish.

"From all I can make out, she was a fine type of woman. She'd done a lot for people. For unlucky children, for all sorts of charities. She's the sort of person that oughtn't to have been killed. Yes. I'd like to know. Even if we can never get enough evidence to satisfy the D.P.P. I'd still like to *know*."

"Well, I wish you the best of luck, Huish," said the Chief Constable. "Fortunately we've nothing very much on just now, but don't be discouraged if you can't get anywhere. It's a very cold trail. Yes, it's a very cold trail."

CHAPTER **6 . . .**

THE LIGHTS went up in the cinema. Advertisements flashed on to the screen. The cinema usherettes walked round with cartons of lemonade and of ice cream. Arthur Calgary scrutinised them. A plump girl with brown hair, a tall dark one and a small, fair-haired one. That was the one he had come to see. Jacko's wife. Jacko's widow, now the wife of a man called Joe Clegg. It was a pretty, rather vapid little face, plastered with make-up, eyebrows plucked, hair hideous and stiff in a cheap perm. Arthur Calgary bought an ice-cream carton from her. He had her home address and he meant to call there, but he had wanted to see her first while she was unaware of him. Well, that was that. Not the sort of daughter-in-law, he thought, that Mrs. Argyle, from all accounts, would have cared about very much. That, no doubt, was why Jacko had kept her dark.

He sighed, concealed the ice-cream carton carefully under his chair, and leaned back as the lights went out and a new picture began to flash on the screen. Presently he got up and left the cinema.

At eleven o'clock the next morning he called at the address he had been given. A sixteen-year-old boy opened the door, and in answer to Calgary's enquiry, said:

"Cleggs? Top floor."

Calgary climbed the stairs. He knocked at a door and Maureen Clegg opened it. Without her smart uniform and her make-up, she looked a different girl. It was a silly little face, good-natured but with nothing particularly interesting about it. She looked at him doubtfully, frowned suspiciously.

"My name is Calgary. I believe you have had a letter from Mr. Marshall about me."

Her face cleared.

"Oh, so you're the one! Come in, do." She moved back to let him enter. "Sorry the place is in such a mess. I haven't had time to get around to things yet." She swept some untidy clothes off a chair and pushed aside the remains of a

48

breakfast consumed some time ago. "Do sit down. I'm sure it's ever so good of you to come."

"I felt it was the least I could do," said Calgary.

She gave a little embarrassed laugh, as though not really taking in what he meant.

"Mr. Marshall wrote me about it," she said. "About that story that Jackie made up—how it was all true after all. That someone *did* give him a lift back that night to Drymouth. So it was you, was it?"

"Yes," said Calgary. "It was I."

"I really can't get over it," said Maureen. "Talked about it half the night, Joe and I did. Really, I said, it might be something on the pictures. Two years ago, isn't it, or nearly?"

"About that, yes."

"Just the sort of thing you do see on the pictures, and of course you say to yourself that sort of thing's all nonsense, it wouldn't happen in real life. And now there it is! It does happen! It's really quite exciting in a way, isn't it?"

"I suppose," said Calgary, "that it might be thought of like that." He was watching her with a vague kind of pain.

She chattered on quite happily.

"There's poor old Jackie dead and not able to know about it. He got pneumonia, you know, in prison. I expect it was the damp or something, don't you?"

She had, Calgary realised, a definite romantic image of prison in her mind's eye. Damp underground cells with rats gnawing one's toes.

"At the time, I must say," she went on, "him dying seemed all for the best."

"Yes, I suppose so. . . . Yes, I suppose it must have done."

"Well, I mean, there he was, shut up for years and years and years. Joe said I'd better get a divorce and I was just setting about it."

"You wanted to divorce him?"

"Well, it's no good being tied to a man who's going to be in prison for years, is it? Besides, you know, although I was fond of Jackie and all that, he wasn't what you call the steady type. I never did think really that our marriage would last."

"Had you actually started proceedings for divorce when he died?"

"Well, I had in a kind of way. I mean, I'd been to a lawyer. Joe got me to go. Of course, Joe never could stand Jackie."

"Joe is your husband?"

"Yes. He works in the electricity. Got a very good job and they think a lot of him. He always told me Jackie was no good, but of course I was just a kid and silly then. Jackie had a great way with him, you know."

"So it seems from all I've heard about him."

"He was wonderful at getting round women—I don't know why, really. He wasn't good-looking or anything like that. Monkey-face, I used to call him. But all the same, he'd got a way with him. You'd find you were doing anything he wanted you to do. Mind you, it came in useful once or twice. Just after we were married he got into trouble at the garage where he was working over some work done on a customer's car. I never understood the rights of it. Anyway, the boss was ever so angry. But Jackie got round the boss's wife. Quite old, she was. Must have been near on fifty, but Jackie flattered her up, played her off this way and that until she didn't know whether she was on her head or her heels. She'd have done anything for him in the end. Got round her husband, she did, and got him to say as he wouldn't prosecute if Jackie paid the money back. But he never knew where the money came from! It was his own wife what provided it. That really gave us a laugh, Jackie and me!"

Calgary looked at her with faint repulsion. "Was it—so very funny?"

"Oh, I think so, don't you? Really, it was a scream. An old woman like that crazy about Jackie and raking out her savings for him."

Calgary sighed. Things were never, he thought, the way you imagined them to be. Every day he found himself less attracted to the man whose name he had taken such trouble to vindicate. He was almost coming to understand and share the point of view which had so astounded him at Sunny Point.

"I only came here, Mrs. Clegg," he said, "to see if there was anything I could—well, do for you to make up for what had happened."

Maureen Clegg looked faintly puzzled.

"Very nice of you, I'm sure," she said. "But why should you? We're all right. Joe is making good money and I've got my own job. I'm an usherette, you know, at the Picture-drome."

"Yes, I know."

"We're going to get a telly next month," the girl went on proudly.

"I'm very glad," said Arthur Calgary, "more glad than I can say that this—this unfortunate business hasn't left any —well, permanent shadow."

He was finding it more and more difficult to choose the right words when talking to this girl who had been married to Jacko. Everything he said sounded pompous, artificial. Why couldn't he talk naturally to her?

"I was afraid it might have been a terrible grief to you."

She stared at him, her wide, blue eyes not understanding in the least what he meant.

"It was horrid at the time," she said. "All the neighbours talking and the worry of it all, though I must say the police were very kind, all things considered. Talked to me very politely and spoke very nice about everything."

He wondered if she had had any feeling for the dead man. He asked her a question abruptly.

"Did you think he'd done it?" he said.

"Do you mean, do I think he'd done his mother in?"

"Yes. Just that."

"Well, of course—well—well—yes, I suppose I did in a way. Of course, he *said* he hadn't, but I mean you never could believe anything Jackie said, and it did seem as though he must have done. You see, he could get very nasty, Jackie could, if you stood up against him. I knew he was in a hole of some kind. He wouldn't say much to me, just swore at me when I asked him about it. But he went off that day and he said that it was going to be all right. His mother, he said, would stump up. She'd have to. So of course I believed him."

"He had never told his family about your marriage, I understand. You hadn't met them?"

"No. You see, they were classy people, had a big house and all that. I wouldn't have gone down very well. Jackie thought it best to keep me dark. Besides, he said if he took me along his mother'd want to run my life as well as his. She couldn't help running people, he said, and he'd had enough of it— we did very well as we were, he said."

She appeared to display no resentment, but to think, indeed, that her husband's behaviour had been natural.

"I suppose it was a great shock to you when he was arrested?"

"Well, naturally. However *could* he do such a thing? I

said to myself, but then, you can't get away from things. He always had a very nasty temper when anything upset him."

Calgary leaned forward.

"Let's put it like this. It really seemed to you not at all a surprising thing that your husband should have hit his mother on the head with a poker and stolen a large quantity of money from her?"

"Well, Mr.—er—Calgary, if you'll excuse me, that's putting it in rather a nasty way. I don't suppose he meant to hit her so hard. Don't suppose he meant to do her in. She just refused to give him some money, he caught up the poker and he threatened her, and when she stuck it out he lost control of himself and gave her a swipe. I don't suppose he meant to kill her. That was just his bad luck. You see, he needed the money very badly. He'd have gone to prison if he hadn't got it."

"So—you don't blame him?"

"Well, of course I blamed him. . . . I don't like all that nasty violent behaviour. And your own mother, too! No, I don't think it was a nice thing to do at all. I began to think as Joe was right in telling me I oughtn't to have had anything to do with Jackie. But, you know how it is. It's ever so difficult for a girl to make up her mind. Joe, you see, was always the steady kind. I've known him a long time. Jackie was different. He'd got education and all that. He seemed very well off, too, always splashing his money about. And of course he had a way with him, as I've been telling you. He could get round anybody. He got round me all right. 'You'll regret it, my girl,' that's what Joe said. I thought that was just sour grapes and the green-eyed monster, if you understand what I mean. But Joe turned out to be quite right in the end."

Calgary looked at her. He wondered if she still failed to understand the full implications of his story.

"Right in exactly what way?" he asked.

"Well, landing me up in the proper mess he did. I mean, we've always been respectable. Mother brought us up very careful. We've always had things nice and no talk. And there was the police arresting my husband! And all the neighbours knowing. In all the papers it was. *News of the World* and all the rest of them. And ever so many reporters coming round and asking questions. It put me in a very nasty position."

"But, my dear child," said Arthur Calgary, "you do realise now that he didn't do it?"

For a moment the fair, pretty face looked bewildered.

"Of course! I was forgetting. But all the same—well, I mean, he did go there and kick up a fuss and threaten her and all that. If he hadn't done that he wouldn't have been arrested at all, would he?"

"No," said Calgary, "no. That is quite true."

Possibly, he thought, this pretty, silly child was more of a realist than he was.

"Oo, it was awful," went on Maureen. "I didn't know *what* to do. And then Mum said better go over right away and see his people. They'd have to do something for me, she said. After all, she said, you've got your rights and you'd best show them as you know how to look after them. So off I went. It was that foreign lady help what opened the door to me and at first I couldn't make her understand. Seemed as if she couldn't believe it. 'It's impossible,' she kept saying. 'It's quite impossible that Jacko should be married to *you.*' Hurt my feelings a bit that did. 'Well married we are,' I said, 'and not in a registry office neither. In a church.' It was the way my Mum wanted! And she said, 'It's not true. I don't believe it.' And then Mr. Argyle came and *he* was ever so kind. Told me not to worry more than I could help, and that everything possible would be done to defend Jackie. Asked me how I was off for money—and sent me a regular allowance every week. He keeps it up, too, even now. Joe doesn't like me taking it, but I say to him, 'Don't be silly. They can spare it, can't they?' Sent me a very nice cheque for a wedding present as well, he did, when Joe and I got married. And he said he was very glad and that he hoped this marriage would be happier than the last one. Yes, he's ever so nice, Mr. Argyle is."

She turned her head as the door opened.

"Oh. Here's Joe now."

Joe was a thin-lipped, fair-haired young man. He received Maureen's explanations and introduction with a slight frown.

"Hoped we'd done with all that," he said disapprovingly. "Excusing me for saying so, sir. But it does no good to go raking up the past. That's what I feel. Maureen was unlucky, that's all there is to say about it—"

"Yes," said Calgary. "I quite see your point of view."

"Of course," said Joe Clegg, "she ought never to have taken up with a chap like that. *I* knew he was no good. There'd been stories about him already. He'd been under a Probation Officer twice. Once they begin like that, they go on. First it's embezzling, or swindling women out of their savings and in the end it's murder."

"But this," said Calgary, "wasn't murder."

"So you say, sir," said Joe Clegg. He sounded himself completely unconvinced.

"Jack Argyle has a perfect alibi for the time the crime was committed. He was in my car being given a lift to Drymouth. So you see, Mr. Clegg, he could not possibly have committed this crime."

"Possibly not, sir," said Clegg. "But all the same it's a pity raking it all up, if you'll excuse me. After all, he's dead now, and it can't matter to him. And it starts the neighbours talking again and making them think things."

Calgary rose. "Well, perhaps from your point of view that is one way of looking at it. But there is such a thing as justice, you know, Mr. Clegg."

"I've always understood," said Clegg, "that an English trial was as fair a thing as can be."

"The finest system in the world can make a mistake," said Calgary. "Justice is, after all, in the hands of men, and men are fallible."

After he had left them and was walking down the street he felt more disturbed in his own mind than he could have thought possible. Would it really have been better, he said to himself, if my memory of that day had never come back to me? After all, as that smug, tight-lipped fellow has just said, the boy is dead. He's gone before a judge who makes no mistake. Whether he's remembered as a murderer or merely as a petty thief, it can make no difference to him now.

Then a sudden wave of anger rose in him. "But it ought to make a difference to someone!" he thought. *"Someone* ought to be glad. Why aren't they? This girl, well, I can understand it well enough. She may have had an infatuation for Jacko, but she never loved him. Probably isn't capable of loving anybody. But the others. His father. His sister, his nurse . . . They should have been glad. They should have spared a thought for him before they began to fear for themselves. . . . Yes—someone should have cared."

"Miss Argyle? At the second desk there."

Calgary stood for a moment watching her.

Neat, small, very quiet and efficient. She was wearing a dark blue dress with white collar and cuffs. Her blue-black hair was coiled neatly in her neck. Her skin was dark, darker than an English skin could ever be. Her bones, too, were smaller. This was the half-caste child that Mrs. Argyle had taken as a daughter into the family.

The eyes that looked up and met his were dark, quite opaque. They were eyes that told you nothing.

Her voice was low and sympathetic.

"Can I help you?"

"You are Miss Argyle? Miss Christina Argyle?"

"Yes."

"My name is Calgary, Arthur Calgary. You may have heard—"

"Yes. I have heard about you. My father wrote to me."

"I would like very much to talk to you."

She glanced up at the clock.

"The library closes in half an hour. If you could wait until then?"

"Certainly. Perhaps you would come and have a cup of tea with me somewhere?"

"Thank you." She turned from him to a man who had come up behind him. "Yes. Can I help you?"

Arthur Calgary moved away. He wandered round, examining the contents of the shelves, observant all the time of Tina Argyle. She remained the same, calm, competent, unperturbed. The half hour passed slowly for him, but at last a bell rang and she nodded to him.

"I will meet you outside in a few minutes' time."

She did not keep him waiting. She wore no hat, merely a thick dark coat. He asked her where they should go.

"I do not know Redmyn very well," he explained.

"There is a tea place near the Cathedral. It is not good, but for that reason it is less full than the others."

Presently they were established at a small table, and a desiccated bored waitress had taken their order with a complete lack of enthusiasm.

"It will not be a good tea," said Tina apologetically, "but

I thought that perhaps you would like to be reasonably private."

"That is so. I must explain my reasons for seeking you out. You see, I have met the other members of your family, including, I may say, your brother Jacko's wife—widow. You were the only member of the family I had not met. Oh yes, and there is your married sister, of course."

"You feel it necessary to meet us all?"

It was said quite politely—but there was a certain detachment about her voice which made Calgary a little uncomfortable.

"Hardly as a social necessity," he agreed dryly. "And it is not mere curiosity." (But wasn't it?) "It is just that I wanted to express, personally, to all of you, my very deep regret that I failed to establish your brother's innocence at the time of the trial."

"I see . . ."

"If you were fond of him—Were you fond of him?"

She considered a moment, then said:

"No. I was not fond of Jacko."

"Yet I hear from all sides that he had—great charm."

She said clearly, but without passion:

"I distrusted and disliked him."

"You never had—forgive me—any doubts that he had killed your mother?"

"It never occurred to me that there could be any other solution."

The waitress brought their tea. The bread and butter were stale, the jam a curious jellified substance, the cakes garish and unappetizing. The tea was weak.

He sipped his and then said:

"It seems—I have been made to understand—that this information I have brought, which clears your brother of the charge of murder, may have repercussions that will not be so agreeable. It may bring fresh—anxieties to you all."

"Because the case will have to be reopened?"

"Yes. You have already thought about that?"

"My father seems to think it is inevitable."

"I am sorry. I am really sorry."

"Why are you sorry, Dr. Calgary?"

"I hate to be the cause of bringing fresh trouble upon you."

"But would you have been satisfied to remain silent?"

"You are thinking in terms of justice?"

"Yes. Weren't you?"

"Of course. Justice seemed to me to be very important. Now—I am beginning to wonder whether there are things that are more important."

"Such as?"

His thoughts flew to Hester.

"Such as—innocence, perhaps."

The opaqueness of her eyes increased.

"What do you feel, Miss Argyle?"

She was silent for a moment or two, then she said:

"I am thinking of those words in Magna Carta. *'To no man will we refuse justice.'*"

"I see," he said. "That is your answer. . . ."

CHAPTER **7** . . .

DR. MACMASTER was an old man with bushy eyebrows, shrewd grey eyes and a pugnacious chin. He leaned back in his shabby armchair and studied his visitor carefully. He found that he liked what he saw.

On Calgary's side also there was a feeling of liking. For the first time almost, since he had come back to England, he felt that he was talking to someone who appreciated his own feelings and point of view.

"It's very good of you to see me, Dr. MacMaster," he said.

"Not at all," said the doctor. "I'm bored to death since I retired from practice. Young men of my own profession tell me I must sit here like a dummy taking care of my groggy heart, but don't think it comes natural to me. It doesn't. I listen to the wireless, blah—blah—blah—and occasionally my housekeeper persuades me to look at television, flick, flick, flick. I've been a busy man, run off my feet all my life. I don't take kindly to sitting still. Reading tires my eyes. So don't apologise for taking up my time."

"The first thing I've got to make you understand," said Calgary, "is why I'm still concerning myself over all this. Logically speaking, I suppose, I've done what I came to do—told the unpalatable fact of my concussion and loss of memory, vindicated the boy's character. After that, the only sane and logical thing to do would be to go away and try to forget about it all. Eh? Isn't that right?"

"Depends," said Dr. MacMaster. "Something worrying you?" he asked in the ensuing pause.

"Yes," said Calgary. "Everything worries me. You see, my news was not received as I thought it would be."

"Oh well," said Dr. MacMaster, "nothing odd in that. Happens every day. We rehearse a thing beforehand in our own minds, it doesn't matter what it is, consultation with another practitioner, proposal of marriage to a young lady, talk with your boy before going back to school—when the thing comes off, it never goes as you thought it would. You've thought it out, you see; all the things that *you* are going to say and you've usually made up your mind what the answers are going to be. And, of course, that's what throws you off every time. The answers never are what you think they will be. That's what's upset you, I suppose?"

"Yes," said Calgary.

"What did you expect? Expected them to be all over you?"

"I expected"— he considered a moment—"blame? Perhaps. Resentment? Very likely. But also thankfulness."

MacMaster grunted. "And there's no thankfulness, and not as much resentment as you think there ought to be?"

"Something like that," Calgary confessed.

"That's because you didn't know the circumstances until you got there. Why have you come to me, exactly?"

Calgary said slowly:

"Because I want to understand more about the family. I only know the acknowledged facts. A very fine and unselfish woman doing her best for her adopted children, a public-spirited woman, a fine character. Set against that, what's called, I believe, a problem child—a child that goes wrong. The young delinquent. That's all I know. I don't know anything else. I don't know anything about Mrs. Argyle herself."

"You're quite right," said MacMaster. "You're putting your finger on the thing that matters. If you think it over, you know, that's always the interesting part of any murder. What the person was like who was murdered. Everybody's always so busy enquiring into the mind of the murderer. You've been thinking probably, that Mrs. Argyle was the sort of woman who shouldn't have been murdered."

"I should imagine that everyone felt that."

"Ethically," said MacMaster, "you're quite right. But you know"—he rubbed his nose—"isn't it the Chinese who held that beneficence is to be accounted a sin rather than a virtue? They've got something there, you know. Beneficence does things to people. Ties 'em up in knots. We all know what human nature's like. Do a chap a good turn and you feel kindly towards him. You like him. But the chap who's had the good turn done to him, does he feel so kindly to you? Does he really like you? He ought to, of course, but does he?

"Well," said the doctor, after a moment's pause. "There you are. Mrs. Argyle was what you might call a wonderful mother. But she overdid the beneficence. No doubt of that. Or wanted to. Or definitely tried to do so."

"They weren't her own children," Calgary pointed out.

"No," said MacMaster. "That's just where the trouble came in, I imagine. You've only got to look at any normal mother cat. She has her kittens, she's passionately protective of them, she'll scratch anyone who goes near them. And then, in a week or so, she starts resuming her own life. She goes out, hunts a bit, takes a rest from her young. She'll still protect them if anyone attacks them, but she is no longer obsessed by them, all the time. She'll play with them a bit; then when they're a bit too rough, she'll turn on them and give them a spank and tell them she wants to be let alone for a bit. She's reverting, you see, to nature. And as they grow up she cares less and less about them, and her thoughts go more and more to the attractive Toms in the neighbourhood. That's what you might call the normal pattern of female life. I've seen many girls and women, with strong maternal instincts, keen on getting married but mainly, though they mayn't quite know it themselves—because of their urge to motherhood. And the babies come; they're happy and satisfied. Life goes back into proportion for them. They can take an interest in their husbands and in the local affairs and in the gossip that's going round, and of course in their children. But it's all in proportion. The maternal instinct, in a purely physical sense, is satisfied, you see.

"Well, with Mrs. Argyle the maternal instinct was very strong, but the physical satisfaction of bearing a child or children, never came. And so her maternal obsession never really slackened. She wanted children, lots of children. She couldn't have enough of them. Her whole mind, night and day, was on those children. Her husband didn't count any more. He was just a pleasant abstraction in the background. No, everything was the children. Their feeding, their clothing, their playing, everything to do with them. Far too much was done for them. The thing she didn't give them and that they needed, was a little plain, honest-to-goodness neglect. They weren't just turned out into the garden to play like ordinary children in the country. No, they had to have every kind of gadget, artificial climbing things and stepping stones, a house built in the trees, sand brought and a little beach made on the river. Their food wasn't plain, ordinary food. Why, those kids even had their vegetables sieved, up to nearly five years old, *and* their milk sterilised and the water tested and their calories weighed and their vitamins computed! Mind you, I'm not being unprofessional in talking to you like this. Mrs. Argyle was never my patient. If she needed a doctor she went to one in Harley Street. Not that she often went. She was a very robust and healthy woman.

"But I was the local doctor who was called in to see the children, though she was inclined to think I was a bit casual over them. I told her to let 'em eat a few blackberries from the hedges. I told her it wouldn't hurt them to get their feet wet and have an occasional cold in the head, and that there's nothing much wrong with a child who's got a temperature of 99. No need to fuss till it's over 101. Those children were pampered and spoon-fed and fussed over and loved and in many ways it didn't do them any good."

"You mean," said Calgary, "it didn't do Jacko any good?"

"Well, I wasn't really only thinking of Jacko. Jacko to my mind was a liability from the start. The modern label for him is 'a crazy mixed-up kid.' It's just as good as any other label. The Argyles did their best for him; they did everything that could have been done. I've seen a good many Jackos in my lifetime. Later in life, when the boy has gone hopelessly wrong, the parents say, 'If only I'd been stricter with him when he was young,' or else they say, 'I was too harsh, if only I'd been kinder.' I don't think myself it amounts to a penn'orth of difference. There are those who go wrong because they've had an unhappy home and essentially feel unloved. And again there are those who go wrong because at the least stress they're going to go wrong anyway. I put Jacko down as one of the latter."

"So you weren't surprised," said Calgary, "when he was arrested for murder?"

"Frankly, yes, I was surprised. Not because the idea of murder would have been particularly repugnant to Jacko. He was the sort of young man who is conscienceless. But the *kind* of murder he'd done did surprise me. Oh, I know he had a violent temper and all that. As a child he often hurled himself on another child or hit him with some heavy toy or bit of wood. But it was usually a child smaller than himself, and it was usually not so much blind rage as the wish to hurt or get hold of something that he himself wanted. The kind of murder I'd have expected Jacko to do, if he did one, was the type where a couple of boys go out on a raid; then, when the police come after them, the Jackos say, 'Biff him on the head, bud. Let him have it. Shoot him down.' They're willing for murder, ready to incite to murder, but they've not got the nerve to do murder themselves with their own hands. That's what I should have said. Now it seems," added the doctor, "I would have been right."

Calgary stared down at the carpet, a worn carpet with hardly any of its pattern remaining.

"I didn't know," he said, "what I was up against. I didn't realise what it was going to mean to the others. I didn't see that it might—that it must—"

The doctor was nodding gently.

"Yes," he said. "It looks that way, doesn't it? It looks as though you've got to put it right there amongst them."

"I think," said Calgary, "that that's really what I came to talk to you about. There doesn't seem, on the face of it, any real motive for any of them to have killed her."

"Not on the face of it," agreed the doctor. "But if you go a little behind the face of it—oh, yes, I think there's plenty of reason why someone might have wanted to kill her."

"Why?" asked Calgary.

"You feel it's really your business, do you?"

"I think so. I can't help feeling so."

"Perhaps I should feel the same in your place . . . I don't know. Well, what I'd say is that none of them really belonged to themselves. Not so long as their mother—I'll call her that for convenience—was alive. She had a good hold of them still, you know, all of them."

"In what way?"

"Financially she'd provided for them. Provided for them handsomely. There was a large income. It was divided between them in such proportions as the Trustees thought fit. But although Mrs. Argyle herself was not one of the Trustees, nevertheless her wishes, so long as she was alive, were operative." He paused a minute and then went on.

"It's interesting in a way, how they all tried to escape. How they fought not to conform to the pattern that she'd arranged for them. Because she did arrange a pattern, and a very good pattern. She wanted to give them a good home, a good education, a good allowance and a good start in the professions that she chose for them. She wanted to treat them exactly as though they were hers and Leo Argyle's own children. Only of course they weren't hers and Leo Argyle's own children. They had entirely different instincts, feelings, aptitudes and demands. Young Micky now works as a car salesman. Hester more or less ran away from home to go on the stage. She fell in love with a very undesirable type and was absolutely no good as an actress. She had to come home. She had to admit—and she didn't like admitting—that her mother had been right. Mary Durrant insisted on marrying a man during the war whom her mother warned her not to marry. He was a brave and intelligent young man but an absolute fool when it came to business matters. Then he got polio. He was brought as a convalescent to Sunny Point. Mrs. Argyle was putting pressure on them to live there permanently. The husband was quite willing. Mary Durrant was holding out desperately against it. She wanted her home and her husband to herself. But she'd have given in, no doubt, if her mother hadn't died.

"Micky, the other boy, has always been a young man with a chip on his shoulder; he resented bitterly being abandoned by his own mother. He resented it as a child and he never got over it. I think, at heart, he always hated his adopted mother.

"Then there's the Swedish masseuse woman. She didn't like Mrs. Argyle. She was fond of the children and she's fond of Leo. She accepted many benefits from Mrs. Argyle and probably tried to be grateful but couldn't manage it. Still, I hardly think that her feelings of dislike could cause her to hit her benefactor on the head with a poker. After all, *she* could leave at any moment she liked. As for Leo Argyle—"

"Yes. What about him?"

"He's going to marry again," said Dr. MacMaster, "and good luck to him. A very nice young woman. Warm-hearted, kind, good company and very much in love with him. Has been for a long time. What did *she* feel about Mrs. Argyle? You can probably guess just as well as I can. Naturally, Mrs. Argyle's death simplified things a good deal. Leo Argyle's not the type of man to have an affair with his secretary with his wife in the same house. I don't really think he'd have left his wife, either."

Calgary said slowly:

"I saw them both; I talked to them; I can't really believe that either of them—"

"I know" said MacMaster. "One can't believe, can one? And yet—one of that household did it, you know."

"You really think so?"

"I don't see what else there is to think. The police are

63

fairly sure that it wasn't the work of an outsider, and the police are probably right."

"But which of them?" said Calgary.

MacMaster shrugged his shoulders. "One simply doesn't know."

"You've no idea yourself from your knowledge of them all?"

"Shouldn't tell you if I had," said MacMaster. "After all, what have I got to go on? Unless there's some factor that I've missed none of them seems a likely murderer to me. And yet—I can't rule any one of them out as a possibility. No," he added slowly, "my view is that we shall never know. The police will make enquiries and all that sort of thing. They'll do their best, but to get evidence after this time and with so little to go upon——" He shook his head. "No, I don't think that the truth will ever be known. There are cases like that, you know. One reads about them. Fifty—a hundred years ago, cases where one of three or four or five people must have done it but there wasn't enough evidence and no one's ever been able to say."

"Do you think it's going to be like that here?"

"We-ll," said Dr. MacMaster, "yes, I do. . . ." Again he cast a shrewd look at Calgary. "And that's what's so terrible, isn't it?" he said.

"Terrible," said Calgary, "because of the innocent. That's what she said to me."

"Who? Who said what to you?"

"The girl—Hester. She said I didn't understand that it was the innocent who mattered. It's what you've just been saying to me. That we shall never know——"

"—who is innocent?" The doctor finished for him. "Yes, if we could only know the truth. Even if it doesn't come to an arrest or trial or conviction. Just to *know*. Because otherwise——" He paused.

"Yes?" said Calgary.

"Work it out for yourself," said Dr. MacMaster. "No— I don't need to say that—you already have."

He went on:

"It reminds me, you know, of the Bravo Case—nearly a hundred years ago now, I suppose, but books are still being written about it; making out a perfectly good case for his wife having done it, or Mrs. Cox having done it, or Dr. Gully —or even for Charles Bravo having taken the poison in spite of the Coroner's verdict. All quite plausible theories—but no one now can ever know the truth. And so Florence Bravo, abandoned by her family, died alone of drink, and Mrs. Cox, ostracised, and with three little boys, lived to be an old woman with most of the people she knew believing her to be a murderess, and Dr. Gully was ruined professionally and socially—

"Someone was guilty—and got away with it. But the others were innocent—and didn't get away with anything."

"That mustn't happen here," said Calgary. "It mustn't!"

CHAPTER 8 . . .

HESTER ARGYLE was looking at herself in the glass. There was little vanity in her gaze. It was more an anxious questioning with behind it the humility of one who has never really been sure of herself. She pushed up her hair from her forehead, pulled it to one side and frowned at the result. Then, as a face appeared behind hers in the mirror, she started, flinched and swung round apprehensively.

"Ah," said Kirsten Lindstrom, "you are afraid!"

"What do you mean, afraid, Kirsty?"

"You are afraid of me. You think that I come up behind you quietly and that perhaps I shall strike you down."

"Oh, Kirsty, don't be so foolish. Of course I wouldn't think anything like that."

"But you did think it," said the other. "And you are right, too, to think such things. To look at the shadows, to start when you see something that you do not quite understand. Because there is something here in this house to be afraid of. We know that now."

"At any rate, Kirsty darling," said Hester, "I needn't be afraid of *you*."

"How do you know?" said Kirsten Lindstrom. "Did I not read in the paper a short while back of a woman who had lived with another woman for years, and then one day suddenly she kills her. Suffocates her. Tries to scratch her eyes out. And why? Because, she tells the police very gently, for some time she has seen that the devil is inhabiting the woman. She has seen the devil looking out of the other woman's eyes and she knows that she must be strong and brave and kill the devil!"

"Oh, well, I remember *that,*" said Hester. "But that woman was mad."

"Ah," said Kirsten. "But she did not know herself that she was mad. And she did not seem mad to those round her, because no one knew what was going on in her poor, twisted mind. And so I say to you, you do not know what is going on in *my* mind. Perhaps *I* am mad. Perhaps I looked one day at your mother and thought that she was Anti-Christ and that I would kill her."

"But, Kirsty, that's nonsense! Absolute nonsense."

Kirsten Lindstrom sighed and sat down.

"Yes," she admitted, "it is nonsense. I was very fond of your mother. She was good to me, always. But what I am trying to say to you, Hester, and what you have got to understand and believe, is that you cannot say 'nonsense' to anything or anyone. You cannot trust me or anybody else."

Hester turned round and looked at the other woman.

"I really believe you're serious," she said.

"I am very serious," said Kirsten. "We must all be serious and we must bring things out into the open. It is no good pretending that nothing has happened. That man who came here—I wish he had not come, but he did, and now he has made it, I understand, quite plain that Jacko was not a murderer. Very well then, someone else is a murderer, and that someone else must be one of us."

"No, Kirsty, no. It could have been someone who—"

"Who what?"

"Well, who wanted to steal something, or who had a grudge against Mother for some reason in the past."

"You think your mother would let that someone in?"

"She might," said Hester. "You know what she was like. If somebody came with a hard luck story, if someone came to tell her about some child that was being neglected or ill-treated. Don't you think Mother would have let that person in and taken them to her room and listened to what they had to say?"

"It seems to me very unlikely," said Kirsten. "At least it seems to me unlikely that your mother would sit down at a table and let that person pick up a poker and hit her on the back of the head. No, she was at her ease, confident, with someone she knew in the room."

"I wish you wouldn't, Kirsty," cried Hester. "Oh, I wish you wouldn't. You're bringing it so near, so close."

"Because it *is* near, it *is* close. No, I will not say any more now, but I have warned you that though you think you know someone well, though you may think you trust them, you cannot be sure. So be on your guard. Be on your guard against me and against Mary and against your father and against Gwenda Vaughan."

"How can I go on living here and suspecting everybody?"

"If you will take my advice it will be better for you to leave this house."

"I can't just now."

"Why not? Because of the young doctor?"

"I don't know what you mean, Kirsty." Colour flamed up in Hester's cheeks.

"I mean Dr. Craig. He is a very nice young man. A sufficiently good doctor, amiable, conscientious. You could do worse. But all the same I think it would be better if you left here and went away."

"The whole thing's nonsense," Hester cried angrily, "nonsense, nonsense, nonsense. Oh, how I wish Dr. Calgary had never come here."

"So do I," said Kirsten, "with all my heart."

ii.

Leo Argyle signed the last of the letters which Gwenda Vaughan placed in front of him.

"Is that the last?" he asked.

"Yes."

"We've not done too badly today."

After a minute or two when Gwenda had stamped and stacked the letters, she asked:

"Isn't it about time that you—took that trip abroad?"

"Trip abroad?"

Leo Argyle sounded very vague. Gwenda said:

"Yes. Don't you remember you were going to Rome and to Sienna."

"Oh, yes, yes, so I was."

"You were going to see those documents from the archives that Cardinal Massilini wrote to you about."

"Yes, I remember."

"Would you like me to make the reservations by air, or would you rather go by train?"

As though coming back from a long way away, Leo looked at her and smiled faintly.

"You seem very anxious to get rid of me, Gwenda," he said.

"Oh no, darling, oh no."

She came quickly across and knelt down by his side.

"I never want you to leave me, never. But—but I think—

oh, I think it would be better if you went away from here after—after . . ."

"After last week?" said Leo. "After Dr. Calgary's visit?"

"I wish he hadn't come here," said Gwenda. "I wish things could have been left as they were."

"With Jacko unjustly condemned for something he didn't do?"

"He might have done it," said Gwenda. "He might have done it any time, and it's a pure accident, I think, that he didn't do it."

"It's odd," said Leo, thoughtfully. "I never really could believe he did it. I mean, of course, I had to give in to the evidence—but it seemed to me so unlikely."

"Why? He always had a terrible temper, didn't he?"

"Yes. Oh, yes. He attacked other children. Usually children rather smaller than himself. I never really felt that he would have attacked Rachel."

"Why not?"

"Because he was afraid of her," said Leo. "She had great authority, you know. Jacko felt it just like everybody else."

"But don't you think," said Gwenda, "that that was just why—I mean—" She paused.

Leo looked at her questioningly. Something in his glance made the colour come up into her cheeks. She turned away, went over to the fire and knelt down in front of it with her hands to the blaze. "Yes," she thought to herself, "Rachel had authority all right. So pleased with herself, so sure of herself, so much the queen bee bossing us all. Isn't that enough to make one want to take a poker, to make one want to strike her down, to silence her once and for all? Rachel was always right, Rachel always knew best, Rachel always got her own way."

She got up abruptly.

"Leo," she said. "Couldn't we—couldn't we be married quite soon instead of waiting until March?"

Leo looked at her. He was silent for a moment, and then he said:

"No, Gwenda, no. I don't think that would be a good plan."

"Why not?"

"I think," said Leo, "it would be a pity to rush into anything."

"What do you mean?"

She came across to him. She knelt down again beside him.

"Leo, what *do* you mean? You must tell me."

He said:

"My dear, I just think that we mustn't, as I said, rush into anything."

"But we *will* be married in March, as we planned?"

"I hope so. . . . Yes, I hope so."

"You don't speak as though you were sure. . . . Leo, don't you care any more?"

"Oh, my dear," his hands rested on her shoulders, "of course I care. You mean everything in the world to me."

"Well, then," said Gwenda impatiently.

"No." He got up. "No. Not yet. We must wait. We must be sure."

"Sure of what?"

He did not answer. She said:

"You don't think—you can't think—"

Leo said: "I—I don't think anything."

The door opened and Kirsten Lindstrom came in with a tray which she put down on the desk.

"Here is your tea, Mr. Argyle. Shall I bring another cup for you, Gwenda, or will you join the others downstairs?"

Gwenda said:

"I will come down to the dining room. I'll take these letters. They ought to go off."

With slightly unsteady hands she picked up the letters Leo had just signed and went out of the room carrying them. Kirsten Lindstrom looked after her, then she looked back at Leo.

"What have you said to her?" she demanded. "What have you done to upset her?"

"Nothing," said Leo. His voice was tired. "Nothing at all."

Kirsten Lindstrom shrugged her shoulders. Then, without another word, she went out of the room. Her unseen, unspoken criticism, however, could be felt. Leo sighed, leaning back in his chair. He felt very tired. He poured out his tea but he did not drink it. Instead, he sat there in his chair staring unseeingly across the room, his mind busy in the past.

The social club he had been interested in in the East End of London. . . . It was there that he had first met Rachel Konstam. He could see her now clearly in his mind's eye. A girl of medium height, stocky in build, wearing what he had not appreciated at the time were very expensive clothes, but

70

wearing them with a dowdy air. A round-faced girl, serious, warm-hearted, with an eagerness and a naïveté which had appealed to him. So much that needed doing, so much that was worth doing! She had poured out words eagerly, rather incoherently, and his heart had warmed to her. For he, too, had felt that there was much that needed doing, much that was worth doing; though he himself had a gift of natural irony that made him doubtful whether work worth doing was always as successful as it ought to be. But Rachel had had no doubts. If you did this, if you did that, if such and such an institution were endowed, the beneficial results would follow automatically.

She had never allowed, he saw now, for human nature. She had seen people always as cases, as problems to be dealt with. She had never seen that each human being was different, would react differently, had its own peculiar idiosyncrasies. He had said to her then, he remembered, not to expect too much. But she had always expected too much, although she had immediately disclaimed his accusation. She had always expected too much, and so always she had been disappointed. He had fallen in love with her quite quickly, and had been agreeably surprised to find out that she was the daughter of wealthy parents.

They had planned their life together on a basis of high thinking and not precisely plain living. But he could see now clearly what it was that had principally attracted him to her. It was her warmth of heart. Only, and there was the tragedy, that warmth of heart had not really been for him. She had been in love with him, yes. But what she had really wanted from him and from life was children. And the children had not come.

They had visited doctors, reputable doctors, disreputable doctors, even quacks, and the verdict in the end had been one she was forced to accept. She would never have children of her own. He had been sorry for her, very sorry, and he had acquiesced quite willingly in her suggestion that they should adopt a child. They were already in touch with adoption societies when on the occasion of a visit to New York their car had knocked down a child running out from a tenement in the poorer quarter of the city.

Rachel had jumped out and knelt down in the street by the child who was only bruised, not hurt; a beautiful child, golden-haired and blue-eyed. Rachel had insisted on taking her to hospital to make sure there was no injury. She'd interviewed the child's relations; a slatternly aunt and the aunt's husband who obviously drank. It was clear that they had no feeling for the child they had taken in to live with them since her own parents were dead. Rachel had suggested that the child should come and stay with them for a few days, and the woman had agreed with alacrity.

"Can't look after her properly here," she'd said.

So Mary had been taken back to their suite at the hotel. The child had obviously enjoyed the soft bed and the luxurious bathroom. Rachel had bought her new clothes. Then the moment had come when the child had said:

"I don't want to go home. I want to stay here with you."

Rachel had looked at him, looked at him with a sudden passion of longing and delight. She had said to him as soon as they were alone:

"Let's keep her. It'll easily be arranged. We'll adopt her. She'll be our own child. That woman'll be only too pleased to be rid of her."

He had agreed easily enough. The child seemed quiet, wellbehaved, docile. She'd obviously no feeling for the aunt and uncle with whom she lived. If this would make Rachel happy, they'd go ahead. Lawyers were consulted, papers were signed and henceforth Mary O'Shaughnessy was known as Mary Argyle, and sailed with them for Europe. He had thought that at last poor Rachel would be happy. And she had been happy. Happy in an excited, almost feverish kind of way, doting on Mary, giving her every kind of expensive toy. And Mary had accepted placidly, sweetly. And yet, Leo thought, there had always been something that disturbed him a little. The child's easy acquiescence. Her lack of any kind of homesickness for her own place and people. True affection, he hoped, would come later. He could see no real signs of it now. Acceptance of benefits, complacence, enjoyment of all that was provided. But of love for her new adopted mother? No, he had not seen that.

It was from that time onwards, Leo thought, that he had somehow managed to slip to the background of Rachel Argyle's life. She was a woman who was by nature a mother, not a wife. Now with the acquiring of Mary, it was as though her maternal longings were not so much fulfilled as stimulated. One child was not enough for her.

All her enterprises from now on were connected with children. Her interest lay in orphanages, in endowments for crippled children, in cases of backward children, spastics, orthopaedics—always children. It was admirable. He felt all along that it was very admirable, but it had become the centre of her life. Little by little he began to indulge in his own activities. He began to go more deeply into the historical background of economics, which had always interested him. He withdrew more and more into his library. He engaged in research, in the writing of short, well phrased monographs. His wife, busy, earnest, happy, ran the house and increased her activities. He was courteous and acquiescent. He encouraged her. "That is a very fine project, my dear." "Yes, yes, I should certainly go ahead with that." Occasionally a word of caution was slipped in. "You want, I think, to examine the position very thoroughly before you commit yourself. You mustn't be carried away."

She continued to consult him, but sometimes now it was almost perfunctory. As time went on she was more and more an authoritarian. She knew what was right, she knew what was best. Courteously he withdrew his criticism and his occasional admonitions.

Rachel, he thought, needed no help from him, needed no love from him. She was busy, happy, terrifically energetic.

Behind the hurt that he could not help feeling, there was also, queerly enough, a sense of pity for her. It was as though he knew that the path she was pursuing might be a perilous one.

On the outbreak of war in 1939, Mrs. Argyle's activities were immediately redoubled. Once she had the idea of opening a war nursery for children from the London slums, she was in touch with many influential people in London. The Ministry of Health was quite willing to co-operate and she had looked for and found a suitable house for her purpose. A newly built, up to date, house in a remote part of England likely to be free from bombing. There she could accommodate up to eighteen children between the ages of two and seven. The children came not only from poor homes but also from unfortunate ones. They were orphans, or illegitimate children whose mothers had no intention of being evacuated with them and who were bored with looking after them. Children from homes where they had been ill-treated and neglected. Three or four of the children were cripples. For orthopaedic treatment she engaged as well as a staff of domestic workers, a Swedish masseuse and two fully trained hospital nurses. The whole thing was done not only on a comfortable but on a luxurious basis. Once he remonstrated with her.

"You mustn't forget, Rachel, these children will have to go back to the background from which we took them. You mustn't make it too difficult for them."

She had replied warmly:

"Nothing's too good for these poor mites. Nothing!"

He had urged, "Yes, but they've got to go *back*, remember."

But she had waved that aside. "It mayn't be necessary. It may—we'll have to see in the future."

The exigencies of war had soon brought changes. The hospital nurses, restive at looking after perfectly healthy children when there was real nursing to be done, had frequently to be replaced. In the end one elderly hospital nurse and Kirsten Lindstrom were the only two left. The domestic help failed and Kirsten Lindstrom had come to the rescue there also. She had worked with great devotion and selflessness.

And Rachel Argyle had been busy and happy. There had been, Leo remembered, moments of occasional bewilderment. The day when Rachel, puzzled at the way one small boy, Micky, was slowly losing weight, his appetite failing, had called in the doctor. The doctor could find nothing wrong but had suggested to Mrs. Argyle that the child might be homesick. Quickly she'd rebuffed the idea.

"That's impossible! You don't know the home he has come from. He was knocked about, ill-treated. It must have been hell for him."

"All the same," Dr. MacMaster had said, "all the same, I shouldn't be surprised. The thing is to get him to talk."

And one day Micky had talked. Sobbing in his bed, he cried out, pushing Rachel away with his fists:

"I want to go home. I want to go home to our Mom and our Ernie."

Rachel was upset, almost incredulous.

"He *can't* want his mother. She didn't care tuppence for him. She knocked him about whenever she was drunk."

And he had said gently: "But you're up against nature, Rachel. She is his mother and he loves her."

"She was no kind of a mother!"

74

"He is her own flesh and blood. That's what he feels. That's what nothing can replace."

And she had answered: "But by now, surely he ought to look on *me* as his mother."

Poor Rachel, thought Leo. Poor Rachel, who could buy so many things. . . . Not selfish things, not things for herself; who could give to unwanted children love, care, a home. All these things she could buy for them, but not their love for her.

Then the war had ended. The children had begun to drift back to London, claimed by parents or relatives. But not all of them. Some of them had remained unwanted and it was then that Rachel had said:

"You know, Leo, they're like our own children now. This is the moment when we can have a real family of our own. Four—five of these children can stay with us. We'll adopt them, provide for them and they'll really *be* our children."

He had felt a vague uneasiness, why he did not quite know. It was not that he objected to the children, but he had felt instinctively the falseness of it. The assumption that it was easy to make a family of one's own by artificial means.

"Don't you think," he had said, "that it's rather a risk?"

But she had replied:

"A risk? What does it matter if it is a risk? It's worth doing."

Yes, he supposed it was worth doing, only he was not quite as sure as she was. By now he had grown so far away, so aloof in some cold misty region of his own, that is was not in him to object. He said as he had said so many times:

"You must do as you please, Rachel."

She had been full of triumph, full of happiness, making her plans, consulting solicitors, going about things in her usual business-like way. And so she had acquired her family. Mary, that eldest child brought from New York; Micky, the homesick boy who had cried himself to sleep for so many nights, longing for his slum home and his negligent, bad-tempered mother; Tina, the graceful dark half-caste child whose mother was a prostitute and whose father had been a Lascar seaman. Hester, whose young Irish mother had borne an illegitimate child and who wanted to start life again. And Jacko, the engaging, monkey-faced little boy whose antics made them all laugh, who could always talk himself out of punishment, and charm extra sweets even from that disciplinarian, Miss Lindstrom. Jacko, whose father was serving a prison sentence and whose mother had gone off with some other man.

Yes, Leo thought, surely it was a worth while job to take these children, to give them the benefits of a home and love and a father and mother. Rachel, he thought, had had a right to be triumphant. Only it hadn't worked out quite the way it was supposed to do. . . . For these children were not the children that he and Rachel would have had. Within them ran none of the blood of Rachel's hard-working thrifty forebears, none of the drive and ambition by which the less reputable members of her family had gained their assured place in society, none of the vague kindliness and integrity of mind that he remembered in his own father and grandfather and grandmother. None of the intellectual brilliance of his grandparents on the other side.

Everything that environment could do was done for them. It could do a great deal, but it could not do everything. There had been those seeds of weakness which had brought them to the nursery in the first place, and under stress those seeds might bear flower. That was exemplified very fully in Jacko. Jacko, the charming agile Jacko, with his merry quips, his charm, his easy habit of twisting everyone round his finger, was essentially of a delinquent type. It showed very early in childish thieving, in lies; all things that were put down to his original bad upbringing. Things that could be, Rachel said, easily ironed out. But they never did get ironed out.

His record at school was bad. He was sent down from the university and from then it was a long series of painful incidents where he and Rachel, doing the best they could, tried to give the boy assurance of their love and their confidence, tried to find work that would be congenial to him where he could hope for success if he applied himself. Perhaps, Leo thought, they had been too soft with him. But no. Soft or hard, in Jacko's case, he thought the end would have been the same. What he wanted he must have. If he could not get it by any legitimate means he was quite willing to get it by any other means. He was not clever enough to be successful in crime, even petty crime. And so it had come to that last day when he had arrived broke, in fear of prison, angrily demanding money as his right, threatening. He had gone away, shouting out that he was coming back and that she had better have the money ready for him—*or else!*

And so—Rachel had died. How remote all the past seemed to him. All those long years of the war with the boys and girls growing up. And he himself? Also remote, colourless. It was as though that robust energy and zest for life that was Rachel had eaten into him, leaving him limp and exhausted, needing, oh so badly, warmth and love.

Even now he could hardly remember when he had first become aware how close these things were to him. Close at hand . . . not proffered to him, but there.

Gwenda. . . . The perfect, helpful secretary, working for him, always at hand, kind, helpful. There was something about her that had reminded him of what Rachel had been when he first met her. The same warmth, the same enthusiasm, the same warm-heartedness. Only in Gwenda's case, that warmth, that warm-heartedness, that enthusiasm were all for *him*. Not for the hypothetical children that she might one day have, just for him. It had been like warming one's hands at a fire. . . . Hands that were cold and stiff with disuse. When had he first realized that she cared for him? It was difficult to say. It had not been any sudden revelation.

But suddenly—one day—he had known that he loved her. And that as long as Rachel lived, they could never marry.

Leo sighed, sat up in his chair and drank his stone-cold tea.

CHAPTER 9

CALGARY HAD only been gone a few minutes when Dr. Mac-Master received a second visitor. This one was well known to him and he greeted him with affection.

"Ah, Don, glad to see you. Come in and tell me what's on your mind. There is something on your mind. I always know when your forehead wrinkles in that peculiar way."

Dr. Donald Craig smiled at him ruefully. He was a good-looking serious young man who took himself and his work in a serious manner. The old retired doctor was very fond of his young successor though there were times when he wished that it was easier for Donald Craig to see a joke.

Craig refused the offer of a drink and came straight to the point.

"I'm badly worried, Mac."

"Not more vitamin deficiencies, I hope," said Dr. Mac-Master. From his point of view vitamin deficiency had been a good joke. It had once taken a veterinary surgeon to point out to young Craig that the cat belonging to a certain child patient was suffering with an advanced case of ringworm.

"It's nothing to do with the patients," said Donald Craig. "It's my own private affairs."

MacMaster's face changed immediately.

"I'm sorry, my boy. Very sorry. Have you had bad news?"

The young man shook his head.

"It's not that. It's—look here, Mac. I've got to talk to someone about it and you know them all, you've been here for years, you know all about them. And I've got to know too. I've got to know where I stand, what I'm up against."

MacMaster's bushy eyebrows rose slowly up his forehead.

"Let's hear the trouble," he said.

"It's the Argyles. You know—I suppose everyone knows—that Hester Argyle and I—"

The old doctor nodded his head.

"A nice little understanding," he said approvingly. "That's

78

the old-fashioned term they used to use, and it was a very good one."

"I'm terribly in love with her," Donald said simply, "and I think—oh, I'm sure—that she cares too. And now all this happens."

A look of enlightenment came into the older doctor's face.

"Ah yes! Free pardon for Jacko Argyle," he said. "A free pardon that's come too late for him."

"Yes. That's just what makes me feel—I know it's an entirely wrong thing to feel, but I can't help it—that it would have been better if—if this new evidence hadn't come to light."

"Oh, you're not the only one who seems to feel that," said MacMaster. "It's felt, as far as I can find out, from the Chief Constable through the Argyle family down to the man who came back from the Antarctic and supplied the evidence." He added: "He's been here this afternoon."

Donald Craig looked startled.

"Has he? Did he say anything?"

"What did you expect him to say?"

"Did he have any idea of who—"

Slowly Dr. MacMaster shook his head.

"No," he said. "He's no idea. How could he have—coming out of the blue and seeing them all for the first time? It seems," he went on, "that nobody has any idea."

"No. No, I suppose not."

"What's upset you so much, Don?"

Donald Craig drew a deep breath.

"Hester rang me up that evening when this fellow Calgary had been there. She and I were going in to Drymouth after the surgery to hear a lecture on criminal types in Shakespeare."

"Sounds particularly suitable," said MacMaster.

"And then she rang me up. Said she wouldn't be coming. Said there had been news of a peculiar upsetting type."

"Ah. Dr. Calgary's news."

"Yes. Yes, although she didn't mention him at the time. But she was very upset. She sounded—I can't explain to you how she sounded."

"Irish blood," said MacMaster.

"She sounded altogether stricken, terrified. Oh, I can't explain it."

"Well, what do you expect?" the doctor asked. "She's not yet twenty, is she?"

"But *why* is she so upset? I tell you, Mac, she's scared stiff of something."

"M'm, yes, well—yes, that might be so, I suppose," said MacMaster.

"Do you think—what do you think?"

"It's more to the point," MacMaster pointed out, "what you are thinking."

The young man said bitterly:

"I suppose, if I wasn't a doctor, I shouldn't even begin to think of such things. She'd be my girl and my girl could do no wrong. But as it is—"

"Yes—come on. You'd better get it off your chest."

"You see, I know something of what goes on in Hester's mind. She—she's a victim of early insecurity."

"Quite so," said MacMaster. "That's the way we put it nowadays."

"She hasn't had time yet to get properly integrated. She was suffering, at the time of the murder, from a perfectly natural feeling of an adolescent young woman—resentment of authority—an attempt to escape from smother-love which is responsible for so much harm nowadays. She wanted to rebel, to get away. She's told me all this herself. She ran away and joined a fourth-class touring theatrical company. Under the circumstances I think her mother behaved very reasonably. She suggested that Hester should go to London and go to RADA and study acting properly if she wanted to do so. But that wasn't what Hester wanted to do. This running away to act was just a gesture really. She didn't really want to train for the stage, or to take up the profession seriously. She just wanted to show she could be on her own. Anyway, the Argyles didn't try to coerce her. They gave her a quite handsome allowance."

"Which was very clever of them," said MacMaster.

"And then she had this silly love affair with a middle-aged member of the company. In the end she realised for herself that he was no good. Mrs. Argyle came along and dealt with him and Hester came home."

"Having learnt her lesson, as they used to say in my young days," said MacMaster. "But of course one never liked learning one's lesson. Hester didn't."

Donald Craig went on anxiously:

"She was full, still, of pent-up resentment; all the worse because she had to acknowledge secretly, if not openly, that her mother had been perfectly right; that she was no good as an actress and that the man she had lavished her affections on wasn't worth it. And that, anyway, she didn't really care for him. 'Mother knows best.' It's always galling to the young."

"Yes," said MacMaster. "That was one of poor Mrs. Argyle's troubles, though she'd never have thought of it like that. The fact was she *was* nearly always right, that she *did* know best. If she'd been one of those women who run into debt, lose their keys, miss trains, and do foolish actions that other people have to help them out of, her entire family would have been much fonder of her. Sad and cruel, but there's life for you. And she wasn't a clever enough woman to get her own way by guile. She was complacent, you know. Pleased with her own power and judgment and quite, quite sure of herself. That's a very difficult thing to come up against when you're young."

"Oh, I know," said Donald Craig. "I realise all that. It's because I realise it so well that I feel—that I wonder—" He stopped.

MacMaster said gently:

"I'd better say it for you, hadn't I, Don? You're afraid that it was your Hester who heard the quarrel between her mother and Jacko, who got worked up by hearing it, perhaps, and who, in a fit of rebellion against authority, and against her mother's superior assumption of omniscience, went into that room, picked up the poker and killed her. That's what you're afraid of, isn't it?"

The young man nodded miserably.

"Not really. I don't really believe it, but—but I feel—I feel that it *could* have happened. I don't feel Hester has got the poise, the balance to—I feel she's young for her age, uncertain of herself, liable to have brainstorms. I look at that household and I don't feel that any of them are likely to have done such a thing until I come to Hester. And then —then I'm not sure."

"I see," said Dr. MacMaster. "Yes, I see."

"I don't really blame her," said Don Craig quickly. "I don't think the poor child really knew what she was doing. I can't call it murder. It was just an act of emotional defiance, of rebellion, of a longing to be free, of the conviction that she would never be free until—until her mother wasn't there any longer."

"And that last is probably true enough," said MacMaster. "It's the only kind of motive there is, and it's rather a peculiar one. Not the kind that looks strong in the eyes of the law. Wishing to be free. Free from the impact of a stronger personality. Just because none of them inherits a large sum of money on the death of Mrs. Argyle the law won't consider that they had a motive. But even the financial control, I should imagine, was very largely in Mrs. Argyle's hands through her influence with the Trustees. Oh yes, her death set them free all right. Not only Hester, my boy. It set Leo free to marry another woman. It set Mary free to look after her husband in the way she liked, it set Micky free to live his own life in the way he cared about living it. Even little dark horse Tina sitting in her library may have wanted freedom."

"I had to come and talk to you," said Donald. "I had to know what you thought, whether you thought that—that it could be true."

"About Hester?"

"Yes."

"I think it *could* be true," said MacMaster slowly. "I don't know that it is."

"You think it could have happened just as I say?"

"Yes. I think what you've imagined is not far-fetched and has an element of probability about it. But it's by no means certain, Donald."

The young man gave a shuddering sigh.

"But it's *got* to be certain, Mac. That's the one thing I do feel is necessary. I've got to *know*. If Hester tells me, if she tells me herself, then—then it will be all right. We'll get married as soon as possible. I'll look after her."

"It's as well Superintendent Huish can't hear you," said MacMaster dryly.

"I'm a law-abiding citizen as a rule," said Donald, "but you know very well yourself, Mac, how they treat psychological evidence in the law courts. In my view it was a bad accident, not a case of cold-blooded murder, or even hot-blooded murder for that matter."

"You're in love with the girl," said MacMaster.

"I'm talking to you in confidence, mind."

"I understand that," said MacMaster.

"All I'm saying is that if Hester tells me, and I know, we'll live it down together. But she must tell me. I can't go through life not knowing."

"You mean, you're not prepared to marry her with this probability overshadowing things?"

"Would you want to in my place?"

"I don't know. In my day, if it happened to me, and I was in love with the girl, I should probably be convinced she was innocent."

"It's not so much the guilt or innocence that matters, as that I've got to *know*."

"And if she did kill her mother, you're quite prepared to marry her and live happily ever afterwards, as they say?"

"Yes."

"Don't you believe it!" said MacMaster. "You'll be wondering if the bitter taste in your coffee is only coffee and thinking that the poker in the grate is a bit too hefty a size. And she'll see you thinking it. It won't do . . ."

CHAPTER 10

"I'M SURE, Marshall, that you'll appreciate my reasons for asking you to come here and have this conference."

"Yes, certainly," said Mr. Marshall. "The fact is that if you had not proposed it, Mr. Argyle, I should myself have suggested coming down. The announcement was in all the morning papers this morning and there is no doubt at all that it will lead to a revival of interest in the case on the part of the press."

"We've already had a few of them ringing up and asking for interviews," said Mary Durrant.

"Quite so, it was only to be expected, I feel. I should advise that you take up the position that you have no comment to make. Naturally you are delighted and thankful, but you prefer not to discuss the matter."

"Superintendent Huish, who was in charge of the case at the time, has asked to come and have an interview with us tomorrow morning," said Leo.

"Yes. Yes, I'm afraid there will have to be a certain amount of reopening of the case, though I really cannot think that the police can have much hope of arriving at any tangible result. After all, two years have passed and anything that people might have remembered at the time—people in the village, I mean—will by now have been forgotten. A pity, of course, in some ways, but it can't be helped."

"The whole thing seems quite clear," said Mary Durrant. "The house was securely locked up against burglars but if anyone had come appealing to my mother over some special case or pretending to be a friend or friends of hers I have no doubt that person would have been admitted. That, I think, is what must have happened. My father here thought he heard a ring at the bell just after seven o'clock."

Marshall turned his head enquiringly to Leo.

"Yes, I think I did say so," said Leo. "Of course, I can't remember very clearly now, but at the time I was under the impression that I heard the bell. I was ready to go down and then I thought I heard the door open and close. There was no sound of voices or any question of anyone forcing an entry or behaving abusively. That I think I should have heard."

"Quite so, quite so," said Mr. Marshall. "Yes, I think there's no doubt that that is what must have happened. Alas, we know only too well the large number of unprincipled persons gaining admission to a house by a plausible tale of distress, and who having gained admission are willing to cosh the householder and make off with what money they can find. Yes, I think that we must assume now that that is what did happen."

He spoke in too persuasive a voice. He looked round the little assembly as he spoke, noting them carefully, and labelling them in his meticulous mind. Mary Durrant, good-looking, unimaginative, untroubled, even slightly aloof, apparently quite sure of herself. Behind her in his wheel-chair, her husband. An intelligent fellow, Philip Durrant, Marshall thought to himself. A man who might have done a good deal and gone far had it not been for his unreliable judgment in all matters of business. He was not, Marshall thought, taking all this as calmly as his wife was. His eyes were alert and thoughtful. He realised, none better, the implications of the whole matter. Of course, though, Mary Durrant might not be as calm as she appeared to be. Both as a girl and a woman, she had always been able to conceal her feelings.

As Philip Durrant moved slightly in his chair, his bright, intelligent eyes watching the lawyer with a faint mockery in them, Mary turned her head sharply. The complete adoration of the look she gave her husband almost startled the lawyer. He had known, of course, that Mary Durrant was a devoted wife, but he had so long considered her as a calm, rather passionless creature without strong affections or dislikes that he was surprised at this sudden revelation. So that was how she felt about the fellow, was it? As for Philip Durrant, he seemed uneasy. Apprehensive, Marshall thought, about the future. As well he might be!

Opposite the lawyer sat Micky. Young, handsome, bitter. Why had he got to be so bitter, Marshall thought parenthetically? Hadn't everything been done for him always? Why did he have to have this look of one who was perpetually against the world? Beside him sat Tina looking rather like a small elegant black cat. Very dark, soft-voiced, big dark eyes and a rather sinuous grace of movement. Quiet, yet perhaps emotional behind the quietness. Marshall really knew very little about Tina. She had taken up the work suggested to her by Mrs. Argyle, as a librarian in the County library. She had a flat in Redmyn and came home at weekends. Apparently a docile and contented member of the family. But who knew? Anyway, she was out of it or ought to be. She had not been here that evening. Though, for all that, Redmyn was only twenty-five miles away. Still presumably Tina and Micky had been out of it.

Marshall swept a quick glance over Kirsten Lindstrom, who was watching him with a touch of belligerence in her manner. Supposing, he thought, it was *she* who had gone berserk and attacked her employer It wouldn't really surprise him. Nothing really surprised you when you'd been in the law a number of years. They'd have a word for it in the modern jargon. Repressed spinster. Envious, jealous, nursing grievances real or fancied. Oh yes, they had a word for it. And how very convenient it would be, thought Mr. Marshall rather improperly. Yes, very convenient. A foreigner. Not one of the family. But would Kirsten Lindstrom have deliberately framed Jacko; have heard the quarrel and taken advantage of it? That was a great deal more difficult to believe. For Kirsten Lindstrom adored Jacko. She had always been devoted to all the children. No, he could not believe that of her. A pity because—but really he must not let his thoughts go along that line.

His glance went on to Leo Argyle and Gwenda Vaughan. Their engagement had not been announced, which was just as well. A wise decision. He had actually written and hinted as much. Of course it was probably an open secret locally and no doubt the police were on to it. From the point of view of the police it was the right kind of answer. Innumerable precedents. Husband, wife, and the other woman. Only, somehow or other, Marshall could not believe that Leo Argyle had attacked his wife. No, he really couldn't believe it. After all, he had known Leo Argyle for a number of years and he had the highest opinion of him. An intellectual. A man of warm sympathies, deep reading and an aloof philosophical outlook upon life. Not the sort of man to murder his wife with a poker. Of course, at a certain age, when a man fell in love—but no! That was newspaper stuff. Pleasant reading, apparently, for Sundays, all over the British Isles! But really, one could not imagine Leo . . .

What about the woman? He didn't know so much about Gwenda Vaughan. He observed the full lips and the ripe figure. She was in love with Leo all right. Oh yes, probably been in love with him for a long time. What about a divorce, he wondered. What would Mrs. Argyle have felt about divorce? Really he had no idea, but he didn't think the idea would appeal to Leo Argyle, who was one of the old-fashioned type. He didn't think that Gwenda Vaughan was Leo Argyle's mistress, which made it all the more probable that if Gwenda Vaughan had seen a chance to eliminate Mrs. Argyle with the certainty that no suspicion would attach to her—he paused before continuing the thought. Would she have sacrificed Jacko without a qualm? He didn't really think she had ever been very fond of Jacko. Jacko's charm had not appealed to her. And women—Mr. Marshall knew only too well—were ruthless. So one couldn't rule out Gwenda Vaughan. It was very doubtful after this time if the police would ever get any evidence. He didn't see what evidence there could be against her. She had been in the house that day, she had been with Leo in his library, she had said good night to him and left him and gone down the stairs. There was no one who could say whether or not she had gone aside into Mrs. Argyle's sitting room, picked up that poker and walked up behind the unsuspecting woman as she bent over papers on the desk. And then afterwards, Mrs. Argyle having been struck down without a cry, all Gwenda Vaughan had to do was to throw down the poker and let herself out of the front door and go home, just as she always did. He couldn't see any possibility of the police or anyone else finding out if that was what she had done.

His eyes went on to Hester. A pretty child. No, not pretty, beautiful really. Beautiful in a rather strange and uncomfortable way. He'd like to know who her parents had been. Something lawless and wild about her. Yes, one could almost use the word desperate in connection with her. What had she had to be desperate about? She'd run away in a silly way to go on the stage and had had a silly affair with an undesirable man; then she had seen reason, come home with Mrs. Argyle and settled down again. All the same, you couldn't really rule out Hester, because you didn't know how her mind worked. You didn't know what a strange moment of desperation might do to her. But the police wouldn't know either.

In fact, thought Mr. Marshall, it seemed very unlikely

that the police, even if they made up their own minds as to who was responsible, could really do anything about it. So that on the whole the position was satisfactory. Satisfactory? He gave a little start as he considered the word. But was it? Was stalemate really a satisfactory outcome to the whole thing? Did the Argyles know the truth themselves, he wondered. He decided against that. They didn't know. Apart, of course, from one person amongst them who presumably knew only too well. . . . No, they didn't know, but did they suspect? Well, if they didn't suspect now, they soon would, because if you didn't know you couldn't help wondering, trying to remember things. . . . Uncomfortable. Yes, yes, a very uncomfortable position.

All these thoughts had not taken very much time. Mr. Marshall came out of his little reverie to see Micky's eyes fixed on him with a mocking gleam in them.

"So that's your verdict, is it, Mr. Marshall?" Micky said. "The outsider, the unknown intruder, the bad character who murders, robs and gets away with it?"

"It seems," said Mr. Marshall, "as though that is what we will have to accept."

Micky threw himself back in his chair and laughed.

"That's our story, and we're going to stick to it, eh?"

"Well, yes, Michael, that is what I should advise." There was a distinct note of warning in Mr. Marshall's voice.

Micky nodded his head.

"I see," he said. "That's what you advise. Yes. Yes, I dare say you're quite right. But you don't believe it, do you?"

Mr. Marshall gave him a very cold look. That was the trouble with people who had no legal sense of discretion. They insisted on saying things which were much better not said.

"For what it is worth," he said, "that is my opinion."

The finality of his tone held a world of reproof. Micky looked round the table.

"What do we all think?" he asked generally. "Eh, Tina, my love, looking down your nose in your quiet way, haven't you any ideas? Any unauthorised versions, so to speak? And you, Mary? You haven't said much."

"Of course I agree with Mr. Marshall," said Mary rather sharply. "What other solution can there be?"

"Philip doesn't agree with you," said Micky.

Mary turned her head sharply to look at her husband. Philip Durrant said quietly:

"You'd better hold your tongue, Micky. No good ever came of talking too much when you're in a tight place. And we are in a tight place."

"So nobody's going to have any opinions, are they?" said Micky. "All right. So be it. But let's all think about it a bit when we go up to bed tonight. It might be advisable, you know. After all, one wants to know where one is, so to speak. Don't you know a thing or two, Kirsty? You usually do. As far as I remember, you always knew what was going on, though I will say for you, you never told."

Kirsten Lindstrom said, not without dignity:

"I think, Micky, that you should hold your tongue. Mr. Marshall is right. Too much talking is unwise."

"We might put it to the vote," said Micky. "Or write a name on a piece of paper and throw it into a hat. That would be interesting, wouldn't it; to see who got the votes?"

This time Kirsten Lindstrom's voice was louder.

"Be quiet," she said. "Do not be a silly, reckless little boy as you used to be. You are grown up now."

"I only said let's think about it," said Micky, taken aback.

"We shall think about it," said Kirsten Lindstrom.

And her voice was bitter.

CHAPTER **11 . . .**

NIGHT SETTLED down on Sunny Point.

Sheltered by its walls seven people retired to rest, but none of them slept well. . . .

Philip Durrant, since his illness and his loss of bodily activity, had found more and more solace in mental activity. Always a highly intelligent man, he now became conscious of the resources opening out to him through the medium of intelligence. He amused himself sometimes by forecasting the reactions of those around him to suitable stimuli. What he said and did was often not a natural outpouring, but a calculated one, motivated simply and solely to observe the response to it. It was a kind of game that he played; when he got the anticipated response, he chalked up, as it were, a mark to himself.

As a result of this pastime he found himself, for perhaps the first time in his life, keenly observant of the differences and realities of human personality.

Human personalities as such had not previously interested him very much. He liked or disliked, was amused or bored by, the people who surrounded him or whom he met. He had always been a man of action, and not a man of thought. His imagination, which was considerable, had been exercised in devising various schemes for making money. All these schemes had a sound core; but a complete lack of business ability always resulted in their coming to nothing. People, as such, had up till now only been considered by him as pawns in the game. Now, since his illness, cut off from his former active life, he was forced to take account of what people themselves were like.

It had started in the hospital when the love lives of the nurses, the secret warfare and the petty grievances of hospital life had been forced on his attention since there was nothing else to occupy it. And now it was fast becoming a habit with him. People—really that was all that life held for him now. Just people. People to study, to find out about, to sum up. Decide for himself what made them tick and find out if he was right. Really, it could all be very interesting. . . .

Only this very evening, sitting in the library, he had realised how little he really knew about his wife's family. What were they really like? What were they like inside, that is, not their outer appearance which he knew well enough.

Odd, how little you knew about people. Even your own wife?

He had looked thoughtfully over at Mary. How much did he really know about Mary?

He had fallen in love with her because he liked her good looks and her calm serious ways. Also, she had had money and that had mattered to him too. He would have thought twice about marrying a penniless girl. It had all been most suitable and he had married her and teased her and called her Polly and had enjoyed the doubtful look she gave him when he made jokes she could not see. But what, really, did he *know* about her Of what she thought and felt? He knew, certainly, that she loved him with a deep and passionate devotion. And at the thought of that devotion he stirred a little uneasily, twisting his shoulders as though to ease them of a burden. Devotion was all very well when you could get away from it for nine or ten hours of the day. It was a nice thing to come home to. But now he was lapped round with it; watched over, cared for, cherished. It made one yearn for a little wholesome neglect. . . . One had, in fact, to find ways of escape. Mental ways—since none other were possible. One had to escape to realms of fancy or speculation.

Speculation. As to who was responsible for his mother-in-law's death, for instance. He had disliked his mother-in-law, and she had disliked him. She had not wanted Mary to marry him (would she have wanted Mary to marry anybody? he wondered), but she had not been able to prevent it. He and Mary had started life happy and independent—and then things had begun to go wrong. First that South American company—and then the Bicycle Accessories Ltd.—good ideas both of them—but the financing of them had been badly judged—and then there had been the Argentine railway strike which had completed the disasters. All purely bad luck, but in some way he felt that somehow Mrs. Argyle was responsible. She hadn't wished him to succeed. Then had come his illness. It had looked as though their only solution

91

was to come and live at Sunny Point where a welcome was assured to them. He wouldn't have minded particularly. A man who was a cripple, only half a man, what did it matter where he was?—but Mary would have minded.

Oh well, it hadn't been necessary to live permanently at Sunny Point. Mrs. Argyle had been killed. The trustees had raised the allowance made to Mary under the trust and they had set up on their own again.

He hadn't felt any particular grief over Mrs. Argyle's death. Pleasanter, of course, if she had died of pneumonia or something like that, in her bed. Murder was a nasty business with its notoriety and its screaming headlines. Still, as murders go, it had been quite a satisfactory murder—the perpetrator obviously having a screw loose in a way that could be served up decently in a lot of psychological jargon. Not Mary's own brother. One of those "adopted children" with a bad heredity who so often go wrong. But things weren't quite so good now. Tomorrow Superintendent Huish was coming to ask questions in his gentle West Country voice. One ought, perhaps, to think about the answers. . . .

Mary was brushing her long fair hair in front of the mirror. Something about her calm remoteness irritated him.

He said: "Got your story pat for tomorrow, Polly?"

She turned astonished eyes upon him.

"Superintendent Huish is coming. He'll ask you all over again just what your movements were on the evening of November 9th."

"Oh, I see. It's so long ago now. One can hardly remember."

"But *he* can, Polly. That's the point. *He* can. It's all written down somewhere in a nice little police notebook."

"Is it? Do they keep these things?"

"Probably keep everything in triplicate for ten years! Well, your movements are very simple, Polly. There weren't any. You were here with me in this room. And if I were you I shouldn't mention that you left it between seven and seven-thirty."

"But that was only to go to the bathroom. After all," said Mary reasonably, "everyone has to go to the bathroom."

"You didn't mention the fact to him at the time. I do remember that."

"I suppose I forgot about it."

"I thought it might have been an instinct of self-preservation. . . . Anyway, I remember backing you up. We were together here, playing picquet from six-thirty until Kirsty gave the alarm. That's our story and we're sticking to it."

"Very well, darling." Her agreement was placid—uninterested.

He thought: "Has she no imagination? Can't she foresee that we're in for a sticky time?"

He leaned forward.

"It's interesting, you know. . . . Aren't *you* interested in who killed her? We all know—Micky was quite right there—that it's one of us. Aren't you interested to know which?"

"It wasn't you or I," said Mary.

"And that's all that interests you? Polly, you're wonderful!"

She flushed slightly.

"I don't see what's so odd about that?"

"No, I can see you don't. . . . Well, I'm different. I'm curious."

"I don't suppose we ever shall know. I don't suppose the police will ever know."

"Perhaps not. They'll certainly have precious little to go upon. But we're in rather a different position to the police."

"What do you mean, Philip?"

"We'll, we've got a few bits of inside knowledge. We know our little lot from inside—have a fairly good idea of what makes them tick. You should have, anyway. You've grown up with them all. Let's hear your views. Who do *you* think it was?"

"I've no idea, Philip."

"Then just make a guess."

Mary said sharply:

"I'd rather not know who did it. I'd rather not even think about it."

"Ostrich," said her husband.

"Honestly, I don't see the point of—guessing. It's much better not to know. Then we can all go on as usual."

"Oh no, we can't," said Philip. "That's where you're wrong, my girl. The rot's set in already."

"What do you mean?"

"Well, take Hester and her young man—earnest young Doctor Donald. Nice chap, serious, worried. He doesn't really think she did it—but he's not really sure she didn't do it! And so he looks at her, anxiously, when he thinks she isn't noticing. But she notices all right. So there you are!

Perhaps she *did* do it—you'd know better than I would—but if she didn't, what the hell can she do about her young man? Keep on saying: 'Please, it wasn't me?' But that's what she'd say anyway."

"Really, Philip, I think you're imagining things."

"*You* can't imagine at all, Polly. Then take poor old Leo. Marriage bells with Gwenda are receding into the distance. The girl's horribly upset about it. Haven't you noticed?"

"I really don't see what Father wants to marry again for at his age."

"He sees all right! But he also sees that any hint of a love affair with Gwenda gives both of them a first-class motive for murder. Awkward!"

"It's fantastic to think for a moment that Father murdered Mother!" said Mary. "Such things don't happen."

"Yes, they do. Read the papers."

"Not our sort of people."

"Murder is no snob, Polly. Then there's Micky. Something's eating him all right. He's a queer, bitter lad. Tina seems in the clear, unworried, unaffected. But she's a little poker face if ever there was one. Then there's poor old Kirsty—"

A faint animation came into Mary's face.

"Now that *might* be a solution!"

"Kirsty?"

"Yes. After all, she's a foreigner. And I believe she's had very bad headaches the last year or two. . . . It seems much more likely that she should have done it than any of us."

"Poor devil," said Philip. "Don't you see that that's just what she is saying to herself? That we'll all agree together that she's the one? For convenience. Because she's not a member of the family. Didn't you see tonight that she was worried stiff? And she's in the same position as Hester. What can she say or do? Say to us all: 'I did *not* kill my friend and employer'? What weight can that statement carry? It's worse hell for her, perhaps, than for anyone else. . . . Because she's alone. She'll be going over in her mind every word she's ever said, every angry look she ever gave your mother—thinking that it will be remembered against her. Helpless to prove her innocence."

"I wish you'd calm down, Phil. After all, what can *we* do about it?"

"Only try to find out the truth."

"But how is that possible?"

"There might be ways. I'd rather like to try."

Mary looked uneasy.

"What sort of ways?"

"Oh, saying things—watching how people react—one could think up things"—he paused, his mind working—"things that would mean something to a guilty person, but not to an innocent one. . . ." Again he was silent, turning ideas over in his mind. He looked up and said: "Don't you want to help the innocent, Mary?"

"No." The word came out explosively. She came over to him and knelt by his chair. "I don't want you to mix yourself up in all this, Phil. Don't start saying things and laying traps. Leave it all alone. Oh, for God's sake, leave it *alone!*"

Philip's eyebrows rose.

"We-ell," he said. And he laid a hand on the smooth golden head.

ii.

Michael Argyle lay sleepless, staring into darkness.

His mind went round and round like a squirrel in a cage, going over the past. Why couldn't he leave it behind him? Why did he have to drag the past with him all through his life? What did it all matter anyway? Why did he have to remember so clearly the frowsty, cheerful room in the London slum, and he "our Micky." The casual exciting atmosphere! Fun in the streets! Ganging up on other boys! His mother with her bright golden head (cheap rinse, he thought, in his adult wisdom), her sudden furies when she would turn and lambaste him (gin, of course!) and the wild gaiety she had when she was in a good mood. Lovely suppers of fish and chips, and she'd sing songs—sentimental ballads. Sometimes they'd go to the pictures. There were always the Uncles, of course—that's what he always had to call them. His own dad had walked out before he could remember him. . . . But his mother wouldn't stand for the Uncle of the day laying a hand on him. "You leave our Micky alone," she'd say.

And then there had come the excitement of the war. Expecting Hitler's bombers—abortive sirens. Moaning Minnies. Going down into the Tubes and spending the nights there. The fun of it! The whole street was there with their sandwiches and their bottles of pop. And trains rushing through practically all night. That had been life, that had! In the thick of things!

And then he'd come down here—to the country. A dead and alive place where nothing ever happened!

"You'll come back, love, when it's all over," his mother had said, but lightly as though it wasn't really true. She hadn't seemed to care about his going. And why didn't she come too? Lots of the kids in the street had been evacuated with their Mums. But his mother hadn't wanted to go. She was going to the North (with the current Uncle, Uncle Harry!) to work in munitions.

He must have known then, in spite of her affectionate farewell. She didn't really care. . . . Gin, he thought, that was all she cared for, gin and the Uncles. . . .

And he'd been here, captured, a prisoner, eating tasteless, unfamiliar meals; going to bed, incredibly, at six o'clock, after a silly supper of milk and biscuits (milk and biscuits!), lying awake, crying, his head pushed down under the blankets, crying for Mom and home.

It was that woman! She'd got him and she wouldn't let him go. A lot of sloppy talk. Always making him play silly games. Wanting something from him. Something that he was determined not to give. Never mind. He'd wait. He'd be patient! And one day—one glorious day, he'd go *home*. Home to the streets, and the boys, and the glorious red buses and the Tube, and fish and chips, and the traffic and the area cats —his mind went longingly over the catalogue of delights. He must wait. The war couldn't go on forever. Here he was stuck in this silly place with bombs falling all over London and half London on fire—too! What a blaze it must make, and people being killed and houses crashing down.

He saw it in his mind all in glorious technicolor.

Never mind. When the war was over he'd go back to Mom. She'd be surprised to see how he'd grown.

In the darkness Micky Argyle expelled his breath in a long hiss.

The war *was* over. They'd licked Hitler and Musso. . . . Some of the children were going back. Soon, now. . . . And then *She* had come back from London and had said that he was going to stay at Sunny Point and be her own little boy. . . .

He had said: "Where's my Mom? Did a bomb get her?"

If she had been killed by a bomb—well, that would be not too bad. It happened to boys' mothers.

But Mrs. Argyle said "No," she hadn't been killed. But she had some rather difficult work to do and couldn't look after a child very well—that sort of thing, anyway; soft soap, meaning nothing. . . . His Mom didn't love him, didn't want him back—he'd got to stay here, forever. . . .

He'd sneaked round after that, trying to overhear conversations, and at last he did hear something, just a fragment between Mrs. Argyle and her husband. "Only too pleased to get rid of him—absolutely indifferent"—and something about a hundred pounds. So then he knew—his mother had sold him for a hundred pounds. . . .

The humiliation—the pain—he'd never got over it. . . . And *She* had bought him! He saw her, vaguely, as embodied Power, someone against whom he, in his puny strength, was helpless. But he'd grow up, he'd be strong one day, a man. And then he'd kill her. . . .

He felt better once he'd made that resolution.

Later, when he went away to school, things were not so bad. But he hated the holidays—because of Her. Arranging everything, planning, giving him all sorts of presents. Looking puzzled, because he was so undemonstrative. He hated being kissed by her. . . . And later still, he'd taken a pleasure in thwarting her silly plans for him. Going into a bank! An oil company. Not he. He'd go and find work for himself.

It was when he was at the university that he'd tried to trace his mother. She'd been dead for some years, he discovered—in a car crash with a man who'd been driving roaring drunk. . . .

So why not forget it all? Why not just have a good time and get on with life? He didn't know why not.

And now—what was going to happen now? *She* was dead, wasn't she? Thinking she'd bought him for a miserable hundred pounds. Thinking she could buy anything—houses and cars—and children since she hadn't any of her own. Thinking she was God Almighty!

Well, she wasn't. Just a crack on the head with a poker and she was a corpse like any other corpse! (Like the golden haired corpse in a car smash on the Great North Road. . . .)

She was dead, wasn't she? Why worry?

What was the matter with him? Was it—that he couldn't hate her any more because she was dead?

So that was Death. . . .

He felt lost without his hatred—lost and afraid.

CHAPTER 12 . . .

IN HER SPOTLESSLY kept bedroom, Kirsten Lindstrom plaited her grizzled blonde hair into two unbecoming plaits and prepared for bed.

She was worried and afraid.

The police didn't like foreigners. She had been in England so long that she herself did not feel foreign. But the police could not know that.

That Dr. Calgary—why did he have to come and do this to her?

Justice had been done. She thought of Jacko—and repeated to herself that justice had been done.

She thought of him as she had known him from a small boy.

Always, yes, always, a liar and a cheat! But so charming, so engaging. Always one forgave him. Always one tried to shield him from punishment.

He lied so well. That was the horrible truth. He lied so well that one believed him—that one couldn't help believing him. Wicked, cruel Jacko.

Dr. Calgary might think he knew what he was talking about! But Dr. Calgary was wrong. Places and times and alibis indeed! Jacko could arrange things of that kind easily enough. Nobody really knew Jacko as *she* had known him.

Would anybody believe her if she told them just exactly what Jacko was like? And now—tomorrow, what was going to happen? The police would come. And everyone so unhappy, so suspicious. Looking at each other. . . . Not sure what to believe.

And she loved them all so much . . . so much. She knew more about them all than anyone else could know. Far more than Mrs. Argyle had ever known. For Mrs. Argyle had been blinded by her intense maternal possessiveness. They were her children—she saw them always as belonging to her. But Kirsten had seen them as individuals—as themselves —with all their faults and virtues. If she had had children of her own, she might have felt possessive about them, she supposed. But she was not pre-eminently a maternal woman. Her principal love would have been for the husband she had never had.

Women like Mrs. Argyle were difficult for her to understand. Crazy about a lot of children who were not her own, and treating her husband as though he were not there! A good man, too, a fine man, none better. Neglected, pushed aside. And Mrs. Argyle too self-absorbed to notice what was happening under her nose. That secretary—a good-looking girl and every inch a woman. Well. It was not too late for Leo—or was it too late now? Now with murder raising its head from the grave in which it had been laid? Would those two ever dare to come together?

Kirsten sighed unhappily. What was going to happen to them all? To Micky, who had borne that deep, almost pathological grudge against his adopted mother. To Hester, so unsure of herself, so wild. Hester, who had been on the point of finding peace and security with that nice stolid young doctor. To Leo and Gwenda, who had had motive and, yes, it had to be faced, opportunity, as they both must realise. To Tina, that sleek little catlike creature. To selfish, cold-hearted Mary, who until she had married had never shown affection for anybody.

Once, Kirsten thought, she herself had been full of affection for her employer, full of admiration. She couldn't remember exactly when she had begun to dislike her, when she had begun to judge her and find her wanting. So sure of herself, benevolent, tyrannical—a kind of living walking embodiment of MOTHER KNOWS BEST. And not really even a mother! If she *had* ever borne a child, it might have kept her humble.

But why go on thinking of Rachel Argyle? Rachel Argyle was dead.

She had to think of herself—and the others.

And of what might happen tomorrow.

ii.

Mary Durrant woke with a start.

She had been dreaming—dreaming that she was a child, back again in New York.

How odd. She hadn't thought of those days for years.

It was really surprising that she could remember anything at all. How old had she been? Five? Six?

She had dreamed that she was being taken home to the tenement from the hotel. The Argyles were sailing for England and not taking her with them after all. Anger and rage filled her heart for a moment or two until the realisation came that it had only been a dream.

How wonderful it had been. Taken into the car, going up in the elevator of the hotel to the eighteenth floor. The big suite, that wonderful bathroom; the revelation of what things there were in the world—if you were rich! If she could stay here, if she could keep all this—for ever . . .

Actually, there had been no difficulty at all. All that was needed was a show of affection; never easy for her, for she was not affectionate by disposition, but she had managed it. And there she was, established for life! A rich father and mother, clothes, cars, ships, aeroplanes, servants to wait on her, expensive dolls and toys. A fairy tale come true . . .

A pity that all those other children had had to be there, too. That was the war, of course. Or would it have happened anyway? That insatiable mother love! Really something un-natural in it. So *animal*.

She had always felt a faint contempt for her adopted mother. Stupid in any case to choose the children she had chosen. The under-privileged! Criminal tendencies like Jacko's. Unbalanced like Hester. A savage like Micky. And Tina, a half-caste! No wonder they had all turned out badly. Though she couldn't really blame them for rebelling. She, herself, had rebelled. She remembered her meeting with Philip, a dashing young pilot. Her mother's disapproval. "These hurried marriages. Wait until the war is over." But she hadn't wanted to wait. She had as strong a will as her mother's, and her father had backed her up. They had mar-ried, and the war had ended soon afterwards.

She had wanted to have Philip all to herself—to get away out of her mother's shadow. It was Fate that had defeated her, not her mother. First the failure of Philip's financial schemes and then that horrifying blow—polio of the paralytic type. As soon as Philip was able to leave hospital they had come to Sunny Point. It had seemed inevitable that they would have to make their home there. Philip himself had seemed to think it inevitable. He had gone through all his money and her allowance from the Trust was not so very big. She had asked for a larger one, but the answer had been that perhaps for a while it would be wise to live at Sunny Point.

But she wanted Philip to herself, all to herself, she didn't want him to be the last of Rachel Argyle's "children." She had not wanted a child of her own—she only wanted Philip.

But Philip himself had seemed quite agreeable to the idea of coming to Sunny Point.

"Easier for you," he said. "And people always coming and going there makes a distraction. Besides, I always find your father very good company."

Why didn't he want only to be with her as she wanted only to be with him? Why did he crave for other company—her father's, Hester's?

And Mary had felt a wave of futile rage sweep over her. Her mother, as usual, would get her own way.

But she hadn't got her own way . . . she had died.

And now it was going to be all raked up again. Why, oh, why?

And why was Philip being so trying about it all? Questioning, trying to find out, mixing himself up in what was none of his business?

Laying traps . . .

What *kind* of traps?

iii.

Leo Argyle watched the morning light fill the room slowly with dim grey light.

He had thought out everything very carefully.

It was quite clear to him—exactly what they were up against, he and Gwenda.

He lay looking at the whole thing as Superintendent Huish would look at it. Rachel coming in and telling them about Jacko—his wildness and his threats. Gwenda had tactfully gone into the next room, and he had tried to comfort Rachel, had told her she was quite right to have been firm, that helping Jacko in the past had done no good—that for better or worse he must take what was coming to him. And she had gone away easier in her mind.

And then Gwenda had come back into the room, and gathered up the letters for the post and had asked if there was anything that she could do, her voice saying more than the actual words. And he had thanked her and said no. And she had said good night and gone out of the room. Along the passage and down the stairs and past the room where Rachel was sitting at her desk and so out of the house with no one to watch her go. . . .

And he himself had sat on alone in the library, and there had been nobody to check whether he left it and went down to Rachel's room.

It was like that—opportunity for either of them.

And motive, because already by then he loved Gwenda and she loved him.

And there was nobody, ever, who could prove the guilt or innocence of either of them.

iv.

A quarter of a mile away, Gwenda lay dry-eyed and sleepless.

Her hands clenched, she was thinking how much she had hated Rachel Argyle.

And now in the darkness, Rachel Argyle was saying: *"You thought you could have my husband once I was dead. But you can't—you can't. You will never have my husband."*

v.

Hester was dreaming. She dreamt that she was with Donald Craig and that he had left her suddenly at the edge of an abyss. She had cried out in fear and then, on the other side of it, she saw that Arthur Calgary was standing holding out his hands to her.

She cried out to him reproachfully.

"Why have you done this to me?" and he answered:

"But I've come to *help* you . . ."

vi.

Lying quietly in the small spare-room bed, Tina breathed gently and regularly, but sleep did not come.

She thought of Mrs. Argyle, without gratitude and without resentment—simply with love. Because of Mrs. Argyle she had had food and drink and warmth and toys and comfort. She had loved Mrs. Argyle. She was sorry she was dead. . . .

But it wasn't quite as simple as that.

It hadn't mattered when it was Jacko. . . .

But now?

CHAPTER 13

SUPERINTENDENT HUISH looked round on them all, gently and politely. His tone when he spoke was persuasive and apologetic.

"I know it must be very painful to you all," he said, "to have to go over the whole thing again. But really, we've no choice in the matter. You saw the notice, I expect? It was in all the morning papers."

"A free pardon," said Leo.

"The phraseology always grates on people," said Huish. "An anachronism, like so much of legal terminology. But its meaning is quite clear."

"It means that you made a mistake," said Leo.

"Yes," Huish acknowledged it simply. "We made a mistake." He added, after a minute, "Of course, without Dr. Calgary's evidence it was really inevitable."

Leo said coldly:

"My son told you, when you arrested him, that he had been given a lift that night."

"Oh, yes, He told us. And we did our best to check—but we couldn't find any confirmation of the story. I quite realise, Mr. Argyle, that you must feel exceedingly bitter about the whole business. I'm not making excuses and apologies. All we police officers have to do is to collect the evidence. The evidence goes to the Public Prosecutor and he decides if there is a case. In this case he decided there was. If it's possible, I'd ask you to put as much bitterness as you can out of your mind and just run over the facts and times again."

"What's the use now?" Hester spoke up sharply. "Whoever did it is miles away and you'll never find him."

Superintendent Huish turned to look at her.

"That may be—and it may not," he said mildly. "You'd be surprised at the times we do get our man—sometimes after several years. It's patience does it—patience and never letting up."

Hester turned her head away, and Gwenda gave a quick

shiver as though a cold wind had passed over her. Her lively imagination felt the menace behind the quiet words.

"Now if you please," said Huish. He looked expectantly at Leo. "We'll start with you, Mr. Argyle."

"What do you want to know exactly? You must have my original statement? I shall probably be less accurate now. Exact times are apt to slip one's memory."

"Oh, we realise that. But there's always the chance that some little fact may come to light, something overlooked at the time."

"Isn't it even possible," asked Philip, "that one might see things in better proportion looking back after the lapse of years?"

"It's a possibility, yes," said Huish, turning his head to look at Philip with some interest.

"Intelligent chap," he thought. "I wonder if he's got any ideas of his own about this. . . ."

"Now, Mr. Argyle, if you'll just run through the sequence of events. You'd had tea?"

"Yes. Tea had been in the dining room at five o'clock as usual. We were all there for it with the exception of Mr. and Mrs. Durrant. Mrs. Durrant took tea for herself and her husband up to their own sitting room."

"I was even more of a cripple then than I am now," said Philip. "I'd only just got out of hospital."

"Quite so." Huish turned back to Leo. "All of you—being—?"

"My wife and myself, my daughter Hester, Miss Vaughan and Miss Lindstrom."

"And then? Just tell me in your own words."

"After tea I came back in here with Miss Vaughan. We were at work upon a chapter of my book on Medieval Economics which I was revising. My wife went to her sitting room and office, which is on the ground floor. She was, as you know, a very busy woman. She was looking over some plans for a new children's playground which she was intending to present to the Council here."

"Did you hear your son Jack's arrival?"

"No. That is, I did not know that it was he. I heard, we both heard, the front-door bell. We did not know who it was."

"Who did you think it was, Mr. Argyle?"

Leo looked faintly amused.

"I was in the fifteenth century at the time, not the twentieth. I didn't think at all. It could have been anybody or anything. My wife and Miss Lindstrom and Hester and possibly one of our daily helps would all be downstairs. Nobody," said Leo simply, "ever expected *me* to answer a bell."

"After that?"

"Nothing. Until my wife came in a good deal later."

"How much later?"

Leo frowned.

"By now I really couldn't tell you. I must have given you my estimate at the time. Half an hour—no, more—perhaps three-quarters."

"We finished tea just after half past five," said Gwenda. "I think it was about twenty minutes to seven when Mrs. Argyle came into the library."

"And she said?"

Leo sighed. He spoke distastefully.

"We have had all this so many times. She said Jacko had been with her, that he was in trouble, that he had been violent and abusive, demanding money and saying that unless he had some money at once it would be a matter of prison. That she had refused definitely to give him a penny. She was worried as to whether she had done right or not."

"Mr. Argyle, may I ask a question. Why, when the boy made these demands for money, did your wife not call you? Why only tell you afterwards? Did that not seem odd to you?"

"No, it did not."

"It seems to me that that would have been the natural thing to do. You were not—on bad terms?"

"Oh no. It was simply that my wife was accustomed to dealing with all practical decisions single-handed. She would often consult me beforehand as to what I thought and she usually discussed the decisions she had taken with me afterwards. In this particular matter she and I had talked very seriously together about the problem of Jacko—what to do for the best. So far, we had been singularly unfortunate in our handling of the boy. She had paid out very considerable sums of money several times to protect him from the consequences of his actions. We had decided that if there was a next time, it would be best for Jacko to learn the hard way."

"Nevertheless, she was upset?"

"Yes. She was upset. If he had been less violent and threatening, I think she might have been broken down and helped him once more, but his attitude only stiffened her resolution."

"Had Jacko left the house by then?"

"Oh, yes."

"Do you know that of your own knowledge, or did Mrs. Argyle tell you?"

"She told me. She said he had gone away swearing, and threatening to come back, and that he'd said she'd better have some cash ready for him then."

"Were you—this is important—were you alarmed at the thought of the boy's return?"

"Of course not. We were quite used to what I can only call Jacko's bluster."

"It never entered your head that he would return and attack her."

"No. I told you so at the time. I was dumbfounded."

"And it seems you were quite right," said Huish softly. "It *wasn't* he who attacked her. Mrs. Argyle left you—when exactly?"

"That I do remember. We've been over it so often. Just before seven—about seven minutes to."

Huish turned to Gwenda Vaughan.

"You confirm that?"

"Yes."

"And the conversation went as Mr. Argyle has just said? You can't add to it? There is nothing he has forgotten?"

"I didn't hear all of it. After Mrs. Argyle had told us about Jacko's demands I thought I'd better remove myself in case they felt it embarrassing to talk freely before me. I went in there"—she pointed to the door at the back of the library—"to the small room where I type. When I heard Mrs. Argyle leave I came back."

"And that was at seven minutes to seven?"

"Just before five to seven, yes."

"And after that, Miss Vaughan?"

"I asked Mr. Argyle if he wanted to continue work, but he said his chain of thought was interrupted. I asked if there was any more I could do, but he said no. So I cleared up my things and went."

"The time?"

"Five minutes past seven."

"You went downstairs and through the front door?"

"Yes."

"Mrs. Argyle's sitting room was immediately to the left of the front door?"

"Yes."

"Was the door open?"

"It was not closed—it was about a foot ajar."

"You didn't go inside or say good night to her?"

"No."

"Didn't you usually do so?"

"No. It would have been silly to disturb her at what she was doing, just to say good night."

"If you had gone in—you might have discovered her body lying there dead."

Gwenda shrugged her shoulders.

"I suppose so. . . . But I imagine—I mean we all imagined at the time, that she was killed later. Jacko would hardly have been able to—"

She stopped.

"You are still thinking on the lines of Jacko having killed her. But that is not so now. So she *might* have been there then, dead?"

"I suppose—yes."

"You left the house and went straight home?"

"Yes. My landlady spoke to me when I came in."

"Just so. And you didn't meet anyone on the way—near the house?"

"I don't think so . . . no." Gwenda frowned. "I can't really remember now. . . . It was cold and dark and this road is a cul-de-sac. I don't think I passed anyone until I came to the Red Lion. There were several people about there."

"Any cars pass you?"

Gwenda looked startled.

"Oh, yes, I do remember a car. It splashed my skirt. I had to wash the mud off when I got home."

"What kind of car?"

"I don't remember. I didn't notice. It passed me just at the entrance to our road. It might have been going to any of the houses."

Huish turned back to Leo.

"You say you heard a ring at the bell some time after your wife left the room?"

"Well—I think I did. I've never been quite sure."

"What time was that?"

"I've no idea. I didn't look."

"Didn't you think it might be your son Jacko come back?"

"I didn't think. I was—at work again."

"One more point, Mr. Argyle. Did you have any idea that your son was married?"

"No idea at all."

"His mother didn't know, either? You don't think she knew but had not told you?"

"I'm quite sure she had no idea of such a thing. She would have come to me about it at once. It was the greatest shock to me when the wife turned up the next day. I could hardly believe it when Miss Lindstrom came into this room and said 'There is a young woman downstairs—a girl—who says she is Jacko's wife. It can't be *true*.' She was terribly upset, weren't you, Kirsty?"

"I could not believe it," said Kirsten. "I made her say it twice and then I came up to Mr. Argyle. It seemed incredible."

"You were very kind to her, I understand," said Huish to Leo.

"I did what I could. She's married again, you know. I'm very glad. Her husband seems a nice steady sort of chap."

Huish nodded. Then he turned to Hester.

"Now, Miss Argyle, just tell me again what you did after tea that day."

"I don't remember now," said Hester sulkily. "How can I? It's two years ago. I might done anything."

"Actually I believe you helped Miss Lindstrom to wash up tea."

"That is quite right," said Kirsten. "And then," she added, "you went upstairs to your bedroom. You were going out later, you remember. You were going to see an amateur performance of *Waiting for Godot* at the Drymouth Playhouse."

Hester was still looking sullen and unco-operative.

"You've got it all written down," she said to Huish. "Why go on about it?"

"Because you never know what might be helpful. Now then, Miss Argyle, what time did *you* leave the house?"

"Seven o'clock—or thereabouts."

"Had you heard the altercation between your mother and your brother Jack?"

"No, I didn't hear anything. I was upstairs."

"But you saw Mrs. Argyle before you left the house?"

"Yes. I wanted some money. I was right out. And I remembered the petrol in my car was nearly down to empty. I'd have to fill up on the way to Drymouth. So when I was ready to start I went in to Mother and asked her for some money—just a couple of pounds—that's all I needed."

"And she gave them to you?"

"Kirsty gave them to me."

Huish looked slightly surprised.

"I don't remember that in the original statement."

"Well, that's what happened," said Hester defiantly. "I went in and said could I have some cash, and Kirsten heard me from the hall and called out that she'd got some and would give it to me. She was just going out herself. And Mother said, 'Yes, get it from Kirsty.' "

"I was just going down to the Women's Institute with some books on Flower Arrangement," said Kirsten. "I knew Mrs. Argyle was busy and didn't want to be disturbed."

Hester said in an aggrieved voice:

"What does it matter who gave me the money? You wanted to know when I last saw Mother alive. That was when. She was sitting at the table poring over a lot of plans. And I said I wanted cash, and then Kirsten called out that she'd give it to me. I took it from her and then went into Mother's room again and said good night to Mother and she said she hoped I'd enjoy the play, and to be careful driving. She always said that. And I went out to the garage and got the car out."

"And Miss Lindstrom."

"Oh, she went off as soon as she'd given me the money."

Kirsten Lindstrom said quickly: "Hester passed me in the car just as I got to the end of our road. She must have started almost immediately after me. She went on up the hill to the main road whilst I turned left to the village."

Hester opened her mouth as though to speak, then quickly shut it again.

Huish wondered. Was Kirsten Lindstrom trying to establish that Hester would not have had time to commit the crime? Wasn't it possible that instead of Hester's saying a quiet good night to Mrs. Argyle, there had been an argument—a quarrel, and that Hester had struck her down?

Smoothly he turned to Kirsten and said:

"Now, Miss Lindstrom, let's have your account of what you remember."

She was nervous. Her hands twisted uncomfortably.

"We had tea. It was cleared away. Hester helped me. Then she went upstairs. Then Jacko came."

"You heard him?"

"Yes. I let him in. He said he had lost his key. He went straight in to his mother. He said at once, 'I'm in a jam. You've got to get me out of it.' I did not hear any more. I went back into the kitchen. There were things to prepare for supper."

"Did you hear him leave?"

"Yes, indeed. He was shouting. I came from the kitchen. He was standing there in the front hall—very angry—shouting out that he'd come back, that his mother had better have the money ready for him. Or else! That is what he said: 'Or else!' It was a threat."

"And then?"

"He went off banging the door. Mrs. Argyle came out in the hall. She was very pale and upset. She said to me, 'You heard?'

"I said: 'He is in trouble?'

"She nodded. Then she went upstairs to the library to Mr. Argyle. I laid the table for supper, and then I went up to put my outdoor things on. The Women's Institute were having a Flower Arrangement Competition next day. There were some Flower Arrangement books we had promised them."

"You took the books to the Institute—what time did you return to the house?"

"It must have been about half past seven. I let myself in with my key. I went in at once to Mrs. Argyle's room—to give her a message of thanks and a note—she was at the desk, her head forward on her hands. And there was the poker, flung down—and drawers of the bureau pulled out. There had been a burglar, I thought. She had been attacked. And I was right. *Now* you know that I was *right!* It *was* a burglar—someone from outside!"

"Someone whom Mrs. Argyle herself let in?"

"Why not?" said Kirsten defiantly. "She was kind—always very kind. And she was not afraid—of people or things. Besides it is not as though she were alone in the house. There were others—her husband, Gwenda, Mary. She had only to call out."

"But she didn't call out," Huish pointed out.

"No. Because whoever it was must have told her some

very plausible story. She would always listen. And so, she sat down again at the desk—perhaps to look for her cheque-book—because she was unsuspicious—so he had the chance to snatch up the poker and hit her. Perhaps, even, he did not mean to kill her. He just wanted to stun her and look for money and jewellery and go."

"He didn't look very far—just turned out a few drawers."

"Perhaps he heard sounds in the house—or lost his nerve. Or found, perhaps, that he had killed her. And so, quickly, in panic, he goes."

She leaned forward.

Her eyes were both frightened and pleading.

"It *must* have been like that—it must!"

He was interested in her insistence. Was it fear for her-self? She *could* have killed her employer there and then, pulling out the drawers to lend verisimilitude to the idea of a burglar. Medical evidence could not put the time of death closer than between seven and seven thirty.

"It seems as though it must be so," he acquiesced pleas-antly. A faint sigh of relief escaped her. She sat back. He turned to the Durrants.

"You didn't hear anything, either of you?"

"Not a thing."

"I took a tray with tea up to our room," said Mary. "It's rather shut off from the rest of the house. We were there un-til we heard someone screaming. It was Kirsten. She'd just found Mother dead."

"You didn't leave the room at all until then?"

"No." Her limpid gaze met his. "We were playing picquet."

Philip wondered why he felt slightly discomposed. Polly was doing what he had told her to do. Perhaps it was the perfection of her manner, calm, unhurried, carrying complete conviction.

"Polly, love, you're a wonderful liar!" he thought.

"And I, Superintendent," he said, "was then, and am still, quite incapable of any comings and goings."

"But you're a good deal better, aren't you, Mr. Dur-rant," said the superintendent cheerfully. "One of these days we'll have you walking again."

"It's a long job."

Huish turned towards the other two members of the fam-ily who up to now had sat without making a sound. Micky had sat with his arms folded and a faint sneer on his face.

Tina, small and graceful, leaned back in her chair, her eyes moving occasionally from face to face.

"Neither of you two were in the house, I know," he said. "But perhaps you'll just refresh my memory as to what you were doing that evening?"

"Does your memory really need refreshing?" asked Micky with his sneer even more pronounced. "I can still say my piece. I was out testing a car. Clutch trouble. I gave it a good long test. From Drymouth up Minchin Hill, along the Moor Road and back through Ipsley. Unfortunately cars are dumb, they can't testify."

Tina had turned her head at last. She was staring straight at Micky. Her face was still expressionless.

"And you, Miss Argyle? You work at the library at Redmyn?"

"Yes. It closes at half past five. I did a little shopping in the High Street. Then I went home. I have a flat—flatlet really—in Morecombe Mansions. I cooked my own supper and enjoyed a quiet evening playing gramophone records."

"You didn't go out at all?"

There was a slight pause before she said:

"No, I didn't go out."

"Quite sure about that, Miss Argyle?"

"Yes. I am sure."

"You have a car, haven't you?"

"Yes."

"She has a bubble," said Micky. "Bubble, bubble, toil and trouble."

"I have a bubble, yes," said Tina, grave and composed.

"Where do you keep it?"

"In the street. I have no garage. There is a side street near the flats. There are cars parked all along it."

"And you've—nothing helpful you can tell us?"

Huish hardly knew himself why he was so insistent.

"I do not think there is anything I could possibly tell you."

Micky threw her a quick glance.

Huish sighed.

"I'm afraid this hasn't helped you much, Superintendent," said Leo.

"You never know, Mr. Argyle. You realise, I suppose, one of the oddest things about the whole business?"

"I—? I'm not quite sure that I follow you."

"The money," said Huish. "The money Mrs. Argyle drew

from the bank including that fiver with Mrs. Bottleberry, 17 Bangor Road written on the back of it. A strong part of the case was that that fiver and others were found on Jack Argyle when he was arrested. He swore he got the money from Mrs. Argyle, but Mrs. Argyle definitely told you and Miss Vaughan that she didn't give Jacko any money—so how did he get that fifty pounds? He couldn't have come back here—Dr. Calgary's evidence makes that quite clear. So he must have had it with him when he left here. Who gave it to him? Did you?"

He turned squarely on Kirsten Lindstrom, who flushed indignantly.

"Me? No, of course not. How could I?"

"Where was the money kept that Mrs. Argyle had drawn from the bank?"

"She usually kept it in a drawer of her bureau," said Kirsten.

"Locked?"

Kirsten considered.

"She would probably lock the drawer before she went up to bed."

Huish looked at Hester.

"Did you take the money from the drawer and give it to your brother?"

"I didn't even know he was there. And how could I take it without Mother knowing?"

"You could have taken it quite easily when your mother went up to the library to consult your father," Huish suggested.

He wondered whether she would see and avoid the trap. She fell straight into it.

"But Jacko had already left by then. I—" She stopped, dismayed.

"I see you *do* know when your brother left," said Huish.

Hester said quickly and vehemently, "I—I—know now— I didn't then. I was up in my room, I tell you. I didn't hear anything at all. And anyway I wouldn't have wanted to give Jacko any money."

"And I tell you this," said Kirsten. Her face was red and indignant. "If I had given Jacko money—it would have been my own money! I would not have stolen it!"

"I'm sure you wouldn't," said Huish. "But you see where

that leads us. Mrs. Argyle, in spite of what she told *you*," he looked at Leo, "must have given him that money *herself*."

"I can't believe it. Why not tell me if she had done so?"

"She wouldn't be the first mother to be softer about her son than she wanted to admit."

"You're wrong, Huish. My wife never indulged in evasion."

"I think she did this time," said Gwenda Vaughan. "In fact she must have done . . . as the superintendent says, it's the only answer."

"After all," said Huish softly. "We've got to look at the whole thing from a different point of view now. At the time of the arrest we thought Jack Argyle was lying. But now we find he spoke the truth about the hitchhike he had from Calgary, so presumably he was speaking the truth about the money too. He said that his mother gave it to him. Therefore presumably she did."

There was silence—an uncomfortable silence.

Huish got up. "Well, thank you. I'm afraid the trail is pretty cold by now, but you never know."

Leo escorted him to the door. When he came back he said with a sigh, "Well, that's over. For the present."

"For always," said Kirsten. "They will never know."

"What's the good of that to us?" cried Hester.

"My dear." Her father went over to her. "Calm down, child. Don't be so strung up. Time heals everything."

"Not some things. What shall we do? Oh! What shall we *do?*"

"Hester, come with me." Kirsten put a hand on her shoulder.

"I don't want anybody." Hester ran out of the room. A moment later they heard the front door bang.

Kirsten said:

"All this! It is not good for her."

"I don't think it's really true, either," said Philip Durrant thoughtfully.

"What isn't true?" asked Gwenda.

"That we shall never know the truth. . . . I feel a kind of pricking in my thumbs."

His face, faun-like and almost mischievous, lit up with a queer smile.

"Please, Philip, be careful," said Tina.

He looked at her in surprise.

"Little Tina. And what do you know about it all?"

"I hope," said Tina very clearly and distinctly, "that I do not know anything."

"DON'T SUPPOSE you got anything?" said the Chief Constable.

"Nothing definite, sir," said Huish. "And yet—the time wasn't altogether wasted."

"Let's hear about it all."

"Well, our main times and premises are the same. Mrs. Argyle was alive just before seven, talked with her husband and Gwenda Vaughan, was seen afterwards downstairs by Hester Argyle. Three people can't be in cahoots. Jacko Argyle is now accounted for, so it means that she could have been killed by her husband, any time between five past seven and half past, by Gwenda Vaughan at five minutes past seven on her way out, by Hester just before that, by Kirsten Lindstrom when she came in later—just before half past seven, say. Durrant's paralysis gives him an alibi, but his wife's alibi depends on his word. She could have gone down and killed her mother if she wanted to between seven and half past if her husband was prepared to back her up. Don't see why she should, though. In fact, as far as I can see, only two people have got a real motive for the crime. Leo Argyle and Gwenda Vaughan."

"You think it's one of them—or both of them together?"

"I don't think they were in it together. As I see it, it was an impulsive crime—not a premeditated one. Mrs. Argyle comes into the library, tells them both about Jacko's threats and demands for money. Put it that, later, Leo Argyle goes down to speak to her about Jacko, or about something else. The house is quiet, nobody about. He goes into her sitting-room. There she is, her back to him, sitting at the desk. And there's the poker, still perhaps where Jacko threw it down after threatening her with it. Those quiet, repressed men do break out sometimes. A handkerchief over his hand so as not to leave prints, up with the poker, down with it on her head and it's done. Pull out a drawer or two to suggest a search

117

for money. Then upstairs again till someone finds her. Or put it that Gwenda Vaughan on her way out looks into the room, and the urge comes over her. Jacko will be the perfect scape-goat, and the way to marriage with Leo Argyle is open."

Major Finney nodded thoughtfully.

"Yes. Could be. And of course they were careful not to announce an engagement too soon. Not till that poor little devil Jacko was safely convicted of murder. Yes, that seems fair enough. Crimes are very monotonous. Husband and third party, or wife and third party—always the same old pattern. But what can *we* do about it, Huish, eh? What can we do about it?"

"I don't see, sir," said Huish slowly, "what we can do about it. *We* may be sure—but where's the evidence? Nothing to stand up in court."

"No—no. But you are sure, Huish? Sure in your own mind?"

"Not as sure as I'd like to be," said Superintendent Huish, sadly.

"Ah! Why not?"

"The kind of man he is—Mr. Argyle, I mean."

"Not the kind to do murder?"

"It's not that so much—not the murder part of it. It's the boy. I don't see him deliberately framing the boy."

"It wasn't his own son, remember. He may not have cared much for the boy—he may even have been resentful—of the affection his wife lavished on him."

"That may be so. Yet he seems to have been fond of all the children. He looks fond of them."

"Of course," said Finney, thoughtfully. "He knew the boy wouldn't be hanged. . . . That might make a difference."

"Ah, you may have something there, sir. He may have thought that ten years in prison, which is what a life sentence amounts to, might have done the boy no harm."

"What about the young woman—Gwenda Vaughan?"

"If she did it," said Huish, "I don't suppose she'd have any qualms about Jacko. Women are ruthless."

"But you're reasonably satisfied it's between those two?"

"Reasonably satisfied, yes."

"But no more?" the Chief Constable pressed him.

"No. There's *something* going on. Undercurrents, as you might say."

"Explain yourself, Huish."

"What I'd really like to know is what they think themselves. About each other."

"Oh, I see, I get you now. You're wondering if they themselves know who it was?"

"Yes. I can't make up my mind about it. Do they *all* know? And are they all agreed to keep it dark? I don't think so. I think it's even possible that they may all have different ideas. There's the Swedish woman—she's a mass of nerves. Right on edge. That may be because she did it herself. She's the age when women go slightly off their rocker in one way or another. She may be frightened for herself or for somebody else. I've the impression, I may be wrong, it's for somebody else."

"Leo?"

"No, I don't think it's Leo she's upset about. I think it's the young one—Hester."

"Hester, h'm? Any chance that it might have been Hester?"

"No ostensible motive. But she's a passionate, perhaps slightly unbalanced type."

"And Lindstrom probably knows a good deal more about the girl than we do."

"Yes. Then there's the little dark one who works in the County Library."

"She wasn't in the house that night, was she?"

"No. But I think she knows something. Knows who did it, maybe."

"Guesses? Or knows?"

"She's worried. I don't think it's only guessing."

He went on: "And there's the other boy. Micky. He wasn't there, either, *but* he was out in a car, nobody with him. He *says* he was testing the car up towards the moor and Minchin Hill. We've only his word for it. He could have driven over, gone into the house, killed her and driven away again. Gwenda Vaughan said something that wasn't in her original statement. She said a car passed her, just at the entrance to the private road. There are fourteen houses in the road, so it might have been going to any one of them and nobody will remember after two years—but it means there's just a possibility that the car was Micky's."

"Why should he want to kill his adopted mother?"

"No reason that we know about—but there might be one."

"Who would know?"

"They'd all know," said Huish. "But they wouldn't tell us. Not if they knew they were telling us, that is."

"I perceive your devilish intention," said Major Finney. "Who are you going to work on?"

"Lindstrom, I think. If I can break down her defences. I also hope to find out if she herself had a grudge against Mrs. Argyle.

"And there's the paralysed chap," he added. "Philip Durrant."

"What about him?"

"Well, I think he's beginning to have a few ideas about it all. I don't suppose he'll want to share them with me, but I may be able to get an inkling of the way his mind is working. He's an intelligent fellow, and I should say pretty observant. He may have noticed one or two rather interesting things."

ii.

"Come out, Tina, and let's get some air."

"Air?" Tina looked up at Micky doubtfully. "But it's so cold, Micky." She shivered a little.

"I believe you hate fresh air, Tina. That's why you're able to stand being cooped up in that library all day long."

Tina smiled.

"I do not mind being cooped up in winter. It is very nice and warm in the library."

Micky looked down on her.

"And there you sit, all cuddled up like a cosy little kitten in front of the fire. But it'll do you good to get out, all the same. Come on, Tina. I want to talk to you. I want to—oh, to get some air into my lungs, forget all this bloody police business."

Tina got up from her chair with a lazy, graceful movement not unlike that of the kitten to which Micky had just compared her.

In the hall she wrapped a fur-collared tweed coat round her and they went out together.

"Aren't you even going to put a coat on, Micky?"

"No. I never feel the cold."

"Brrr," said Tina gently. "How I hate this country in the winter. I would like to go abroad. I would like to be somewhere where the sun was always shining and the air was moist and soft and warm."

"I've just been offered a job out in the Persian Gulf," said Micky, "with one of the oil companies. The job's looking after motor transport."

"Are you going?"

"No, I don't think so. . . . What's the good?"

They walked round to the back of the house and started down a zigzag path through trees which led finally to the beach on the river below. Halfway down there was a small summer house sheltered from the wind. They did not at once sit down but stood in front of it, gazing out over the river.

"It's beautiful here, isn't it?" said Micky.

Tina looked at the view with incurious eyes.

"Yes," she said, "yes, perhaps it is."

"But you don't really know, do you?" said Micky, looking at her affectionately, "you don't realise the beauty, Tina, you never have."

"I do not remember," said Tina, "in all the years we lived here that you ever enjoyed the beauty of this place. You were always fretting, longing to go back to London."

"That was different," said Micky shortly. "I didn't belong here."

"That is what is the matter, isn't it?" said Tina. "You do not belong anywhere."

"I don't belong anywhere," said Micky in a dazed voice. "Perhaps that's true. My goodness, Tina, what a frightening thought. Do you remember that old song? Kirsten used to sing it to us, I believe. Something about a dove. *O fair dove, O fond dove, O dove with the white, white breast.* Do you remember?"

Tina shook her head.

"Perhaps she sang it to you, but—no, I do not remember."

Micky went on, half speaking, half humming.

"*O maid most dear, I am not here. I have no place, no part, No dwelling more by sea nor shore, but only in thy heart.*" He looked at Tina. "I suppose that could be true."

Tina put a small hand on his arm.

"Come, Micky, sit down here. It is out of the wind. It is not so cold."

As he obeyed her she went on:

"Must you be so unhappy always?"

"My dear girl, you don't begin to understand the first thing about it."

"I understand a good deal," said Tina. "Why can't you forget about her, Micky?"

"Forget about her? Who are you talking about?"

"Your mother," said Tina.

"Forget about her!" said Micky bitterly. "Is there much chance of forgetting after this morning—after the questions! If anyone's been murdered, they don't let you 'forget about her'!"

"I did not mean that," said Tina. "I meant your real mother."

"Why should I think about her? I never saw her after I was six years old."

"But, Micky, you did think about her. All the time."

"Did I ever tell you so?"

"Sometimes one knows about these things," said Tina.

Micky turned and looked at her.

"You're such a quiet, soft little creature, Tina. Like a little black cat. I want to stroke your fur the right way. Nice pussy! Pretty little pussy!" His hand stroked the sleeve of her coat.

Tina, sitting still, smiled at him as he did so. Micky said:

"*You* didn't hate her, did you, Tina? All the rest of us did."

"That was very unkind," said Tina. She shook her head at him and went on with some energy: "Look what she gave you, all of you. A home, warmth, kindness, good food, toys to play with, people to look after you and keep you safe—"

"Yes, yes," said Micky, impatiently. "Saucers of cream and lots of fur-stroking. That was all you wanted, was it, little pussy cat?"

"I was grateful for it," said Tina. "None of you were grateful."

"Don't you understand, Tina, that one can't be grateful when one ought to be? In some ways it makes it worse, feeling the obligation of gratitude. I didn't *want* to be brought here. I didn't *want* to be given luxurious surroundings. I didn't *want* to be taken away from my own home."

"You might have been bombed," Tina pointed out. "You might have been killed."

"What would it matter? I wouldn't mind being killed. I'd have been killed in my own place, with my own people about me. Where I belonged. There you are, you see. We're back to it again. There's nothing so bad as not belonging. But you, little pussy cat, you only care for material things."

"Perhaps that is true in a way," said Tina. "Perhaps that is why I do not feel like the rest of you. I do not feel that odd resentment that you all seem to feel—you most of all, Micky. It is easy for me to be grateful because, you see, I did *not* want to be *myself*. I did *not* want to be where I was. I wanted to escape from myself. I wanted to be someone else. And she made me into someone else. She made me into Christina Argyle with a home and with affection. Secure. Safe. I loved Mother because she gave me all those things."

"What about your own mother? Don't you ever think of her?"

"Why should I? I hardly remember her. I was only three years old, remember, when I came here. I was always frightened—terrified—with her. All those noisy quarrels with seamen, and she herself—I suppose, now that I am old enough to remember properly, that she must have been drunk most of the time." Tina spoke in a detached, wondering voice. "No, I do not think about her, or remember her. Mrs. Argyle was my mother. This is my home."

"It's so easy for you, Tina," said Micky.

"And why is it hard for you? Because you make it so! It was not Mrs. Argyle you hated, Micky, it was your own mother. Yes, I know that what I am saying is true. And if you killed Mrs. Argyle, as you may have done, then it was your own mother you wanted to kill."

"Tina! What the hell are you talking about?"

"And now," went on Tina, talking calmly, "you have nobody to hate any longer. And that makes you quite lonely, doesn't it? But you've got to learn to live without hate, Micky. It may be difficult, but it can be done."

"I don't know what you're talking about. What did you mean by saying that I may have killed her? You know perfectly well I was nowhere near here that day. I was testing out a customer's car up on the Moor Road, by Minchin Hill."

"Were you?" said Tina.

She got up and stepped forward till she stood at the Lookout Point from where you could look down to the river below.

"What are you getting at?" Micky came up behind her.

Tina pointed down to the beach.

"Who are those two people down there?"

Micky gave a quick cursory glance.

"Hester and her doctor pal, I think," he said. "But Tina, what did you mean? For God's sake don't stand there right at the edge."

"Why—do you want to push me over? You could. I'm very small, you know."

Micky said hoarsely:

"Why do you say I may have been here that evening?"

Tina did not answer. She turned and began walking back up the path to the house.

"Tina!"

Tina said in her quiet, soft voice:

"I'm worried, Micky. I'm very worried about Hester and Don Craig."

"Never mind about Hester and her boy-friend."

"But I do mind about them. I am afraid that Hester is very unhappy."

"We're not talking about them."

"*I* am talking about them. They matter, you see."

"Have you believed all along, Tina, that I was here the night Mother was killed?"

Tina did not reply.

"You didn't say anything at the time."

"Why should I? There was no need. I mean, it was so obvious that Jacko had killed her."

"And now it's equally obvious that Jacko didn't kill her."

Again Tina nodded.

"And so?" Micky asked. "And so?"

She did not answer him, but continued to walk up the path to the house.

iii.

On the little beach by the point, Hester scuffled the sand with the point of her shoe.

"I don't see what there is to talk about," she said.

"You've got to talk about it," said Don Craig.

"I don't see why. . . . Talking about a thing never does any good—it never makes it any better."

"You might at least tell me what happened this morning."

"Nothing," said Hester.

"What do you mean—nothing? The police came along, didn't they?"

"Oh yes, they came along."

"Well, then, did they question you all?"

"Yes," said Hester, "they questioned us."

"What sort of questions?"

"All the usual ones," said Hester. "Really just the same as before. Where we were and what we did, and when we last saw Mother alive. Really, Don, I don't want to talk about it any more. It's over now."

"But it isn't over, dearest. That's just the point."

"I don't see why *you* need to fuss," said Hester. "*You're* not mixed up in this."

"Darling, I want to help you. Don't you understand?"

"Well, talking about it doesn't help me. I just want to forget. If you'd help me to forget, that would be different."

"Hester, dearest, it's no good running away from things. You must face them."

"I've been facing them, as you call it, all the morning."

"Hester, I love you. You know that, don't you?"

"I suppose so," said Hester.

"What do you mean, you suppose so?"

"Going on and on about it all."

"But I have to do that."

"I don't see why. *You're* not a policeman."

"Who was the last person to see your mother alive?"

"I was," said Hester.

"I know. That was just before seven, wasn't it, just before you came out to meet me."

"Just before I came out to go to Drymouth—to the Playhouse," said Hester.

"Well, I was at the Playhouse, wasn't I?"

"Yes, of course you were."

"You did know then, didn't you, Hester, that I loved you?"

"I wasn't sure," said Hester. "I wasn't even sure then that I was beginning to love you."

"You'd no reason, had you, no earthly reason for doing away with your mother?"

"No, not really," said Hester.

"What do you mean by not really?"

"I often thought about killing her," said Hester in a matter-of-fact voice. "I used to say 'I wish she was dead, I wish

125

she was dead.' Sometimes," she added, "I used to dream that I killed her."

"In what way did you kill her in your dream?"

For a moment Don Craig was no longer the lover but the interested young doctor.

"Sometimes I shot her," said Hester cheerfully, "and sometimes I banged her on the head."

Dr. Craig groaned.

"That was just dreaming," said Hester. "I'm often *very* violent in dreams."

"Listen, Hester." The young man took her hand in his. "You've got to tell me the truth. You've got to trust me."

"I don't understand what you mean," said Hester.

"The truth, Hester. I want the *truth*. I love you—and I'll stand by you. If—if you killed her I—I think I can find out the reasons why. I don't think it will have been exactly your fault. Do you understand? Certainly I'd never go to the police about it. It will be between you and me only. Nobody else will suffer. The whole thing will die down for want of evidence. But I've got to *know*." He stressed the last word strongly.

Hester was looking at him. Her eyes were wide, almost unfocused.

"What do you want me to say to you?" she said.

"I want you to tell me the truth."

"You think you know the truth already, don't you? You think—I killed her."

"Hester, darling, don't look at me like that." He took her by the shoulders and shook her gently. "I'm a doctor. I know the reasons behind these things. I know that people can't always be held responsible for their actions. I know you for what you are—sweet and lovely and essentially all right. I'll help you. I'll look after you. We'll get married, then we'll be happy. You need never feel lost, unwanted, tyrannised over. The things we do often spring from reasons most people don't understand."

"That's very much what we all said about Jacko, isn't it?" said Hester.

"Never mind Jacko. It's you I'm thinking about. I love you so very much, Hester, but I've got to know the truth."

"The truth?" said Hester.

A very slow, mocking smile curved the corners of her mouth upwards.

"Please, darling."

Hester turned her head and looked up.

"Hester!"

"Would you believe me if I told you I didn't kill her?"

"Of course I'd—I'd believe you."

"I don't think you would," said Hester.

She turned sharply away from him and began running up the path. He made a movement to follow her, then abandoned it.

"Oh, hell," said Donald Craig. "Oh, *hell!*"

CHAPTER **15** ...

"BUT I DON'T want to go home just yet," said Philip Durrant. He spoke with plaintive irritability.

"But, Philip, really, there's nothing to stay here for, any longer. I mean, we had to come to see Mr. Marshall to discuss the thing, and then wait for the police interviews. But now there's nothing to stop us going home right away."

"I think your father's quite happy for us to stop on for a bit," said Philip. "He likes having someone to play chess with in the evenings. My word, he's a wizard at chess. I thought I wasn't bad, but I never get the better of him."

"Father can find someone else to play chess with," said Mary shortly.

"What—whistle someone up from the Women's Institute?"

"And anyway, we ought to go home," said Mary. "Tomorrow is Mrs. Carden's day for doing the brasses."

"Polly, the perfect housewife!" said Philip laughing. "Anyway, Mrs. Whatsaname can do the brasses without you, can't she? Or if she can't, send her a telegram and tell her to let them moulder for another week."

"You don't understand, Philip, about household things, and how difficult they are."

"I don't see that any of them are difficult unless you make them difficult. Anyway, *I* want to stop on."

"Oh, Philip," Mary spoke with exasperation, "I do so hate it here."

"But why?"

"It's so gloomy, so miserable and—and all that's happened here. The murder and everything."

"Now, come, Polly, don't tell me you're a mass of nerves over things of that kind. I'm sure you could take murder without turning a hair. No, you want to go home because you want to see to the brasses and dust the place and make sure no moths have got into your fur coat—"

"Moths don't go into fur coats in winter," said Mary.

"Well, you know what I mean, Polly. The general idea.

But you see, from my point of view, it's so much more interesting here."

"More interesting than being in our own home?" Mary sounded both shocked and hurt.

Philip looked at her quickly.

"I'm sorry, darling, I didn't put it very well. Nothing could be nicer than our own home, and you've made it really lovely. Comfortable, neat, attractive. You see, it'd be quite different if—if I were like I used to be. I mean, I'd have lots of things to do all day. I'd be up to my ears in schemes. And it would be perfect coming back to you and having our own home, talking about everything that had happened during the day. But you see, it's different now."

"Oh, I know it's different in *that* way," said Mary. "Don't think I ever forget that, Phil. I do mind. I mind most terribly."

"Yes." said Philip, and he spoke almost between his teeth. "Yes, you mind too much, Mary. You mind so much that sometimes it makes me mind more. All I want is distraction and—no"—he held up his hand—"don't tell me that I can get distraction from jigsaw puzzles and all the gadgets of occupational therapy and having people to come and give me treatment, and reading endless books. I want so badly sometimes to get my teeth into something! And here, in this house, there *is* something to get one's teeth into."

"Philip," Mary caught her breath, "you're not *still* harping on—on that idea of yours?"

"Playing at Murder Hunt?" said Philip. "Murder, murder, who did the murder? Yes, Polly, you're not far off. I want desperately to know who did it."

"But why? And how can you know? If somebody broke in or found the door open—"

"Still harping on the outsider theory?" asked Philip. "It won't wash, you know. Old Marshall put a good face upon it. But actually he was just helping *us* to keep face. Nobody believes in that beautiful theory. It just isn't true."

"Then you must see, if it *isn't* true," Mary interrupted him, "if it isn't true—if it was, as you put it, one of us—then I don't want to know. Why should we know? Aren't we —aren't we a hundred times better not knowing?"

Philip Durrant looked up at her questioningly.

"Putting your head in the sand, eh, Polly? Haven't you any natural curiosity?"

"I tell you I don't want to know! I think it's all horrible. I want to forget it and not think about it."

"Didn't you care enough for your mother to want to know who killed her?"

"What good would it do, knowing who killed her? For two years we've been quite satisfied that Jacko killed her."

"Yes," said Philip, "lovely the way we've all been satisfied." His wife looked at him doubtfully.

"I don't—I really don't know what you mean, Philip."

"Can't you see, Polly, that in a way this is a challenge to me? A challenge to my intelligence? I don't mean that I've felt your mother's death particularly keenly or that I was particularly fond of her. I wasn't. She'd done her very best to stop you marrying me, but I bore her no grudge for that because I succeeded in carrying you off all right. Didn't I, my girl? No, it's not a wish for revenge, it's not even a passion for justice. I think it's—yes, mainly curiosity, though perhaps there's a better side to it than that."

"It's the sort of thing you oughtn't to meddle about with," said Mary. "No good can come of your meddling about with it. Oh, Philip, please, please *don't*. Let's go home and forget all about it."

"Well," said Philip, "you can pretty well cart me anywhere you like, can't you? But I want to stay here. Don't you sometimes want me to do what *I* want to do?"

"I want you to have everything in the world you want," said Mary.

"You don't really, darling. You just want to look after me like a baby in arms and know what's best for me every day and in every possible way." He laughed.

Mary said, looking at him doubtfully: —

"I never know when you're serious or not."

"Apart from curiosity," said Philip Durrant, "somebody ought to find out the truth, you know."

"Why? What good can it do? Having someone else sent to prison. I think it's a horrible idea."

"You don't quite understand," said Philip. "I didn't say that I'd turn in whoever it was (if I discovered who it was) to the police. I don't think that I would. It depends, of course, on the circumstances. Probably it wouldn't be any use my turning them over to the police because I still think that there couldn't be any real evidence."

"Then if there isn't any real evidence," said Mary, "how are you going to find out anything?"

"Because," said Philip, "there are lots of ways of finding out things, of knowing them quite certainly once and for all. And I think, you know, that that's becoming rather necessary. Things aren't going very well in this house and very soon they'll be getting worse."

"What do you mean?"

"Haven't you noticed anything, Polly? What about your father and Gwenda Vaughan?"

"What about them? Why my father should want to marry again at his age—"

"I can understand that," said Philip. "After all, he had rather a raw deal in marriage. He's got a chance now of real happiness. Autumn happiness, if you like, but he's got it. Or, shall we say, he had it. Things aren't going too well between them now."

"I suppose, all this business—" said Mary vaguely.

"Exactly," said Philip. "All this business. It's shoving them farther apart every day. And there could be two reasons for that. Suspicion or guilt."

"Suspicion of whom?"

"Well, let's say of each other. Or suspicion on one side and consciousness of guilt on the other and vice versa and as you were and as you like it."

"Don't, Philip, you're confusing me." Suddenly a faint trace of animation came into Mary's manner. "So you think it was Gwenda?" she said. "Perhaps you're right. Oh, what a blessing it would be if it was Gwenda."

"Poor Gwenda. Because she's one removed from the family, you mean?"

"Yes," said Mary. "I mean then it wouldn't be one of us."

"That's all you feel about it, is it?" said Philip. "How it affects us."

"Of course," said Mary.

"Of course, of course," said Philip irritably. "The trouble with you is, Polly, you haven't got any imagination. You can't put yourself in anyone else's place."

"Why should one?" asked Mary.

"Yes, why should one?" said Philip. "I suppose if I'm honest I'd say to pass the time away. But I can put myself in your father's place, or in Gwenda's, and if they're innocent, what hell it must be. What hell for Gwenda to be held suddenly at arms' length. To know in her heart that she's not going to be able to marry the man she loves after all. And then put yourself in your father's place. He knows, he can't help knowing, that the woman he is in love with had an opportunity to do the murder and had a motive, too. He *hopes* she didn't do it, he *thinks* she didn't do it, but he isn't *sure*. And what's more he never will be sure."

"At his age—" began Mary.

"Oh, at his age, at his age," said Philip impatiently. "Don't you realise it's worse for a man of that age? It's the last love of his life. He's not likely to have another. It goes deep. And taking the other point of view," he went on, "suppose Leo came out of the mists and shadows of the self-contained world that he's managed to live in so long. Suppose it was he who struck down his wife? One can almost feel sorry for the poor devil, can't one? Not," he added meditatively, "that I really can imagine his doing anything of the sort for a moment. But I've no doubt the police can imagine it all right. Now, Polly, let's hear your views. Who do you think did it?"

"How can I possibly know?" said Mary.

"Well, perhaps you can't know," said Philip, "but you might have a very good idea—if you thought."

"I tell you I refuse to think about the thing at all."

"I wonder why. . . . Is that just distaste? Or is it—perhaps—because you *do* know? Perhaps in your own cool, calm mind you're quite sure. . . . So sure that you don't want to think about it, that you don't want to tell *me*? Is it Hester you've got in mind?"

"Why on earth should Hester want to kill Mother?"

"No real reason, is there?" said Philip meditatively. "But you know, you do read of those things. A son or a daughter fairly well looked after, indulged, and then one day some silly little thing happens. Fond parent refuses to stump up for the cinema or for buying a new pair of shoes or says when you're going out with the boy-friend you've got to be in at ten. It mayn't be anything very important but it seems to set a match to a train that's already laid, and suddenly the adolescent in question has a brainstorm and up with a hammer or an axe, or possibly a poker, and that's that. Always hard to explain, but it happens. It's the culmination of a long train of repressed rebellion. That's a pattern which would fit Hester. You see, with Hester the trouble is that one doesn't know what goes on in that rather lovely head of hers. She's weak, of course, and she resents being weak. And your mother was the sort of person who would make her feel conscious of her weakness. Yes," said Philip, leaning forward with some animation, "I think I could make out quite a good case for Hester."

"Oh, will you stop talking about it," cried Mary.

"Oh, I'll stop talking," said Philip. "Talking won't get me anywhere. Or will it? After all, one has to decide in one's own mind what the pattern of the murder might be, and apply that pattern to each of the different people concerned. And then when you've got it taped out the way it must have been, *then* you start laying your little pitfalls and see if they tumble into them."

"There were only four people in the house," said Mary. "You speak as though there were half a dozen or more. I agree with you that Father couldn't possibly have done it, and it's absurd to think that Hester could have any real reason for doing anything of that kind. That leaves Kirsty and Gwenda."

"Which of them do you prefer?" asked Philip, with faint mockery in his tone.

"I can't really imagine Kirsty doing such a thing," said Mary. "She's always been so patient and good-tempered. Really quite devoted to Mother. I suppose she *could* go queer suddenly. One does hear of such things, but she's never *seemed* at all queer."

"No," said Philip thoughtfully, "I'd say Kirsty is a very normal woman, the sort of woman who'd have liked a normal woman's life. In a way she's something of the same type as Gwenda, only Gwenda is good-looking and attractive and poor old Kirsty is plain as a currant bun. I don't suppose any man's ever looked at her twice. But she'd have liked them to. She'd have liked to have fallen in love and married. It must be pretty fair hell to be born a woman and to be born plain and unattractive, especially if that isn't compensated for by having any special talent or brain. The truth is she'd been here far too long. She ought to have left after the war, gone on with her profession as masseuse. She might have hooked some well off elderly patient."

"You're like all men," said Mary. "You think women think of nothing but getting married."

Philip grinned.

"I still think it's all women's first choice," he said. "Hasn't Tina any boy-friends, by the way?"

"Not that I know of," said Mary. "But she doesn't talk much about herself."

"No, she's a quiet little mouse, isn't she? Not exactly pretty, but very graceful. I wonder what she knows about this business?"

"I don't suppose she knows anything," said Mary.

"Don't you?" said Philip. "I do."

"Oh, you just imagine things," said Mary.

"I'm not imagining this. Do you know what the girl said? She said she hoped she didn't know anything. Rather a curious way of putting things. I bet she *does* know something."

"What sort of thing?"

"Perhaps there's something that ties in somewhere, but she herself doesn't quite realise where it does tie in. I hope to get it out of her."

"Philip!"

"It's no good, Polly. I've got a mission in life. I've persuaded myself that it's very much in the public interest that I should get down to it. Now where shall I start? I rather think I'll work on Kirsty first. In many ways she's a simple soul."

"I wish—oh, how I wish," said Mary, "that you'd give all this crazy idea up and come home. We were so happy. Everything was going along so well—" Her voice broke as she turned away.

"Polly!" Philip was concerned. "Do you really mind so much? I didn't realise you were quite so upset."

Mary wheeled round, a hopeful look in her eye.

"Then you will come home and forget about it all?"

"I couldn't forget about it all," said Philip. "I'd only go on worrying and puzzling and thinking. Let's stay here till the end of the week anyway, Mary, and then, well, we'll see."

CHAPTER **16...**

"Do you mind if I stay on a bit, Dad?" asked Micky.

"No, of course not. I'm delighted. Is it all right with your firm?"

"Yes," said Micky. "I rang 'em up. I needn't be back until after the week-end. They've been very decent about it. Tina's staying over the week-end too," he said.

He went to the window, looked out, walked across the room with hands in his pockets, gazing up at the bookshelves. He spoke then in a jerky, awkward voice.

"You know, Dad, I do appreciate really all you've done for me. Just lately I've seen—well, I've seen how ungrateful I've always been."

"There's never been any question of gratitude," said Leo Argyle. "You are my son, Micky. I have always regarded you as such."

"An odd way of treating a son," said Micky. "You never bossed me about."

Leo Argyle smiled, his remote, far-away smile.

"Do you really think that's the only function of a father?" he said. "To boss his children about?"

"No," said Micky, "no. I suppose it isn't." He went on, speaking in a rush. "I've been a damned fool," he said. "Yes. A damned fool. It's comic in a way. Do you know what I'd like to do, what I'm thinking of doing? Taking a job with an oil company out in the Persian Gulf. That was what Mother wanted to put me into to begin with—an oil company. But I wasn't having any then! Flung off on my own."

"You were at the age," said Leo, "when you wanted to choose for yourself, and you hated the idea of anything being chosen for you. You've always been rather like that, Micky. If we wanted to buy you a red sweater, you insisted you wanted a blue one, but all the time it was probably a red one you wanted."

"True enough," said Micky, with a short laugh. "I've been an unsatisfactory sort of creature always."

"Just young," said Leo. "Just kicking up your heels. Apprehensive of the bridle, of the saddle, of control. We all feel like that at one time in our lives, but we have to come to it in the end."

"Yes, I suppose so," said Micky.

"I'm very glad," said Leo, "that you have got this idea for the future. I don't think, you know, that just working as a car salesman and demonstrator is quite good enough for you. It's all right, but it doesn't lead anywhere."

"I like cars," said Micky. "I like getting the best out of them. I can do a line of talk when I have to. Patter, patter, all the smarmy bits, but I don't enjoy the life, blast it. This is a job to do with motor transport, anyway. Controlling the servicing of cars. Quite an important job."

"You know," said Leo, "that at any time you might want to finance yourself, to buy yourself into any business you thought worth while, the money is there, available. You know about the Discretionary Trust. I am quite prepared to authorise any necessary sum provided always that the business details are passed and acceptable. We would get expert opinion on that. But the money is there, ready for you if you want it."

"Thanks, Dad, but I don't want to sponge on you."

"There's no question of sponging, Micky, it's *your* money. Definitely made over to you in common with the others. All I have is the power of appointment, the when and the how. But it's not my money and I'm not giving it to you. It's yours."

"It's Mother's money really," said Micky.

"The Trust was made several years ago," said Leo.

"I don't want any of it!" said Micky. "I don't want to touch it! I couldn't! As things are, I *couldn't*." He flushed suddenly as he met his father's eye. He said uncertainly: "I didn't—I didn't quite mean to say that."

"Why can't you touch it?" said Leo. "We adopted you. That is, we took full responsibility for you, financial and otherwise. It was a business arrangement that you should be brought up as our son and properly provided for in life."

"I want to stand on my own feet," Micky repeated.

"Yes. I see you do. . . . Very well, then, Micky, but if you change your mind, remember the money is there, waiting."

"Thanks, Dad. It's good of you to understand. Or at least, not to understand, to let me have my way. I wish I could explain better. You see, I don't want to profit by—I can't profit by—oh, dammit all, it's all too difficult to talk about."

There was a knock on the door which was almost more a bump.

"That's Philip, I expect," said Leo Argyle. "Will you open the door for him, Micky."

Micky went across to open the door, and Philip, working his invalid chair, propelled himself into the room. He greeted them both with a cheerful grin.

"Are you very busy, sir?" he asked Leo. "If so, say so. I'll keep quiet and not interrupt you and just browse along the bookshelves."

"No," said Leo, "I have nothing to do this morning."

"Gwenda not here?" asked Philip.

"She rang up to say she had a headache and couldn't come today," said Leo. His voice was expressionless.

"I see," said Philip.

Micky said:

"Well, I shall go and dig out Tina. Make her go for a walk. That girl hates fresh air."

He left the room, walking with a light, springy step.

"Am I wrong," asked Philip, "or is there a change in Micky lately? Not scowling at the world as much as usual, is he?"

"He's growing up," said Leo. "It's taken rather a long time for him to do so."

"Well, he's chosen a curious time to cheer up," said Philip. "Yesterday's session with the police wasn't exactly encouraging, did you think so?"

Leo said quietly:

"It's painful, of course, to have the whole case reopened."

"A chap like Micky now," said Philip, working his way along the bookshelves, pulling out a volume or two in a desultory manner, "would you say he had much of a conscience?"

"That's an odd question, Philip."

"No, not really. I was just wondering about him. It's like being tone deaf. Some people can't really feel any pangs of guilt or remorse, or even regret for their actions. Jacko didn't."

"No," said Leo, "Jacko certainly didn't."

"And I wondered about Micky," said Philip. He paused, and then went on in a detached voice. "Do you mind if I ask

137

you a question, sir? How much really do you know about the background of all this adopted family of yours?"

"Why do you want to know, Philip?"

"Just curiosity, I suppose. One always wonders, you know, how much there is in heredity."

Leo did not answer. Philip observed him with bright-eyed interest.

"Perhaps," he said, "I'm bothering you asking these questions." ·

"Well," said Leo, rising, "after all, why shouldn't you ask them? You're one of the family. They are at the moment, one can't disguise it, very pertinent questions to ask. But our family, as you put it, were not adopted in the usual regular sense of the term. Mary, your wife, was formally and legally adopted, but the others came to us in a much more informal manner. Jacko was an orphan and was handed over to us by an old grandmother. She was killed in the blitz and he stayed with us. It was as simple as that. Micky was illegitimate. His mother was only interested in men. She wanted £100 down and got it. We've never known what happened to Tina's mother. She never wrote to the child, she never claimed her after the war, and it was quite impossible to trace her."

"And Hester?"

"Hester was illegitimate too. Her mother was a young Irish hospital nurse. She married an American G.I. shortly after Hester came to us. She begged us to keep the child. She did not propose to tell her husband anything about its birth. She went to the States with her husband at the end of the war and we've never heard any more from her."

"All tragic histories in a way," said Philip. "All poor unwanted little devils."

"Yes," said Leo. "That's what made Rachel feel so passionately about them all. She was determined to make them feel wanted, to give them a real home, be a real mother to them."

"It was a fine thing to do," said Philip.

"Only—only it can never work out exactly as she hoped it might," said Leo. "It was an article of faith with her that the blood tie didn't matter. But the blood tie *does* matter, you know. There is usually something in one's own children, some kink of temperament, some way of feeling that you recognise and can understand without having to put into words. You haven't got that tie with children you adopt. One has no *in*-

stinctive knowledge of what goes on in their minds. You judge them, of course, by yourself, by your own thoughts and feelings, but it's wise to recognise that those thoughts and feelings may be very widely divergent from theirs."

"You understood that, I suppose, all along," said Philip.

"I warned Rachel about it," said Leo, "but of course she didn't believe it. Didn't want to believe it. She wanted them to be her own children."

"Tina's always the dark horse, to my mind," said Philip. "Perhaps it's the half of her that isn't white. Who was the father, do you know?"

"He was a seaman of some kind, I believe. Possibly a Lascar. The mother," added Leo dryly, "was unable to say."

"One doesn't know how she reacts to things, or what she thinks about. She says so little." Philip paused, and then shot out a question: "What does she know about this business that she isn't telling?"

He saw Leo Argyle's hand, that had been turning over papers, stop. There was a moment's pause, and then Leo said:

"Why should you think she isn't telling everything she knows?"

"Come now, sir, it's pretty obvious, isn't it?"

"It's not obvious to me," said Leo.

"She knows something," said Philip. "Something damaging, do you think, about some particular person?"

"I think, Philip, if you'll forgive me for saying so, that it is rather unwise to speculate about these things. One can easily imagine so much."

"Are you warning me off, sir?"

"Is it really your business, Philip?"

"Meaning I'm not a policeman?"

"Yes, that's what I meant. Police have to do their duty. They have to enquire into things."

"And you don't want to enquire into them?"

"Perhaps *you* know who did it. Do you, sir?"

"No."

The abruptness and vigour of Leo's reply startled Philip.

"No," said Leo, bringing his hand down on the desk. He was suddenly no longer the frail, attenuated, withdrawn personality that Philip knew so well. "I don't know who did it! D'you hear? I don't know. I haven't the least idea. I don't— I don't *want* to know."

CHAPTER **17** . . .

"AND WHAT are *you* doing, Hester, my love?" asked Philip.

In his wheeled-chair he was propelling himself along the passage. Hester was leaning out of the window halfway along it. She started and drew her head in.

"Oh, it's you," she said.

"Are you observing the universe, or considering suicide?" asked Philip.

She looked at him defiantly.

"What makes you say a thing like that?"

"Obviously it was in your mind," said Philip. "But, frankly, Hester, if you are contemplating such a step, that window is no good. The drop's not deep enough. Think how unpleasant it would be for you with a broken arm and a broken leg, say, instead of the merciful oblivion you are craving?"

"Micky used to climb down the magnolia tree from this window. It was his secret way in and out. Mother never knew."

"The things parents never know! One could write a book about it. But if it's suicide you are contemplating, Hester, just by the summerhouse would be a better place to jump from."

"Where it juts out over the river? Yes, one would be dashed on the rocks below!"

"The trouble with you, Hester, is that you're so melodramatic in your imaginings. Most people are quite satisfied with arranging themselves tidily in the gas oven or measuring themselves out an enormous number of sleeping pills."

"I'm glad you're here," said Hester unexpectedly. "You don't mind talking about things, do you?"

"Well, actually, I haven't much else to do nowadays," said Philip. "Come into my room and we'll do some more talking." As she hesitated, he went on: "Mary's downstairs, gone to prepare me some delicious little morning mess with her own fair hands."

"Mary wouldn't understand," said Hester.

"No," Philip agreed, "Mary wouldn't understand in the least."

Philip propelled himself along and Hester walked beside him. She opened the door of the sitting room and he wheeled himself in. Hester followed.

"But you understand," said Hester. "Why?"

"Well, there's a time, you know, when one thinks about such things. . . . When this business first happened to me, for instance, and I knew that I might be a cripple for life . . ."

"Yes," said Hester, "that must have been terrible. Terrible. And you were a pilot, too, weren't you? You flew."

"Up above the world so high, like a tea-tray in the sky," agreed Philip.

"I'm terribly sorry," said Hester. "I am really. I ought to have thought about it more, and been more sympathetic!"

"Thank God you weren't," said Philip. "But anyway, that phase is over now. One gets used to anything, you know. That's something, Hester, that you don't appreciate at the moment. But you'll come to it. Unless you do something very rash and very silly first. Now come on, tell me all about it. What's the trouble? I suppose you've had a row with your boy-friend, the solemn young doctor. Is that it?"

"It wasn't a row," said Hester. "It was much worse than a row."

"It will come right," said Philip.

"No, it won't," said Hester. "It can't—ever."

"You're so extravagant in your terms. Everything's black and white to you, isn't it, Hester? No half-tones."

"I can't help being like that," said Hester. "I've always been like it. Everything I thought I could do or wanted to do has always gone wrong. I wanted to have a life of my own, to be someone, to do something. It was all no good. I was no good at *anything*. I've often thought of killing myself. Ever since I was fourteen."

Philip watched her with interest. He said in a quiet, matter-of-fact voice:

"Of course people do kill themselves a good deal, between fourteen and nineteen. It's an age in life when things are very much out of proportion. Schoolboys kill themselves because they don't think they can pass examinations and girls kill themselves because their mothers won't let them go to the pictures with unsuitable boy-friends. It's a kind of period where everything appears to be in glorious technicolour. Joy or despair. Gloom or unparalleled happiness. One snaps out of it. The trouble with you is, Hester, it's taken you longer to snap out of it than most people."

"Mother was always right," said Hester. "All the things she wouldn't let me do and I wanted to do. She was right about them and I was wrong. I couldn't bear it, I simply couldn't bear it! So I thought I'd got to be brave. I'd got to go off on my own. I'd got to test myself. And it all went wrong. I wasn't any good at acting."

"Of course you weren't," said Philip. "You've got no discipline. You can't, as they say in theatrical circles, take production. You're too busy dramatising yourself, my girl. You're doing it now."

"And then I thought I'd have a proper love affair," said Hester. "Not a silly, girlish thing. An older man. He was married, and he'd had a very unhappy life."

"Stock situation," said Philip, "and he exploited it, no doubt."

"I thought it would be a—oh, a grand passion. You're not laughing at me?" She stopped, looking at Philip suspiciously.

"No, I'm not laughing at you, Hester," said Philip gently. "I can see quite well that it must have been hell for you."

"It wasn't a grand passion," said Hester bitterly. "It was just a silly, cheap little affair. None of the things he told me about his life, or his wife, were true. I—I'd just thrown myself at his head. I'd been a fool, a silly, cheap little fool."

"You've got to learn a thing, sometimes, by experience," said Philip. "None of that's done you any harm, you know, Hester. It's probably helped you to grow up. Or it would help you if you let it."

"Mother was so—so competent about it all," said Hester, in a tone of resentment. "She came along and settled everything and told me that if I really wanted to act I'd better go to the dramatic school and do it properly. But I didn't really want to act, and I knew by that time I was no good. So I came home. What else could I do?"

"Probably heaps of things," said Philip. "But that was the easiest."

"Oh, yes," said Hester with fervour. "How well you understand. I'm terribly weak, you see. I always do want to do the easy thing. And if I rebel against it, it's always in some silly way that doesn't really work."

"You're terribly unsure of yourself, aren't you?" said Philip gently.

"Perhaps that's because I'm only adopted," said Hester. "I didn't find out about that, you know, not till I was nearly sixteen. I knew the others were and then I asked one day, and —I found that I was adopted too. It made me feel so awful, as though I didn't belong *anywhere*."

"What a terrible girl you are for dramatising yourself," said Philip.

"She wasn't my mother," said Hester. "She never really understood a single thing I felt. Just looked at me indulgently and kindly and made plans for me. Oh! I hated her. It's awful of me, I know it's awful of me, but I hated her!"

"Actually, you know," said Philip, "most girls go through a short period of hating their own mothers. There wasn't really anything very unusual about that."

"I hated her because she was right," said Hester. "It's so awful when people are always right. It makes you feel more and more inadequate. Oh, Philip, everything's so terrible. What am I going to do? What can I do?"

"Marry that nice young man of yours," said Philip, "and settle down. Be a good little G.P.'s wife. Or isn't that magnificent enough for you?"

"He doesn't want to marry me now," said Hester mournfully.

"Are you sure? Did he tell you so? Or are you only imagining it?"

"He thinks I killed Mother."

"Oh," said Philip, and paused a minute. "Did you?" he asked.

She wheeled round at him.

"Why do you ask me that? Why?"

"I thought it would be interesting to know," said Philip. "All in the family, so to speak. Not for passing on to the authorities."

"If I did kill her, do you think I'd tell you?" said Hester.

"It would be much wiser not to," agreed Philip.

"He told me he knew I'd killed her," said Hester. "He told me that if I'd only admit it, if I'd confess it to him, that it would be all right, that we'd be married, that he'd look after me. That—that he wouldn't let it matter between us."

Philip whistled.

"Well, well, well," he said.

143

"What's the good?" asked Hester. "What's the good of telling him I didn't kill her? He wouldn't believe it, would he?"

"He ought to," said Philip, "if you tell him so."

"I didn't kill her," said Hester. "You understand? I didn't kill her. I didn't, I didn't, I didn't." She broke off. "That sounds unconvincing," she said.

"The truth often does sound unconvincing," Philip encouraged her.

"We don't know," said Hester. "Nobody knows. We all *look* at each other. Mary looks at me. And Kirsten. She's so kind to me, so protective. She thinks it's me, too. What chance have I? That's it, don't you see? What chance have I? It would be better, much better, to go down to the Point, throw myself over. . . ."

"For God's sake, don't be a fool, Hester. There are other things to do."

"What other things? How can there be? I've lost everything. How can I go on living day after day?" She looked at Philip. "You think I'm wild, unbalanced. Well, perhaps I did kill her. Perhaps it's remorse gnawing at me. Perhaps I can't forget—*here*." She put her hand dramatically to her heart.

"Don't be a little idiot," said Philip. He shot out an arm and pulled her to him.

Hester half fell across his chair. He kissed her.

"What you need is a husband, my girl," he said. "Not that solemn young ass, Donald Craig, with his head full of psychiatry and jargon. You're silly and idiotic and—completely lovely, Hester."

The door opened. Mary Durrant stood abruptly still in the doorway. Hester struggled to an upright position and Philip gave his wife a sheepish grin.

"I'm just cheering up Hester, Polly," he said.

"Oh," said Mary.

She came in carefully, placing the tray on a small table. Then she wheeled the table up beside him. She did not look at Hester. Hester looked uncertainly from husband to wife.

"Oh well," she said, "perhaps I'd better go and—go and—" She didn't finish.

She went out of the room, shutting the door behind her.

"Hester's in a bad way," said Philip. "Contemplating suicide. I was trying to dissuade her," he added.

Mary did not answer.

He stretched out a hand towards her. She moved away from him.

"Polly, have I made you angry? Very angry?"

She did not reply.

"Because I kissed her, I suppose? Come, Polly, don't grudge me one silly little kiss. She was so lovely and so silly—and I suddenly felt—well, I felt it would be fun to be a gay dog again and have a flirtation now and then. Come, Polly, kiss me. Kiss and make friends."

Mary Durrant said:

"Your soup will get cold if you don't drink it."

She went through the door to the bedroom and shut it behind her.

CHAPTER **18...**

"THERE'S A YOUNG lady down below wanting to see you, sir."

"A young lady?" Calgary looked surprised. He could not think who was likely to visit him. He looked at the work which littered his desk, and frowned. The voice of the hall porter spoke again, discreetly lowered.

"A real young lady, sir, a very nice young lady."

"Oh, well. Show her up then."

Calgary could not help smiling to himself slightly. The discreet undertones and the assurance tickled his sense of humour. He wondered who it could be who wanted to see him. He was completely astonished when his door bell buzzed and on going to open it he was confronted by Hester Argyle.

"You!" The exclamation came out with full surprise. Then, "Come in, come in," he said. He drew her inside and shut the door.

Strangely enough, his impression of her was almost the same as the first time he had seen her. She was dressed with no regard to the conventions of London. She was hatless, her dark hair hanging round her face in a kind of elf lock disarray. The heavy tweed coat showed a dark green skirt and sweater underneath. She looked as though she had just come in breathless from a walk on the moor.

"Please," said Hester, "please you've got to help me."

"To help you?" He was startled. "In what way? Of course I'll help you if I can."

"I didn't know what to do," said Hester. "I didn't know who to come to. But someone's got to help me. I can't go on, and you're the person. You started it all."

"You're in trouble of some kind? Bad trouble?"

"We're all in trouble," said Hester. "But one's so selfish, isn't one? I mean, I only think of myself."

"Sit down, my dear," he said gently.

He cleared papers off an armchair and settled her there. Then he went over to his corner cupboard.

"You must have a glass of wine," he said. "A glass of dry sherry. Will that suit you?"

"If you like. It doesn't matter."

"It's very wet and cold out. You need something."

He turned, decanter and glass in hand. Hester was slumped down in the chair with a queer kind of angular grace that touched him by its complete abandonment.

"Don't worry," he said gently, as he put the glass by her side and filled it. "Things are never quite so bad as they seem, you know."

"People say that, but it's not true," said Hester. "Sometimes they're worse than they seem." She sipped the wine, then she said accusingly, "We were all right till you came. Quite all right. Then—then it all started."

"I won't pretend," said Arthur Calgary, "that I don't know what you mean. It took me completely aback when you first said that to me, but now I understand better what my—my information must have brought to you."

"So long as we thought it was Jacko—" Hester said and broke off.

"I know, Hester, I know. But you've got to go behind that, you know. What you were living in was a false security. It wasn't a real thing, it was only a thing of make-believe, of cardboard—a kind of stage scenery. Something that represented security but which was not really, and could never be, security."

"You're saying, aren't you," said Hester, "that one must have courage, that it's no good snatching at a thing because it's false and easy?" She paused a minute and then said: "*You* had courage! I realise that. To come and tell us yourself. Not knowing how we'd feel, how we'd react. It was brave of you. I admire bravery because, you see, I'm not really very brave myself."

"Tell me," said Calgary gently, "tell me just what the trouble is now. It's something special, isn't it?"

"I had a dream," said Hester. "There's someone—a young man—a doctor—"

"I see," said Calgary. "You are friends, or, perhaps, more than friends?"

"I thought," said Hester, "we were more than friends. . . . And he thought so too. But you see, now that all this has come up—"

"Yes?" said Calgary.

147

"He thinks I did it," said Hester. Her words came with a rush. "Or perhaps he doesn't think I did it but he's not sure. He can't be sure. He thinks—I can see he thinks—that I'm the most likely person. Perhaps I am. Perhaps we all think that about each other. And I thought, somebody has got to help us in the terrible mess we're in, and I thought of you because of the dream. You see, I was lost and I couldn't find Don. He'd left me and there was a great big sort of ravine thing—an abyss. Yes, that's the word. An abyss. It sounds so deep, doesn't it? So deep and so—so unbridgeable. And you were there on the other side and you held out your hands and said 'I want to help you.'" She drew a deep breath. "So I came to you. I ran away and I came here because you've got to help us. If you don't help us, I don't know what's going to happen. You *must* help us. You brought all this. You'll say, perhaps, that it's nothing to do with you. That having once told us—told us the truth about what happened—that it's no business of yours. You'll say—"

"No," said Calgary, interrupting her. "I shall not say anything of the kind. It is my business, Hester. I agree with you. When you start a thing you have to go on with it. I feel that every bit as much as you do."

"Oh!" Colour flamed up into Hester's face. Suddenly, as was the way with her, she looked beautiful. "So I'm not alone!" she said. "There *is* someone."

"Yes, my dear, there is someone—for what he's worth. So far I haven't been worth very much, but I'm trying and I've never stopped trying to help." He sat down and drew his chair nearer to her. "Now tell me all about it," he said. "Has it been very bad?"

"It's one of us you see," said Hester. "We all know that. Mr. Marshall came and we pretended it must have been someone who got in, but he knew it wasn't. It's one of us."

"And your young man—what's-his-name?"

"Don. Donald Craig. He's a doctor."

"Don thinks it's you?"

"He's afraid it's me," said Hester. She twisted her hands in a dramatic gesture. She looked at him. "Perhaps you think it's me, too?"

"Oh, no," said Calgary. "Oh, no, I know quite well that you're innocent."

"You say that as though you were really quite sure."

"I am quite sure," said Calgary.

148

"But why? How can you be so sure?"

"Because of what you said to me when I left the house after telling all of you. Do you remember? What you said to me about innocence. You couldn't have said that—you couldn't have felt that way—unless you were innocent."

"Oh," cried Hester. "Oh—the relief! To know there's someone who really feels like that!"

"So now," said Calgary, "we can discuss it calmly, can't we?"

"Yes," said Hester. "It feels—it feels quite different now."

"Just as a matter of interest," said Calgary, "and keeping firmly in mind that you know what I feel about it, why should anyone for one moment think that you would kill your adopted mother?"

"I might have done," said Hester. "I often felt like it. One does sometimes feel just mad with rage. One feels so futile, so—so helpless. Mother was always so calm and so superior and knew everything, and was right about everything. Sometimes I would think, 'Oh! I would like to kill her.'" She looked at him. "Do you understand? Didn't you ever feel like that when you were young?"

The last words gave Calgary a sudden pang, the same pang perhaps that he had felt when Micky in the hotel at Drymouth had said to him, "You look older!" "When he was young?" Did it seem so very long ago to Hester? He cast his mind back. He remembered himself at nine years old consulting with another small boy in the gardens of his prep school, wondering ingeniously what would be the best way to dispose of Mr. Warborough, their form master. He remembered the helplessness of rage that had consumed him when Mr. Warborough had been particularly sarcastic in his comments. That, he thought, was what Hester had felt too. But whatever he and young—what was his name now?— Porch, yes, Porch had been the boy's name—although he and young Porch had consulted and planned, they had never taken any active steps to bring about the demise of Mr. Warborough.

"You know," he said to Hester, "you ought to have got over those sort of feelings a good many years ago. I can understand them, of course."

"It was just that Mother had that effect upon me," said Hester. "I'm beginning to see now, you know, that it was my own fault. I feel that if only she'd lived a little longer, just lived till I was a little older, a little more settled, that—that we'd have been friends in a curious way. That I'd have been glad of her help and her advice. But—but as it was I couldn't bear it; because, you see, it made me feel so ineffectual, so stupid. Everything I did went wrong and I could see for myself that the things I did were foolish things. That I'd only done them because I wanted to rebel, wanted to prove that I was myself. And I wasn't *anybody*. I was fluid. Yes, that's the word," said Hester. "It's exactly the word. Fluid. Never taking a shape for long. Just trying on shapes—shapes—shapes of other people that I admired. I thought, you see, if I ran away and went on the stage and had an affair with someone, that—"

"That you would feel yourself, or at any rate, feel somebody?"

"Yes," said Hester. "Yes, that's just it. And of course really I see now that I was just behaving like a silly child. But you don't know how I wish, Dr. Calgary, that Mother was alive now. Because it's so unfair—unfair on her, I mean. She did so much for us and gave us so much. We didn't give her anything back. And now it's too late." She paused. "That's why," she said, with a sudden renewal of vigour, "I've determined to stop being silly and childish. And you'll help me, won't you?"

"I've already said I'll do anything in the world to help you."

She gave him a quick, rather lovely smile.

"Tell me," he said, "exactly what has been happening."

"Just what I thought would happen," said Hester. "We've all been looking at each other and wondering and we don't know. Father looks at Gwenda and thinks perhaps it was her. She looks at father and isn't sure. I don't think they're going to get married now. It's spoilt everything. And Tina thinks Micky had something to do with it. I don't know why because he wasn't there that evening. And Kirsten thinks I did it and tries to protect me. And Mary—that's my older sister who you didn't meet—Mary thinks Kirsten did it."

"And who do you think did it, Hester?"

"Me?" Hester sounded startled.

"Yes, you," said Calgary. "I think, you know, it's rather important to know that."

Hester spread out her hands. "I don't know," she wailed. "I just don't know. I'm—it's an awful thing to say—but I'm frightened of everybody. It's as though behind each face there was another face. A—sinister sort of face that I don't know. I don't feel sure that Father's Father, and Kirsten keeps saying that I shouldn't trust anybody—not even her. And I look at Mary and I feel I don't know anything about her. And Gwenda—I've always liked Gwenda. I've been glad that Father was going to marry Gwenda. But now I'm not sure about Gwenda any more. I see her as somebody different, ruthless and—and revengeful. I don't know what anybody's like. There's an awful feeling of unhappiness."

"Yes," said Calgary, "I can well imagine that."

"There's so much unhappiness," said Hester, "that I can't help feeling perhaps there's the murderer's unhappiness too. And that might be the worst of all. . . . Do you think that's likely?"

"It's possible, I suppose," said Calgary, "and yet I doubt —of course I'm not an expert—I doubt if a murderer is ever really unhappy."

"But why not? I should think it would be the most terrible thing to be, to know you'd killed someone."

"Yes," said Calgary, "it is a terrible thing and therefore I think a murderer must be one of two kinds of people. Either a person to whom it has *not* been terrible to kill anyone, the kind of person who says to himself, 'Well, of course it was a pity to have to do that but it was necessary for my own well being. After all, it's not my fault. I just—well, just had to do it.' Or else—"

"Yes?" said Hester. "What's the other kind of murderer?"

"I'm only guessing, mind you, I don't know, but I think if you were what you call the other kind of murderer, you wouldn't be able to live with your unhappiness over what you'd done. You'd either have to confess it or else you'd have to rewrite the story for yourself, as it were. Putting the blame on someone else, saying 'I should never have done such a thing unless—' such and such a thing had happened. 'I'm not really a murderer because I didn't mean to do it. It just happened, and so really it was fate and not myself.' Do you understand a little what I am trying to say?"

"Yes," said Hester, "and I think it's very interesting." She half-closed her eyes. "I'm just trying to think—"

"Yes, Hester," said Calgary, "think. Think as hard as you can because if I'm ever going to be able to help you I've got to see things through your mind."

"Micky hated Mother," said Hester slowly. "He always did . . . I don't know why. Tina, I think, loved her. Gwenda didn't like her. Kirsten was always loyal to Mother though she didn't always think that Mother was right in all the things she did. Father—" she paused for a long time.

"Yes?" Calgary prompted her.

"Father's gone a long way away again," said Hester. "After Mother died, you know, he was quite different. Not so—what shall I call it—remote. He's been more human, more alive. But now he's gone back to some—some sort of shadowy place where you can't get at him. I don't know what he felt about Mother, really. I suppose he loved her when he married her. They never quarrelled, but I don't know what he felt about her. Oh"—her hands flew out again—"one doesn't know what anyone feels, does one, really? I mean, what goes on behind their faces, behind their nice everyday words? They may be ravaged with hate or love or despair, and one wouldn't *know!* It's frightening. . . . Oh, Dr. Calgary, it's frightening!"

He took both her hands in his.

"You're not a child any longer," he said. "Only children are frightened. You're grown-up, Hester. You're a woman." He released her hands and said in a matter-of-fact tone: "Is there anywhere you can stay in London?"

Hester looked slightly bewildered.

"I suppose so. I don't know. Mother usually stayed at Curtis's."

"Well, that's a very nice, quiet hotel. I should go there and book a room if I were you."

"I'll do anything you tell me to do," said Hester.

"Good girl," said Calgary. "What's the time?" He looked up at the clock. "Hallo, it's about seven o'clock already. Supposing you go and book yourself a room, and I'll come along about quarter to eight to take you out to dinner. How would that suit you?"

"It sounds wonderful," said Hester. "Do you really mean it?"

"Yes," said Calgary, "I really mean it."

"But after that? What's going to happen next? I can't go on staying, can I, at Curtis's for ever?"

"Your horizon always seems bounded by infinity," said Calgary.

"Are you laughing at me?" she asked him doubtfully.

"Just a little," he said, and smiled.

Her expression wavered and then she, too, smiled.

"I suppose really," she said confidentially, "I've been dramatising myself again."

"It's rather a habit of yours, I suspect," said Calgary.

"That's why I thought I should do well on the stage," said Hester. "But I didn't. I was no good at all. Oh, I was a lousy actress."

"You'll get all the drama you want out of ordinary life, I should say," said Calgary. "Now I'm going to put you in a taxi, my dear, and you go off to Curtis's. And wash your face and brush your hair," he went on. "Have you got any luggage with you?"

"Oh, yes. I've got a sort of overnight bag."

"Good." He smiled at her. "Don't worry, Hester," he said again. "We'll think of something."

CHAPTER 19

"I WANT TO talk to you, Kirsty," said Philip.

"Yes, of course, Philip."

Kirsten Lindstrom paused in her task. She had just brought in some washing which she was putting away in the chest of drawers.

"I want to talk to you about all this business," said Philip. "You don't mind, do you?"

"There is too much talk already," said Kirsten. "That is my view."

"But it would be as well, wouldn't it," said Philip, "to come to some conclusion among ourselves. You know what's going on at present, don't you?"

"Things are going wrong everywhere," said Kirsten.

"Do you think Leo and Gwenda will ever get married now?"

"Why not?"

"Several reasons," said Philip. "First of all, perhaps, because Leo Argyle, being an intelligent man, realises that a marriage between him and Gwenda will give the police what they want. A perfectly good motive for the murder of his wife. Or, alternatively, because Leo suspects that Gwenda is the murderer. And being a sensitive man, he doesn't really like taking as a second wife the woman who killed his first wife. What do you say to that?" he added.

"Nothing," said Kirsten. "What should I say?"

"Playing it very close to your chest, aren't you, Kirsty?"

"I don't understand you."

"Who are you covering up for, Kirsten?"

"I am not 'covering up,' as you call it, for anyone. I think there should be less talk and I think people should not stay on in this house. It is not good for them. I think you, Philip, should go home with your wife to your own home."

"Oh, you do, do you? Why, in particular?"

"You are asking questions," said Kirsten. "You are trying to find out things. And your wife does not want you to do it. She is wiser than you are. You might find out something you did not want to find out, or that she did not want you to find out. You should go home, Philip. You should go soon."

"I don't want to go home," said Philip. He spoke rather like a petulant small boy.

"That is what children say," said Kirsten. "They say I don't want to do this and I don't want to do that, but those who know more of life, who see better what is happening, have to coax them to do what they do not want to do."

"So this is your idea of coaxing, is it?" said Philip. "Giving me orders."

"No, I do not give you orders. I only advise you." She sighed. "I would advise all of them the same way. Micky should go back to his work as Tina has gone back to her library. I am glad Hester has gone. She should be somewhere where she is not continually reminded of all this."

"Yes," said Philip. "I agree with you there. You're right about Hester. But what about you yourself, Kirsten? Oughtn't you to go away, too?"

"Yes," said Kirsten with a sigh. "I ought to go away."

"Why don't you?"

"You would not understand. It is too late for me to go."

Philip looked at her thoughtfully. Then he said:

"There are so many variations, aren't there—variations on a single theme. Leo thinks Gwenda did it, Gwenda thinks Leo did it. Tina knows something that makes her suspect who did it. Micky knows who did it but doesn't care. Mary thinks Hester did it." He paused and then went on, "But the truth is, Kirsty, that those are only variations on a theme as I said. We know who did it quite well, don't we, Kirsty. You and I?"

She shot a quick, horrified glance at him.

"I thought as much," said Philip exultantly.

"What do you mean? said Kirsten. "What are you trying to say?"

"I *don't* really know who did it," said Philip. *"But you do.* You don't only think you know who did it, you actually *do know.* I'm right, aren't I?"

Kirsten marched to the door. She opened it, then turned back and spoke.

"It is not a polite thing to say, but I will say it. You are a fool, Philip. What you are trying to do is dangerous. You understand one kind of danger. You have been a pilot. You have faced death up there in the sky. Can you not see that if you get anywhere near the truth, you are in just as great danger as you ever were in the war?"

"And what about you, Kirsty? If you know the truth, aren't you in danger too?"

"I can take care of myself," said Kirsten grimly. "I can be on my guard. But you, Philip, are in an invalid chair and helpless. Think of that! Besides," she added, "I do not air my views. I am content to let things be—because I honestly think that that is best for everyone. If everyone would go away and attend to their own business, then there would be no further trouble. If I am asked, I have my official view. I say still that it was Jacko."

"Jacko?" Philip stared.

"Why not? Jacko was clever. Jacko could plan a thing and be sure he would not suffer from the consequences. Often he did that as a child. After all, to fake an alibi. Is that not done every day?"

"He couldn't have faked this one. Dr. Calgary—"

"Dr. Calgary—Dr. Calgary," said Kirsten with impatience, "because he is well known, because he has a famous name, you say, 'Dr. Calgary' as though he were God! But let me tell you this. When you have had concussion as he had concussion, things may be quite different from the way you remember them. It may have been a different day—a different time—a different place!"

Philip looked at her, his head slightly on one side.

"So that's your story," he said. "*And* you're sticking to it. A very creditable attempt. But you don't believe it yourself, do you, Kirsty?"

"I've warned you," said Kirsten, "I can't do more."

She turned away, then popped her head in again to say in her usual matter-of-fact voice:

"Tell Mary I have put the clean washing away in the second drawer there."

Philip smiled a little at the anti-climax, then the smile died away. . . .

His sense of inner excitement grew. He had a feeling he was getting very near indeed. His experiment with Kirsten had been highly satisfactory, but he doubted that he would get any more out of her. Her solicitude for him irritated him. Just because he was a cripple did not mean that he was as vulnerable as she made out. He, too, could be on his guard—and for heaven's sake, wasn't he watched over incessantly? Mary hardly ever left his side.

He drew a sheet of paper towards him and began to write. Brief notes, names, question marks. . . . A vulnerable spot to probe. . . .

Suddenly he nodded his head and wrote: *Tina . . .*

He thought about it. . . .

Then he drew another sheet of paper towards him.

When Mary came in, he hardly looked up.

"What are you doing, Philip?"

"Writing a letter."

"To Hester?"

"Hester? No. I don't even know where she's staying. Kirsty just had a postcard from her with London written at the top, that was all."

He grinned at her.

"I believe you're jealous, Polly. Are you?"

Her eyes, blue and cold, looked into his.

"Perhaps."

He felt a little uncomfortable.

"Who are you writing to?" She came a step nearer.

"The Public Prosecutor," said Philip cheerfully, though within him a cold anger stirred. Couldn't a fellow write a letter, even, without being questioned about it?

Then he saw her face and he relented.

"Only a joke, Polly. I'm writing to Tina."

"To Tina? Why?"

"Tina's my next line of attack. Where are you going, Polly?"

"To the bathroom," said Mary as she went out of the room.

Philip laughed. To the bathroom, as on the night of the murder. . . . He laughed again as he remembered their conversation about it.

ii.

"Come on, sonny," said Superintendent Huish encouragingly. "Let's hear all about it."

Master Cyril Green took a deep breath. Before he could speak, his mother interposed.

"As you might say, Mr. Huish, I didn't take much notice at the time. You know what these children are. Always talking and thinking about space ships and things. And he comes home to me and he says, 'Mum, I've seen a sputnik, it's come down.' Well, I mean, before that it was flying saucers. It's always something. It's these Russians that go putting things into their heads."

Superintendent Huish sighed and thought how much easier it would be if mothers would not insist on accompanying their sons and talking for them.

"Come on, Cyril," he said, "you went home and told your Mum—that's right, isn't it?—that you'd seen this Russian sputnik—whatever it was."

"Didn't know no better then," said Cyril. "I was only a kid then. That's two years ago. Course, I know better now."

"Them bubble cars," his mother put in, "was quite new at the time. There hadn't been one about locally, so naturally when he saw it—and bright red too—he didn't realise as it was just an ordinary car. And when we heard the next morning as Mrs. Argyle had been done in, Cyril he says to me, 'Mum,' he says, 'it's them Russians,' he says, 'they come down in that sputnik of theirs and they must have got in and killed her.' 'Don't talk such nonsense,' I said. And then of course later in the day we hear her own son has been arrested for having done it."

Superintendent Huish addressed himself patiently once more to Cyril.

"It was in the evening, I understand? What time, do you remember?"

"I'd had me tea," said Cyril, breathing hard in the effort of rememberance, "and Mum was out at the Institute, so I went out again a bit with the boys and we larked around a bit up that way down the new road."

"And what was you doing there, I'd like to know," his mother put in.

P.C. Good, who'd brought in this promising piece of evidence, interposed. He knew well enough what Cyril and the boys had been doing down the new road. The disappearance of chrysanthemums had been angrily reported from several householders there, and he knew well enough that the bad characters of the village surreptitiously encouraged the younger generation to supply them with flowers which they themselves took to market. This was not the moment, P.C. Good knew, to go into past cases of delinquency. He said heavily:

"Boys is boys, Mrs. Green, they gets larking around."

"Yes," said Cyril, "just having a game or two, we were. And that's where I saw it. 'Coo,' I said, 'what's this?' O' course I know now, I'm not a silly kid any longer. It was just one o' them bubble cars. Bright red, it was."

"And the time?" said Superintendent Huish patiently.

"Well, as I say, I'd had me tea an' we'd gone out there and larked around—must have been near on seven o'clock, because I heard the clock strike and 'Coo,' I thought, 'Mum'll be home and won't she create if I'm not there.' So I went home. I told her then that I thought I'd seen that Russian satellite come down. Mum said it were all lies, but it wasn't. Only o' course, I knows better now. I was just a kid then, see."

Superintendent Huish said that he saw. After a few more questions he dismissed Mrs. Green and her offspring. P.C. Good, remaining behind, put on the gratified expression of a junior member of the force who has shown intelligence and hopes that it will count in his favour.

"It just come to me," said P.C. Good, "what that boy'd been around saying about Russians doing Mrs. Argyle in. I thought to myself, 'Well, that may mean something.'"

"It does mean something," said the superintendent. "Miss Tina Argyle has a red bubble car, and it looks as though I'd have to ask her a few more questions."

iii.

"You were there that night, Miss Argyle?"

Tina looked at the superintendent. Her hands lay loosely in her lap, her eyes, dark, unwinking, told nothing.

"It is so long ago," she said, "really I cannot remember."

"Your car was seen there," said Huish.

"Was it?"

"Come now, Miss Argyle. When we asked you for an account of your movements on that night, you told us that you went home and didn't go out that evening. You made yourself supper and listened to the gramophone. Now, that isn't true. Just before seven o'clock your car was seen in the road quite near to Sunny Point. What were you doing there?"

She did not answer. Huish waited a few moments, then he spoke again.

"Did you go into the house, Miss Argyle?"

159

"No," said Tina.

"But you were there?"

"You say I was there."

"It's not just a question of my saying so. We've got evidence that you were there."

Tina sighed.

"Yes," she said. "I did drive out there that evening."

"But you say you didn't go into the house?"

"No, I didn't go into the house."

"What did you do?"

"I drove back again to Redmyn. Then, as I told you, I made myself some supper and put on the gramophone."

"Why did you drive out there if you didn't go into the house?"

"I changed my mind," said Tina.

"What made you change your mind, Miss Argyle?"

"When I got there I didn't want to go in."

"Because of something you saw or heard?"

She did not answer.

"Listen, Miss Argyle. That was the night that your mother was murdered. She was killed between seven and half past that evening. You were there, your car was there, at some time before seven. How long it was there we do not know. It is possible, you know, that it may have been there for some time. It may be that you went into the house—you have a key, I think—"

"Yes," said Tina, "I have a key."

"Perhaps you went into the house. Perhaps you went into your mother's sitting room and found her there, dead. Or perhaps—"

Tina raised her head.

"Or perhaps I killed her? Is that what you want to say, Superintendent Huish?"

"It is one possibility," said Huish, "but I think it's more likely, Miss Argyle, someone else did the killing. If so, I think you know—or have a very strong suspicion—who the killer was."

"I did not go into the house," said Tina.

"Then you saw something or heard something. You saw someone go into the house or someone leave the house. Someone perhaps who was not known to be there. Was it your brother Michael, Miss Argyle?"

Tina said:

160

"I saw nobody."

"But you heard something," said Huish shrewdly. "What did you hear, Miss Argyle?"

"I tell you," said Tina, "I simply changed my mind."

"You'll forgive me, Miss Argyle, but I don't believe that. Why should you drive out from Redmyn to visit your family, and drive back again without seeing them? Something made you change your mind about that. Something you saw or heard." He leaned forward. "I think you know, Miss Argyle, who killed your mother."

Very slowly she shook her head.

"You know *something*," said Huish. "Something that you are determined not to tell. But think, Miss Argyle, think very carefully. Do you realise what you are condemning your entire family to go through? Do you want them all to remain under suspicion--for that's what's going to happen unless we get at the truth. Whoever killed your mother doesn't deserve to be shielded. For that's it, isn't it? You're shielding some-one."

Again that dark, opaque look met his.

"I know nothing," said Tina. "I didn't hear anything and didn't see anything. I just—changed my mind."

CHAPTER 20

CALGARY AND Huish looked at each other. Calgary saw what seemed to him one of the most depressed and gloomy-looking men he had ever seen. So profoundly disillusioned did he appear that Calgary felt tempted to suppose that Superintendent Huish's career had been one long series of failures. He was surprised to discover on a later occasion that Superintendent Huish had been extremely successful professionally. Huish saw a lean, prematurely grey-haired man with slightly stooping shoulders, a sensitive face and a singularly attractive smile.

"You don't know who I am, I'm afraid," Calgary began.

"Oh, we know all about you, Dr. Calgary," said Huish. "You're the joker in the pack who queered the Argyle case." A rather unexpected smile lifted the corners of his sad-looking mouth.

"You can hardly regard me favourably then," said Calgary.

"It's all in the day's work," said Superintendent Huish. "It seemed a clear case and nobody can be blamed for thinking it so. But these things happen," he went on. "They're sent to try us, so my old mother used to say. We don't bear malice, Dr. Calgary. After all, we do stand for Justice, don't we?"

"So I've always believed, and shall continue to believe," said Calgary. "To no man will we deny Justice," he murmured softly.

"Magna Carta," said Superintendent Huish.

"Yes," said Calgary, "quoted to me by Miss Tina Argyle." Superintendent Huish's eyebrows rose.

"Indeed. You surprise me. That young lady, I should say, has not been particularly active in helping the wheels of justice to turn."

"Now why do you say that?" asked Calgary.

"Frankly," said Huish, "for withholding information. There's no doubt about that."

"Why?" asked Calgary.

"Well, it's a family business," said Huish. "Families stick together. But what was it you wanted to see me about?" he continued.

"I want information," said Calgary.

"About the Argyle case?"

"Yes. I realise that I must seem to you to be butting in in a matter that's not my concern—"

"Well, it is your concern in a way, isn't it?"

"Ah, you do appreciate that. Yes. I feel responsible. Responsible for bringing trouble."

"You can't make an omelette without breaking eggs, as the French say," said Huish.

"There are things I want to know," said Calgary.

"Such as?"

"I'd like a great deal more information about Jacko Argyle."

"About *Jacko* Argyle. Well, now, I didn't expect you to say that."

"He'd got a bad record, I know," said Calgary. "What I want is a few details from it."

"Well, that's simple enough," said Huish. "He'd been on probation twice. On another occasion, for embezzlement of funds, he was just saved by being able to put up the money in time."

"The budding young criminal, in fact?" asked Calgary.

"Quite right, sir," said Huish. "Not a murderer, as you've made clear to us, but a good many other things. Nothing, mind you, on a grand scale. He hadn't got the brains or the nerve to put up a big swindle. Just a small-time criminal. Pinching money out of tills, wheedling it out of women."

"And he was good at that," said Calgary. "Wheedling money out of women, I mean."

"And a very nice safe line it is," said Superintendent Huish. "Women fell for him very easily. Middle-aged or elderly were the ones he usually went for. You'd be surprised how gullible that type of woman can be. He put over a very pretty line. Got them to believe he was passionately in love with them. There's nothing a woman won't believe if she wants to."

"And then?" asked Calgary.

Huish shrugged his shoulders.

"Well, sooner or later they were disillusioned. But they

don't prosecute, you know. They don't want to tell the world that they've been fooled. Yes, it's a pretty safe line."

"Was there ever blackmail?" Calgary asked.

"Not that we know of," said Huish. "Mind you, I wouldn't have put it past him. Not out and out blackmail, I'd say. Just a hint or two, perhaps. Letters. Foolish letters. Things their husbands wouldn't like to know about. He'd be able to keep a woman quiet that way."

"I see," said Calgary.

"Is that all you wanted to know?" asked Huish.

"There's one member of the Argyle family I haven't met yet," said Calgary. "The eldest daughter."

"Ah, Mrs. Durrant."

"I went to her house, but it was shut up. They told me she and her husband were away."

"They are at Sunny Point."

"Still there?"

"Yes. He wanted to stay on. Mr. Durrant," added Huish, "is doing a bit of detecting, I understand."

"He's a cripple, isn't he?"

"Yes, polio. Very sad. He hasn't much to do with his time, poor chap. That's why he's taken up this murder business so eagerly. Thinks he's on to something, too."

"And is he?" asked Calgary.

Huish shrugged his shoulders.

"He might be, at that," he said. "He's a better chance than we have, you know. He knows the family and he's a man with a good deal of intuition as well as intelligence."

"Do you think he'll get anywhere?"

"Possibly," said Huish, "but he won't tell *us* if he does. They'll keep it all in the family."

"Do you yourself know who's guilty, Superintendent?"

"You mustn't ask me things like that, Dr. Calgary."

"Meaning that you do know?"

"One can think one knows a thing," said Huish slowly, "but if you haven't got evidence there's not much you can do about it, is there?"

"And you're not likely to get the evidence you want?"

"Oh! we're very patient," Huish said. "We shall go on trying."

"What's going to happen to them all if you don't succeed?" said Calgary, leaning forward. "Have you thought of that?"

"That's what's worrying you, is it, sir?"

"They've *got* to know," said Calgary. "Whatever else happens, they've got to *know*."

"Don't you think they do know?"

Calgary shook his head.

"No," he said slowly, "that's the tragedy."

ii.

"Oo," said Maureen Clegg, "it's you again!"

"I'm very, very sorry to bother you," said Calgary.

"Oh, but you're not bothering me a bit. Come in. It's my day off."

That fact Calgary had already found out, and was the reason for his being here.

"I'm expecting Joe back in a minute," said Maureen. "I haven't seen any more about Jacko in the papers. I mean not since it said how he got a free pardon and a bit about a question being asked in Parliament and then saying that it was quite clear he didn't do it. But there's nothing more about what the police are doing and who really did it. Can't they find out?"

"Have you still no idea yourself?"

"Well, I haven't really," said Maureen. "I shouldn't be surprised, though, if it was the other brother. Very queer and moody he is. Joe sees him sometimes driving people around. He works for the Bence Group, you know. He's rather good-looking but terribly moody, I should think. Joe heard a rumour he was going out to Persia or somewhere and that looks bad, I think, don't you?"

"I don't see why it should look bad, Mrs. Clegg."

"Well, it's one of those places the police can't get at you, isn't it?"

"You think that he is running away?"

"He may feel he's got to."

"I suppose that's the sort of thing people do say," Arthur Calgary said.

"Lots of rumours flying around," said Maureen. "They say the husband and the secretary were going on together, too. But if it was the husband I should think he would be more likely to poison her. That's what they usually do, isn't it?"

"Well, you see more films than I do, Mrs. Clegg."

"I don't really look at the screen," said Maureen. "If you work there, you know, you get terribly bored with films. Hallo, here's Joe."

Joe Clegg also looked surprised to see Calgary and possibly not too pleased. They talked together for a while and then Calgary came to the purpose of his visit.

"I wonder," he said, "if you'd mind giving me a name and address?"

He wrote it down carefully in his notebook.

iii.

She was about fifty, he thought, a heavy cumbrous woman who could never have been good-looking. She had nice eyes, though, brown and kindly.

"Well, really, Dr. Calgary—" She was doubtful, upset. "Well, really, I'm sure I don't know. . . ."

He leaned forward, trying his utmost to dispel her reluctance, to soothe her, to make her feel the full force of his sympathy.

"It's so long ago now," she said. "It's—I really don't want to be reminded of—of things."

"I do understand that," said Calgary, "and it's not as though there were any question of anything being made public. I do assure you of that."

"You say you want to write a book about it, though?"

"Just a book to illustrate a certain type of character," said Calgary. "Interesting, you know, from a medical or psychological standpoint. No names. Just Mr. A., Mrs. B. That sort of thing."

"You've been to the Antarctic, haven't you?" she said suddenly.

He was surprised at the abruptness with which she had changed the subject.

"Yes," he said, "yes, I was with the Hayes Bentley Expedition."

The colour came up in her face. She looked younger. Just for a moment he could see the girl she had once been. "I used to read about it . . . I've always been fascinated, you know, with anything to do with the Poles. That Norwegian, wasn't it, Amundsen, who got there first? I think the Poles are much more exciting than Everest or any of these satellites, or going to the Moon or anything like that."

He seized on this cue and began to talk to her about the Expedition. Odd that her romantic interest should lie there, in Polar Explorations. She said at last with a sigh:

"It's wonderful hearing about it all from someone who's actually been there." She went on: "You want to know all about—about Jackie?"

"Yes."

"You wouldn't use my name or anything like that?"

"Of course not. I've told you so. You know how these things are done. Mrs. M. Lady Y. That sort of thing."

"Yes. Yes, I've read that kind of book—and I suppose it was, as you said, path—patho—"

"Pathological," he said.

"Yes, Jackie was definitely a pathological case. He could be ever so sweet, you know," she said. "Wonderful, he was. He'd say things and you'd believe every word of it."

"He probably meant them," said Calgary.

" 'I'm old enough to be your mother,' I used to say to him, and he'd say he didn't care for girls. Crude, he used to say girls were. He used to say women who were experienced and mature were what attracted him."

"Was he very much in love with you?" said Calgary.

"He said he was. He seemed to be . . ." Her lips trembled. "And all the time, I suppose, he was just after the money."

"Not necessarily," said Calgary, straining the truth as far as he could. "He may have been genuinely attracted, you know, as well. Only—he just couldn't help being crooked."

The pathetic middle-aged face brightened a little.

"Yes," she said, "it's nice to think that. Well, there it was. We used to make plans; how we'd go away together to France, or Italy, if this scheme of his came off. It just needed a bit of capital, he said."

The usual approach, thought Calgary, and wondered how many pathetic women fell for it.

"I don't know what came over me," she said. "I'd have done anything for him—*anything.*"

"I'm sure you would," said Calgary.

"I dare say," she said bitterly, "I wasn't the only one."

Calgary rose.

"It's been very good of you to tell me all this," he said.

"He's dead now. . . . But I shall never forget him. That monkey-face of his! The way he looked so sad and then laughed. Oh, he had a way with him. He wasn't all bad, I'm sure he wasn't all bad."

She looked at him wistfully.

But for that Calgary had no answer.

CHAPTER 21

THERE HAD been nothing to tell Philip Durrant that this day was different from any other day.

He had no idea that today would decide his future once and for all.

He woke in good health and spirits. The sun, a pale autumnal sun, shone in at the window. Kirsten brought him a telephone message which increased his good spirits.

"Tina's coming over for tea," he told Mary when she came in with his breakfast.

"Is she? Oh, yes, of course, it's her afternoon off, isn't it?" Mary sounded preoccupied.

"What's the matter, Polly?"

"Nothing."

She chipped off the top of his egg for him. At once, he felt irritated.

"I can still use my hands, Polly."

"Oh, I thought it would save you trouble."

"How old do you think I am? Six?"

She looked faintly surprised. Then she said abruptly:

"Hester's coming home today."

"Is she?" He spoke vaguely, because his mind was full of his plans for dealing with Tina. Then he caught sight of his wife's expression.

"For goodness' sake, Polly, do you think I've got a guilty passion for the girl?"

She turned her head aside.

"You're always saying she's so lovely."

"So she is. If you like beautiful bones and a quality of the unearthly." He added dryly: "But I'm hardly cut out to be a seducer, am I?"

"You might wish you were."

"Don't be ridiculous, Polly. I never knew you had this tendency to jealousy."

"You don't know anything about me."

He started to rebut that, but paused. It came to him, with

something of a shock, that perhaps he didn't know very much about Mary.

She went on:

"I want you to myself—all to myself. I want there to be nobody in the world but you and me."

"We'd run out of conversation, Polly."

He had spoken lightly, but he felt uncomfortable. The brightness of the morning seemed suddenly dimmed.

She said: "Let's go home, Philip, please let's go home."

"Very soon we will, but not just yet. Things are coming along. As I told you, Tina's coming this afternoon." He went on, hoping to turn her thoughts into a new channel: "I've great hopes of Tina."

"In what way?"

"Tina knows something."

"You mean—about the murder?"

"Yes."

"But how can she? She wasn't even here that night."

"I wonder now. I think, you know, that she *was*. Funny how odd little things turn up to help. That daily, Mrs. Narracott—the tall one, she told me something."

"What did she tell you?"

"A bit of village gossip. Mrs. Somebody or other's Ernie —no—Cyril. He'd had to go with his mother to the police station. Something he'd seen on the night poor Mrs. Argyle was done in."

"What had he seen?"

"Well, there Mrs. Narracott was rather vague. She hadn't got it out of Mrs. Somebody yet. But one can guess, can't one, Polly? Cyril wasn't inside the house, so he must have seen something outside. That gives us two guesses. He saw Micky or he saw Tina. It's my guess that Tina came out here that night."

"She'd have said so."

"Not necessarily. It sticks out a mile that Tina knows something she isn't telling. Say she drove out that night. Perhaps she came into the house and found your mother dead."

"And went away again without saying anything? Nonsense."

"There may have been reasons. . . . She may have seen or heard something that made her think she knew who'd done it."

"She was never particularly fond of Jacko. I'm sure she wouldn't have wanted to shield him."

"Then perhaps it wasn't Jacko she suspected. . . . But later, when Jacko was arrested, she thought that what she had suspected was quite wrong. Having said she wasn't here, she had to stick to it. But now, of course, it's different."

Mary said impatiently:

"You just imagine things, Philip. You make up a lot of things that can't possibly be true."

"They're quite likely to be true. I'm going to try and make Tina tell me what she knows."

"I don't believe she knows anything. Do you really think she knows who did it?"

"I wouldn't go as far as that. I think she either saw—or heard—something. I want to find out what that something is."

"Tina won't tell if she doesn't want to."

"No, I agree. And she's a great one for keeping things to herself. Little poker face, too. Never shows anything. But she's not really a good liar—not nearly as good a liar as you are, for instance. . . . My method will be to guess. Put my guess to her as a question. To be answered yes or no. Do you know what will happen then? One of three things. She'll either say yes—and that will be that. Or she will say no—and since she isn't a good liar I shall know whether her no is genuine. Or she will refuse to answer and put on her poker face—and that, Poly, will be as good as yes. Come now, you must admit that there are possibilities with this technique of mine."

"Oh, leave it all alone, Phil! Do leave it alone! It will all die down and be forgotten."

"No. This thing has got to be cleared up. Otherwise we'll have Hester throwing herself out of windows and Kirsty having a nervous breakdown. Leo's already freezing up into a kind of stalactite. As for poor old Gwenda, she's on the point of accepting a post in Rhodesia."

"What does it matter what happens to them?"

"Nobody matters but us—that's what you mean?"

His face was stern and angry. It startled Mary. She had never seen her husband look like that before.

She faced him defiantly.

"Why should I care about other people?" she asked.

"You never have, have you?"

"I don't know what you mean."

Philip gave a sharp exasperated sigh. He pushed his breakfast tray aside.

"Take this thing away. I don't want any more."

"But Philip—"

He made an impatient gesture. Mary picked up the tray and carried it out of the room. Philip wheeled himself over to the writing-table. Pen in hand, he stared out of the window. He felt a curious oppression of spirit. He had been so full of excitement a short while ago. Now he felt uneasy and restless.

But presently he rallied. He covered two sheets of paper rapidly. Then he sat back and considered.

It was plausible. It was possible. But he wasn't entirely satisfied. Was he really on the right tack? He couldn't be sure. Motive. Motive was what was so damnably lacking. There was some factor, somewhere, that had escaped him.

He sighed impatiently. He could hardly wait for Tina to arrive. If only this could be cleared up. Just among themselves. That was all that was necessary. Once they *knew*— then they would all be free. Free of this stifling atmosphere of suspicion and hopelessness. They could all, except one, get on with their own lives. He and Mary would go back home and—

His thoughts stopped. Excitement died down again. He faced his own problem. *He didn't want to go home. . . .* He thought of its orderly perfection, its shining chintzes, its gleaming brass. A clean, bright, well-tended cage! And he in the cage, tied to his invalid-chair, surrounded by the loving care of his wife.

His wife. . . . When he thought of his wife, he seemed to see two people. One the girl he had married, fair-haired, blue-eyed, gentle, reserved. That was the girl he had loved, the girl he teased whilst she stared at him with a puzzled frown. That was his Polly. But there was another Mary—a Mary who was hard as steel, who was passionate, but incapable of affection—a Mary to whom nobody mattered but herself. Even he only mattered because he was hers.

A line of French verse passed through his mind—how did it go?

Venus toute entière à sa proie attaché . . .

And that Mary he did not love. Behind the cold blue eyes of that Mary was a stranger—a stranger he did not know. . . .

And then he laughed at himself. He was getting nervy and het up like everybody else in the house. He remembered his mother-in-law talking to him about his wife. About the sweet little fair-haired girl in New York. About the moment when the child had thrown her arms round Mrs. Argyle's neck and had cried out: "I want to stay with you. I don't want to leave you *ever!*"

That had been affection, hadn't it? And yet—how very unlike Mary. Could one change so much between child and woman? How difficult, almost impossible it was for Mary ever to voice affection, to be demonstrative?

Yet certainly on that occasion— His thoughts stopped dead. Or was it really quite simple? Not affection- -just calculation. A means to an end. A show of affection deliberately produced. What was Mary capable of to get what she wanted?

Almost anything, he thought—and was shocked with himself for thinking it.

Angrily he dashed down his pen, and wheeled himself out of the sitting room into the bedroom next door. He wheeled himself up to the dressing table. He picked up his brushes and brushed back his hair from where it was hanging over his forehead. His own face looked strange to him.

Who am I, he thought, and where am I going? Thoughts that had never occurred to him before. . . . He wheeled his chair close to the window and looked out. Down below, one of the daily women stood outside the kitchen window and talked to someone inside. Their voices, softly accented in the local dialect, floated up to him. . . .

His eyes widening, he remained as though tranced.

A sound from the next room awakened him from his preoccupation. He wheeled himself to the connecting door.

Gwenda Vaughan was standing by the writing table. She turned towards him and he was startled by the haggardness of her face in the morning sunshine.

"Hallo, Gwenda."

"Hallo, Philip. Leo thought you might like the *Illustrated London News.*"

"Oh, thanks."

"This is a nice room," said Gwenda, looking round her. "I don't believe I've ever been in it before."

"Quite the Royal Suite, isn't it?" said Philip. "Away from everybody. Ideal for invalids and honeymoon couples."

Just too late he wished he had not used the last two words. Gwenda's face quivered.

"I must get on with things," she said vaguely.

"The perfect secretary."

"Not even that nowadays. I make mistakes."

"Don't we all?" He added deliberately: "When are you and Leo getting married?"

"We probably never shall."

"That would be a real mistake," said Philip.

"Leo thinks it might cause unfavourable comment—from the police!"

Her voice was bitter.

"Dash it all, Gwenda, one has to take some risks."

"I'm willing to take risks," said Gwenda. "I've never minded taking risks. I'm willing to gamble on happiness. But Leo—"

"Yes? Leo?"

"Leo," said Gwenda, "will probably die as he has lived, the husband of Rachel Argyle."

The anger and bitterness in her eyes startled him.

"She might just as well be alive," said Gwenda. "She's *here*—in the house—all the time. . . ."

CHAPTER 22

TINA PARKED her car on the grass by the churchyard wall. She removed the paper carefully from the flowers she had brought, then she walked in through the cemetery gates and along the main path. She did not like the new cemetery. She wished it had been possible for Mrs. Argyle to have been buried in the old churchyard which surrounded the church. There seemed an old-world peace there. The yew tree and the moss-grown stones. In this cemetery, so new, so well arranged, with its main walk and the paths radiating off it, everything seemed as slick and mass-produced as the contents of a supermarket.

Mrs. Argyle's grave was well kept. It had a square marble surround filled with granite chips, a granite cross rising from the back of it.

Tina, holding her carnations, bent to read the inscription. "In loving memory of Rachel Louise Argyle, who departed this life on November 9th, 195—" Below it was the text:

"Her children shall rise up and call her blessed."

There was a footstep behind her and Tina turned her head, startled.

"Micky!"

"I saw your car. I followed you. At least—I was coming here anyway."

"You were coming here? Why?"

"I don't know. Just to say good-bye, perhaps."

"Good-bye to—her?"

He nodded.

"Yes. I've taken that job with the oil company I told you about. I'm going off in about three weeks."

"And you came here to say good-bye to Mother first?"

"Yes. Perhaps to thank her and to say I'm sorry."

"What are you sorry for, Micky?"

"I'm not sorry that I killed her if that's what you're trying to imply. Have you been thinking I killed her, Tina?"

"I was not sure."

"You can't be sure now, either, can you? I mean it's no good my telling you that I didn't kill her."

"Why are you sorry?"

"She did a lot for me," said Micky slowly. "I was never the least bit grateful. I resented every single damn thing she did. I never gave her a kind word, or a loving look. I wish now that I had, that's all."

"When did you stop hating her? After she was dead?"

"Yes. Yes, I suppose so."

"It wasn't her you hated, was it?"

"No—no. You were right about that. It was my own mother. Because I loved her. Because I loved her and she didn't care a button for me."

"And now you're not even angry about that?"

"No. I don't suppose she could help it. After all, you're born what you are. She was a sunny, happy sort of creature. Too fond of men and too fond of the bottle, and she was nice to her kids when she felt like being nice. She wouldn't have let anyone else hurt them. All right, so she didn't care for me! All these years I refused to live with that idea. Now I've accepted it." He stretched out a hand. "Give me just one of your carnations, will you, Tina?" He took it from her and bending down, laid it on the grave below the inscription. "There you are, Mum," he said. "I was a rotten son to you, and I don't think you were a very wise Mother to me. But you meant well." He looked at Tina. "Is that a good enough apology?"

"I think it will do," said Tina.

She bent down and put her own bunch of carnations there.

"Do you often come here and put flowers?"

"I come here once a year," said Tina.

"Little Tina," said Micky.

They turned together and walked back down the cemetery path.

"I didn't kill her, Tina," said Micky. "I swear I didn't. I want you to believe me."

"I was there that night," said Tina.

He wheeled round.

"You were there? You mean at Sunny Point?"

"Yes. I was thinking of changing my job. I wanted to consult Father and Mother about it."

"Well," said Micky, "go on."

When she did not speak, he took her arm and shook her. "Go on, Tina," he said. "You've got to tell me."

"I haven't told anyone so far," said Tina.

"Go on," said Micky again.

"I drove there. I didn't take the car right up to the gate. You know there's a place half-way where it's easier to turn it?"

Micky nodded.

"I got out of the car there and I walked towards the house. I felt unsure of myself. You know how difficult it was in some ways to talk to Mother. I mean, she always had her own ideas. I wanted to put the case as clearly as I could. And so I walked to the house and then back towards the car, and then back again. Thinking things out."

"What time was this?" asked Micky.

"I don't know," said Tina. "I can't remember now. I—time doesn't mean very much to me."

"No, darling," said Micky. "You always have that air of infinite leisure."

"I was under the trees," said Tina, "and walking very softly—"

"Like the little cat you are," said Micky affectionately.

"—When I heard them."

"Heard what?"

"Two people whispering."

"Yes?" Micky's body had tensed. "What did they say?"

"They said—one of them said, 'Between seven and seven-thirty. That's the time. Now remember that and don't make a muck of it. Between seven and seven-thirty.' The other person whispered. 'You can trust me,' and then the first voice said, 'And after that, darling, everything will be wonderful.' "

There was a silence, then Micky said:

"Well—why have you held this up?"

"Because I didn't know," said Tina. "I didn't know who was speaking."

"But surely! Was it a man or a woman?"

"I don't know," said Tina. "Don't you see, when two people are whispering, you don't hear the *voice*. It's just—well, just a whisper. I think, of course I think, it was a man and a woman because—"

"Because of what they said?"

"Yes. But I didn't know who they were."

"You thought," said Micky, "that it might have been Father and Gwenda?"

"It's possible, isn't it?" said Tina. "It might have meant that Gwenda was to leave the house and come back between those times, or it might have been Gwenda telling Father to come down between seven and half past."

"If it was Father and Gwenda, you wouldn't want to turn them over to the police. Is that it?"

"If I were sure," said Tina. "But I'm not sure. It could have been someone else. It could have been—Hester and someone? It could even have been Mary, but not Philip. No, not Philip, of course."

"When you say Hester and someone, who do you mean?"

"I don't know."

"You didn't see him—the man, I mean?"

"No," said Tina. "I didn't see him."

"Tina, I think you're lying. It was a man, wasn't it?"

"I turned back," said Tina, "towards the car, and then someone came by on the other side of the road, walking very fast. He was just a shadow in the darkness. And then I thought—I thought I heard a car start up at the end of the road."

"You thought it was *me* . . ." said Micky.

"I didn't know," said Tina. "It *could* have been you. It was about your size and height."

They reached Tina's little car.

"Come on, Tina," said Micky, "get in. I'm coming with you. We'll drive down to Sunny Point."

"But Micky—"

"It's no use my telling you it wasn't me, is it? What else should I say? Come on, drive to Sunny Point."

"What are you going to do, Micky?"

"Why should you think I'm going to do anything? Weren't you going to Sunny Point anyway?"

"Yes," said Tina, "I was. I had a letter from Philip." She started the little car. Micky, sitting beside her, held himself very taut and rigid.

"Heard from Philip, did you? What had he to say?"

"He asked me to come over. He wanted to see me. He knows this is my half-day."

"Oh. Did he say what he wanted to see you about?"

"He said he wanted to ask me a question and he hoped that I'd give him the answer to it. He said that I needn't tell him anything—he'd tell me. I would only have to say yes or no. He said that whatever I told him he'd hold in confidence."

"So he's up to something, is he?" said Micky. "Interesting."

It was a very short distance to Sunny Point. When they got there. Micky said:

"You go in, Tina. I'm going to walk up and down the garden a bit, thinking of things. Go on. Have your interview with Philip."

Tina said:

"You're not going to—you wouldn't—"

Micky gave a short laugh.

"Suicide from Lover's Leap? Come now, Tina, you know me better than that."

"Sometimes," said Tina, "I think one does not know anybody."

She turned away from him and walked slowly into the house. Micky looked after her, his head thrust forward, his hands in his pockets. He was scowling. Then he walked round the corner of the house looking up at it thoughtfully. All his boyhood memories came back to him. There was the old magnolia tree. He'd climbed up there many a time and through the landing window. There was the small plot of earth that had been supposed to be his own garden. Not that he'd ever taken very kindly to gardens. He'd always preferred taking any mechanical toys he had to pieces. "Destructive little devil," he thought with faint amusement.

Ah well, one didn't really change.

Inside the house, Tina met Mary in the hall. Mary looked startled at seeing her.

"Tina! Have you come over from Redmyn?"

"Yes," said Tina. "Didn't you know I was coming?"

"I'd forgotten," said Mary. "I believe Philip did mention it."

She turned away.

"I'm going into the kitchen," she said, "to see if the Ovaltine has come. Philip likes it last thing at night. Kirsten is just taking him up some coffee. He likes coffee better than tea. He says tea gives him indigestion."

"Why do you treat him like an invalid, Mary?" said Tina. "He's not really an invalid."

There was a touch of cold anger in Mary's eyes.

179

"When you've got a husband of your own, Tina," she said, "you'll know better how husbands like to be treated."

Tina said gently:

"I'm sorry."

"If only we could get out of this house," said Mary. "It's so *bad* for Philip being here. And Hester's coming back to-day," she added.

"Hester?" Tina sounded surprised. "Is she? Why?"

"How should I know? She rang up last night and said so. I don't know what train she's coming by. I suppose it'll be the express, as usual. Someone will have to go in to Drymouth to meet her."

Mary disappeared along the passage to the kitchen. Tina hesitated a moment, then she walked up the stairs. On the landing the first door to the right opened and Hester came through it. She looked startled at seeing Tina.

"Hester! I heard you were coming back but I'd no idea you'd arrived."

"Dr. Calgary drove me down," said Hester. "I came straight up to my room—I don't think anyone knows I've arrived."

"Is Dr. Calgary here now?"

"No. He just dropped me and went on into Drymouth. He wanted to see someone there."

"Mary didn't know you'd arrived."

"Mary never knows anything," said Hester. "She and Philip isolate themselves from everything that goes on. I suppose Father and Gwenda are in the library. Everything seems to be going on just the same as usual."

"Why shouldn't it?"

"I don't really know," said Hester vaguely. "I just suspected that it would all be different somehow."

She moved past Tina and down the stairs. Tina went on past the library and along the passage to the suite at the end which the Durrants occupied. Kirsten Lindstrom, standing just outside Philip's door with a tray in her hand, turned her head sharply.

"Why, Tina, you made me jump," she said. "I was just taking Philip some coffee and biscuits." She raised a hand to knock. Tina joined her.

After knocking, Kirsten opened the door and passed in. She was a little ahead of Tina and her tall angular frame blocked Tina's view, but Tina heard Kirsten's gasp. He arms gave way and the tray crashed to the ground, cup and plates smashing against the fender.

"Oh, no," cried Kirsten, "oh *no!*"

Tina said:

"Philip?"

She passed the other woman and came forward to where Philip Durrant's chair had been brought up to the desk. He had, she supposed, been writing. There was a ball-point pen lying close to his right hand, but his head was dropped forward in a curious twisted attitude. And at the base of his skull she saw something that looked like a bright red lozenge staining the whiteness of his collar.

"He has been killed," said Kirsten. "He has been killed—stabbed. There, through the bottom of the brain. One little stab and it is fatal."

She added, her voice rising:

"I warned him. I did all I could. But he was like a child—enjoying himself playing with tools that were dangerous—not seeing where he was going."

It was like a bad dream, Tina thought. She stood there softly at Philip's elbow, looking down at him whilst Kirsten raised his limp hand and felt the wrist for the pulse that was not there. What had he wanted to ask her? Whatever he wanted, he would never ask it now. Without really thinking objectively, Tina's mind was taking in and registering various details. He had been writing, yes. The pen was there, but there was no paper in front of him. Nothing written. Whoever had killed him had taken away what he'd written. She said, speaking quietly and mechanically:

"We must tell the others."

"Yes, yes, we must go down to them. We must tell your father."

Side by side the two women went to the door, Kirsten's arm round Tina. Tina's eyes went to the dropped tray and the broken crockery.

"That does not matter," said Kirsten. "All that can be cleared up later."

Tina half stumbled and Kirsten's arm restrained her.

"Be careful. You will fall."

They went along the passage. The door of the library opened. Leo and Gwenda came out. Tina said in her clear, low voice:

"Philip has been killed. Stabbed."

It was like a dream, Tina thought. The shocked exclamations of her father and Gwenda flowing past her, going to Philip. . . . To Philip, who was dead. Kirsten left her and hurried down the stairs.

"I must tell Mary. It must be broken to her gently. Poor Mary. It will be a terrible shock."

Tina followed her slowly. More than ever she felt dazed and dreamlike, a strange pain catching at her heart. Where was she going? She did not know. Nothing was real. She came to the open front door and passed through it. It was then she saw Micky coming round the corner of the house. Automatically as though this was where her footsteps had been leading her all the time, she went straight to him.

"Micky," she said. "Oh, Micky!"

His arms were open. She went straight into them.

"It's all right," said Micky. "I've got you."

Tina crumpled slightly in his arms. She dropped to the ground, a small huddled heap, just as Hester came running from the house.

"She's fainted," Micky said helplessly. "I've never known Tina to faint before."

"It's the shock," said Hester.

"What do you mean—the shock?"

"Philip has been killed," said Hester. "Didn't you know?"

"How could I know? When? How?"

"Just now."

He stared at her. Then he picked up Tina in his arms. With Hester accompanying him, he took her into Mrs. Argyle's sitting room and laid her on the sofa.

"Ring up Dr. Craig," he said.

"That's his car now," said Hester, looking out of the window. "Father was calling him on the telephone about Philip. I—" She looked round. "I don't want to meet him."

She ran out of the room and up the stairs.

Donald Craig got out of his car and came in through the open front door. Kirsten came from the kitchen to meet him.

"Good afternoon, Miss Lindstrom. What's this I hear? Mr. Argyle tells me that Philip Durrant has been *killed. Killed?*"

"It is quite true," said Kirsten.

"Has Mr. Argyle rung up the police?"

"I do not know."

"Any chance that he's just wounded?" said Don. He turned to take his medical bag out of the car.

"No," said Kirsten. Her voice was flat and tired. "He is dead. I am quite sure of that. He has been stabbed—here."

She put her hand to the back of her own head.

Micky came out into the hall.

"Hallo, Don, you had better have a look at Tina," he said. "She's fainted."

"Tina? Oh yes, that's the—the one from Redmyn, isn't it? Where is she?"

"She is in there."

"I'll just have a look at her before I go upstairs." As he went into the room he spoke over his shoulder to Kirsten. "Keep her warm," he said. "Get some hot tea or coffee for her as soon as she comes round. But you know the drill—"

Kirsten nodded.

"Kirsty!" Mary Durrant came slowly along the hall from the kitchen—Kirsten went to her—Micky stared at her helplessly.

"It's not true." Mary spoke in a loud harsh voice. "It's not *true!* It's a lie you've made up. He was all right when I left him just now. He was quite all right. He was writing. I told him not to write. I *told* him not to. What made him do it? Why should he be so pig-headed? Why wouldn't he leave this house when I wanted him to?"

Coaxing her, soothing her, Kirsten did her best to make her relax.

Donald Craig strode out of the sitting room.

"Who said that girl had fainted?" he demanded.

Micky stared at him.

"But she did faint," he said.

"Where was she when she fainted?"

"She was with me. . . . She came out of the house and walked to meet me. Then—she just collapsed."

"Collapsed, did she? Yes, she collapsed all right," said Donald Craig grimly. He moved quickly towards the telephone. "I must get hold of an ambulance," he said, "at once."

"An ambulance?" Both Kirsten and Micky stared at him. Mary did not seem to have heard.

"Yes." Donald was dialling angrily. "That girl didn't faint," he said. "She was stabbed. Do you hear? Stabbed in the back. We've got to get her to hospital at once."

CHAPTER 23

IN HIS HOTEL room, Arthur Calgary went over and over the notes he had made.

From time to time, he nodded his head.

Yes . . . he was on the right tack now. To begin with, he had made the mistake of concentrating on Mrs. Argyle. In nine cases out of ten that would have been the right procedure. But this was the tenth case.

All along he had felt the presence of an unknown factor. If he could once isolate and identify that factor, the case would be solved. In seeking it he had been obsessed by the dead woman. But the dead woman, he saw now, was not really important. *Any* victim, in a sense, would have done.

He had shifted his viewpoint—shifted it back to the moment when all this had begun. He had shifted it back to Jacko.

Not just Jacko as a young man unjustly sentenced for a crime he did not commit—but Jacko, the intrinsic human being. Was Jacko, in the words of the old Calvinistic doctrine, "a vessel appointed to destruction?" He'd been given every chance in life, hadn't he? Dr. MacMaster's opinion, at any rate, was that he was one of those who are born to go wrong. No environment could have helped him or saved him. Was that true? Leo Argyle had spoken of him with indulgence, with pity. How had he put it? "One of Nature's misfits." He had accepted the modern psychologocal approach. An invalid, not a criminal. What had Hester said? Bluntly, that Jacko was always awful!

A plain, childish statement. And what was it Kirsten Lindstrom had said? That Jacko was wicked! Yes, she had put it as strongly as that. Wicked! Tina had said: "I never liked him or trusted him." So they all agreed, didn't they, in general terms? It was only in the case of his widow that they'd come down from the general to the particular. Maureen Clegg had thought of Jacko entirely from her own point of view. She had wasted herself on Jacko. She had been carried away by his charm and she was resentful of the fact. Now, securely remarried, she echoed her husband's views. She had given Calgary a forthright account of some of Jacko's dubious dealings, and the methods by which he had obtained money. *Money* . . .

In Arthur Calgary's fatigued brain the word seemed to dance on the wall in gigantic letters. Money! Money! Money! Like a *motif* in an opera, he thought. Mrs. Argyle's money! Money put into trust! Money put into an annuity! Residual estate left to her husband! Money got from the bank! Money in the bureau drawer! Hester rushing out to her car with no money in her purse, getting two pounds from Kirsten Lindstrom. Money found on Jacko, money that he swore his mother had given him.

The whole thing made a pattern—a pattern woven out of irrelevant details about money.

And surely, in that pattern, the unknown factor was becoming clear.

He looked at his watch. He had promised to ring up Hester at an agreed time. He drew the telephone towards him and asked for the number.

Presently her voice came to him, clear, rather childish.

"Hester. Are you all right?"

"Oh, yes, *I'm* all right."

It took him a moment or two to grasp the implication of that accented word. Then he said sharply:

"What has happened?"

"Philip has been killed."

"Philip! Philip Durrant?"

Calgary sounded incredulous.

"Yes. And Tina, too—at least she isn't dead yet. She's in hospital."

"Tell me," he ordered.

She told him. He questioned and re-questioned her narrowly until he got all the facts.

Then he said grimly:

"Hold on, Hester, I'm coming. I'll be with you"—he looked at his watch—"in an hour's time. I've got to see Superintendent Huish first."

ii.

"What exactly do you want to know, Dr. Calgary?" asked Superintendent Huish, but before Calgary could speak the telephone rang on Huish's desk and the superintendent picked it up. "Yes. Yes, speaking. Just a moment." He drew a piece of paper towards him, picked up a pen and prepared to write. "Yes. Go ahead. Yes." He wrote. "What? How do you spell that last word? Oh, I see. Yes, doesn't seem to make much sense yet, does it? Right. Nothing else? Right. Thanks." He replaced the receiver. "That was the hospital," he said.

"Tina?" asked Calgary.

The superintendent nodded.

"She regained consciousness for a few minutes."

"Did she say anything?" asked Calgary.

"I don't really know just why I should tell you that, Dr. Calgary."

"I ask you to tell me," said Calgary, "because I think that I can help you over this business."

Huish looked at him consideringly.

"You've taken all this very much to heart, haven't you, Dr. Calgary?" he said.

"Yes, I have. You see, I felt responsible for reopening the case. I even feel responsible for these two tragedies. Will the girl live?"

"They think so," said Huish. "The blade of the knife missed the heart, but it may be touch and go." He shook his head. "That's always the trouble," he said. "People will *not* believe that a murderer is unsafe. Sounds a queer thing to say, but there it is. They all knew there was a murderer in their midst. They ought to have told what they knew. The only safe thing if a murderer is about is to tell the police anything you know *at once*. Well, they didn't. They held out on me. Philip Durrant was a nice fellow—an intelligent fellow; but he regarded this as a kind of game. He went poking about laying traps for people. And he got somewhere, or he thought he got somewhere. And somebody else thought he was getting somewhere. Result: I get a call to say he's dead, stabbed through the back of the neck. That's what comes of messing about with murder and not realising its dangers." He stopped and cleared his throat.

"And the girl?" asked Calgary.

"The girl knew something," said Huish. "Something she didn't want to tell. It's my opinion," he said, "she was in love with the fellow."

"You're talking about—Micky?"

Huish nodded. "Yes. I'd say, too, that Micky was fond of

her, in a way. But being fond of anyone isn't enough if you're mad with fear. Whatever she knew was probably more deadly than she herself realised. That's why, after she found Durrant dead and she came rushing out straight into his arms, he took his chance and stabbed her."

"That's merely conjecture on your part, isn't it, Superintendent Huish?"

"Not entirely conjecture, Dr. Calgary. The knife was in his pocket."

"The actual knife?"

"Yes. It had blood on it. We're going to test it, but it'll be her blood all right. Her blood and the blood of Philip Durrant!"

"But—it couldn't have been."

"Who says it couldn't have been?"

"Hester. I rang her up and she told me all about it."

"She did, did she? Well, the facts are very simple. Mary Durrant went down to the kitchen, leaving her husband alive, at ten minutes to four—at that time there were in the house Leo Argyle and Gwenda Vaughan in the library, Hester Argyle in her bedroom on the first floor, and Kirsten Lindstrom in the kitchen. Just after four o'clock, Micky and Tina drove up. Micky went into the garden and Tina went upstairs, following close on Kirsten's footsteps, who had just gone up with coffee and biscuits for Philip. Tina stopped to speak to Hester, then went on to join Miss Lindstrom and together they found Philip dead."

"And all this time Micky was in the garden. Surely that's a perfect alibi?"

"What you don't know, Dr. Calgary, is that there's a big magnolia tree growing up by the side of the house. The kids used to climb it. Micky in particular. It was one of his ways in and out of the house. He could have shinned up that tree, gone into Durrant's room, stabbed him, back and out again. Oh, it needed split-second timing, but it's astonishing what audacity will do sometimes. And he was desperate. At all costs he had to prevent Tina and Durrant meeting. To be safe, he had to kill them both."

Calgary thought for a moment or two.

"You said just now, Superintendent, that Tina has recovered consciousness. Wasn't she able to say definitely who stabbed her?"

"She wasn't very coherent," said Huish slowly. "In fact I doubt if she was conscious in the proper sense of the term."

He gave a tired smile.

"All right, Dr. Calgary, I'll tell you exactly what she said. First of all she said a name. *Micky . . .*"

"She has accused him, then," said Calgary.

"That's what it looks like," said Huish, nodding his head. "The rest of what she said didn't make sense. It's a bit fantastic."

"What did she say?"

Huish looked down at the pad in front of him.

"*'Micky.'* Then a pause. Then, *'The cup was empty . . .'* then another pause, and then, *'The Dove on the mast.'*" He looked at Calgary. "Can you make any sense of that?"

"No," said Calgary. He shook his head and said wonderingly: *"The Dove on the mast . . .* That seems a very extraordinary thing to say."

"No masts and no doves as far as we know," said Huish.

"But it meant something to her, something in her own mind. But it mayn't, you know, have been anything to do with the murder. Goodness knows what realms of fancy she's floating in."

Calgary was silent for some moments. He sat thinking things over. He said: "You've arrested Micky?"

"We've detained him. He will be charged within twenty-four hours."

Huish looked curiously at Calgary.

"I gather that this lad, Micky, wasn't *your* answer to the problem?"

"No," said Calgary. "No, Micky wasn't my answer. Even now—I don't know." He got up. "I still think I'm right," he said. "but I quite see that I've not got enough to go on for you to believe me. I must go out there again. I must see them all."

"Well," said Huish, "be careful of yourself, Dr. Calgary. What *is* your idea, by the way?"

"Would it mean anything to you," said Calgary, "if I told you that it is my belief that this was a crime of passion?"

Huish's eyebrows rose.

"There are a lot of passions, Dr. Calgary," he said. "Hate, avarice, greed, fear, they're all passions."

"When I said a crime of passion," said Calgary, "I meant exactly what one usually means by that term."

"If you mean Gwenda Vaughan and Leo Argyle," said Huish, "that's what we've thought all along, you know, but it doesn't seem to fit."

"It's more complicated than that," said Arthur Calgary.

CHAPTER 24

IT WAS AGAIN dusk when Arthur Calgary came to Sunny Point on an evening very like the evening when he had first come there. Viper's Point, he thought to himself as he rang the bell.

Once again events seemed to repeat themselves. It was Hester who opened it. There was the same defiance in her face, the same air of desperate tragedy. Behind her in the hall he saw, as he had seen before, the watchful, suspicious figure of Kirsten Lindstrom. It was history repeating itself.

Then the pattern wavered and changed. The suspicion and the desperation went out of Hester's face. It broke up into a lovely, welcoming smile.

"You," she said. "Oh, I'm so glad you've come!"

He took her hands in his.

"I want to see your father, Hester. Is he upstairs in the library?"

"Yes. Yes, he's there with Gwenda."

Kirsten Lindstrom came forward towards them.

"Why do you come here again?" she said accusingly. "Look at the trouble you brought last time! See what has happened to us all. Hester's life ruined, Mr. Argyle's life ruined—and two deaths. Two! Philip Durrant and little Tina. And it is *your* doing—all your doing!"

"Tina is not dead yet," said Calgary, "and I have something here to do that I cannot leave undone."

"What have you got to do?" Kirsten still stood barring his way to the staircase.

"I've got to finish what I began," said Calgary.

Very gently he put a hand on her shoulder and moved her slightly aside. He walked up the stairs and Hester followed him. He turned back over his shoulder and said to Kirsten: "Come, too, Miss Lindstrom, I would like you all to be here."

In the library, Leo Argyle was sitting in a chair by the desk. Gwenda Vaughan was kneeling in front of the fire, aring into its embers. They looked up with some surprise.

"I'm sorry to burst in upon you," said Calgary, "but as 've just been saying to these two, I've come to finish what began." He looked round. "Is Mrs. Durrant in the house ill? I should like her to be here also."

"She's lying down, I think," said Leo. "She—she's taken things terribly hard."

"I should like her to be here all the same." He looked at Kirsten. "Perhaps you would go and fetch her."

"She may not want to come," said Kirsten sullenly.

"Tell her," said Calgary, "that there are things she may want to hear about her husband's death."

"Oh, go on, Kirsty," said Hester. "Don't be so suspicious and so protective of us all. I don't know what Dr. Calgary's going to say, but we ought all to be here."

"As you please," said Kirsten.

She went out of the room.

"Sit down," said Leo. He indicated a chair on the other side of the fireplace, and Calgary sat there.

"You must forgive me," said Leo, "if I say at this moment that I wish you'd never come here in the first place, Dr. Calgary."

"That's unfair," said Hester fiercely. "That's a terribly unfair thing to say."

"I know what you must feel," said Calgary, "I think in your place I should feel much the same. Perhaps I even shared your view for a short period, but on reflection I still cannot see that there was anything else that I could have done."

Kirsten re-entered the room. "Mary is coming," she said.

They sat in silence waiting and presently Mary Durrant entered the room. Calgary looked at her with interest, since it was the first time he had seen her. She looked calm and composed, neatly dressed, every hair in place. But her face was masklike in its lack of expression and there was an air about her as of a woman who walks in her sleep.

Leo made an introduction. She bowed her head slightly.

"It is good of you to come, Mrs. Durrant," said Calgary. "I thought you ought to hear what I have to say."

"As you please," said Mary. "But nothing that you can say or anyone can say will bring Philip back again."

She went a little way away from them and sat down in a chair by the window. Calgary looked round him.

"Let me first say this: When I came here the first time when I told you that I was able to clear Jacko's name, your reception of my news puzzled me. I understand it now. But the thing that made the greatest impression upon me was what this child here"—he looked at Hester--"said to me as I left. She said that it was not justice that mattered, it was what happened to the innocent. There is a phrase in the latest translation of the Book of Job that describes it. *The calamity of the innocent.* As a result of my news that is what you have all been suffering. The innocent should not suffer and must not suffer, and it is to end the suffering of the innocent that I am here now to say what I have to say."

He paused for a moment or two but no one spoke. In his quiet pedantic voice, Arthur Calgary went on:

"When I came here first, it was not, as I thought, to bring you what might be described as tidings of great joy. You had all accepted Jacko's guilt. You were all, if I may say so, *satisfied* with it. It was the best solution that there could be in the murder of Mrs. Argyle."

"Isn't that speaking a little harshly?" asked Leo.

"No," said Calgary, "it is the truth. Jacko was satisfactory to you all as the criminal since there could be no real question of an outsider having committed the crime, and because in the case of Jacko you could find the necessary excuses. He was unfortunate, a mental invalid, not responsible for his actions, a problem or delinquent boy! All the phrases that we can use nowadays so happily to excuse guilt. You said, Mr. Argyle, that you did not blame him. You said his mother, the victim, would not have blamed him. Only one person blamed him." He looked at Kirsten Lindstrom. "*You* blamed him. You said fairly and squarely that he was wicked. That is the term you used. 'Jacko was wicked,' you said."

"Perhaps," said Kirsten Lindstrom. "Perhaps—yes, perhaps I said that. It was true."

"Yes, it was true. He *was* wicked. If he had not been wicked none of this would have happened. Yet you know quite well," said Calgary, "that my evidence cleared him of the actual crime."

Kirsten said:

"One cannot always believe evidence. You had concussion. I know very well what concussion does to people. They remember things not clearly but in a kind of blur."

192

"So that is still your solution?" said Calgary. "You think that Jacko actually committed that crime and that in some way he managed to fake an alibi? Is that right?"

"I do not know the details. Yes, something of that sort. I still say he did it. All the suffering that has gone on here and the deaths—yes, these terrible deaths—they are all *his* doing. All Jacko's doing!"

Hester cried:

"But Kirsten, you were always devoted to Jacko."

"Perhaps," said Kirsten, "yes, perhaps. But I still say he was wicked."

"There I think you are right," said Calgary, "but in another way you are wrong. Concussion or no concussion, my memory is perfectly clear. On the night of Mrs. Argyle's death I gave Jacko a lift at the stated time. There is no possibility—and I repeat those words strongly—there is no possibility that Jacko Argyle killed his adopted mother that night. His alibi holds."

Leo moved with a trace of restlessness. Calgary went on:

"You think that I'm repeating the same thing over and over again? Not quite. There are other points to be considered. One of them is the statement that I got from Superintendent Huish that Jacko was very glib and assured when giving his alibi. He had it all pat and ready, the times, the place, *almost as though he knew he might need it*. That ties up with the conversation I had about him with Dr. MacMaster, who has had a very wide experience of borderline delinquent cases. He said he was not so surprised at Jacko having the seeds of murder in his heart, but he was surprised that he had actually carried one out. He said the type of murder he would have expected was one where Jacko egged on *someone else* to commit the crime. So I came to the point where I asked myself this: Did Jacko know that a crime was to be committed that night? Did he know that he would need an alibi and did he deliberately go about giving himself one? If so, *someone else* killed Mrs. Argyle, *but*— Jacko knew she was going to be killed and one may fairly say that he was the instigator of the crime."

He said to Kirsten Lindstrom:

"*You feel that, don't you? You still feel it, or you want to feel it? You feel that it was Jacko who killed her, not you. . . . You feel it was under his orders and under his influence you did it. Therefore you want all the blame to be his!*"

"I?" said Kirsten Lindstrom. "I? What are you saying?"

"I'm saying," said Calgary, "that there was only one person in this house who could in any way fit into the role of Jacko Argyle's accomplice. And that is *you*, Miss Lindstrom. Jacko had a record behind him, a record of being able to inspire passion in middle-aged women. He employed that power deliberately. He had the gift of making himself believed." He leaned forward. "He made love to you, didn't he?" he said gently. "He made you believe that he cared for you, that he wanted to marry you, that after this was over and he'd got more control of his mother's money, you would be married and go away somewhere. That is right, isn't it?"

Kirsten stared at him. She did not speak. It was as though she were paralysed.

"It was done cruelly and heartlessly and deliberately," said Arthur Calgary. "He came here that night desperate for some money, with the shadow over him of arrest and a jail sentence. Mrs. Argyle refused to give him money. When he was refused by her he applied to you."

"Do you think," said Kirsten Lindstrom, "do you think that I would have taken Mrs. Argyle's money to give him instead of giving him my own?"

"No," said Calgary, "you would have given him your own if you'd had any. But I don't think you had. . . . You had a good income from the annuity which Mrs. Argyle had bought for you, but I think he'd already milked you dry of that. So he was desperate that evening and when Mrs. Argyle had gone up to her husband in the library, you went outside the house where he was waiting and he told you what you had to do. First you must give him the money and then, before the theft could be discovered, Mrs. Argyle had to be killed. Because she would not have covered up the theft. He said it would be easy. You had just to pull out the drawers to make it look as though a burglar had been there and to hit her on the back of the head. It would be painless, he said. She would not feel anything. He himself would establish an alibi, so that you must be careful to do this thing within the right time limits, between seven and seven-thirty."

"It's not true," said Kirsten. She had begun to tremble. "You are mad to say such things."

Yet there was no indignation in her voice. Strangely enough, it was mechanical and weary.

"Even if what you say is true," she said, "do you think I would let him be accused of the murder?"

"Oh yes," said Calgary. "After all, he had told you he would have an alibi. You expected him, perhaps, to be arrested and then to prove his innocence. That was all part of the plan."

"But when he couldn't prove his innocence," said Kirsten. "Would I not have saved him then?"

"Perhaps," said Calgary, "perhaps—but for one fact. The fact that on the morning after the murder *Jacko's wife turned up here*. You didn't know he was married. The girl had to repeat the statement two or three times before you would believe her. At that moment your world crashed round you. You saw Jacko for what he was—heartless, scheming, without a particle of affection for you. You realised what he had made you do."

Suddenly Kirsten Lindstrom was speaking. The words came rushing out incoherently.

"I loved him. . . . I loved him with all my heart. I was a fool, a credulous middle-aged doting fool. He made me think it—he made be believe it. He said he had never cared for girls. He said—I cannot tell you all the things he said. I loved him. I tell you I loved him. And then that silly, simpering child came here, that common little thing. I saw it was all lies, all wickedness, wickedness. . . . *His* wickedness, not mine."

"The night I came here," said Calgary, "you were afraid, weren't you? You were afraid of what was going to happen. You were afraid for the others. Hester, whom you loved, Leo, whom you were fond of. You saw, perhaps, a little of what this might do to them. But principally you were afraid for *yourself*. And you see where fear has led you. . . . You have two more deaths on your hands now."

"You are saying I killed Tina and Philip?"

"Of course you killed them," said Calgary. "Tina has recovered consciousness."

Kirsten's shoulders dropped in the sagging of despair.

"So she has told that I stabbed her. I did not think she even knew. I was mad, of course. I was mad by then, mad with terror. It was coming so close—so close."

"Shall I tell you what Tina said when she regained consciousness?" said Calgary. "She said 'The cup was empty.' I knew what that meant. You pretended to be taking up a cup of coffee to Philip Durrant, but actually you had already stabbed him and were coming *out* of that room when you heard Tina coming. So you turned round and pretended you were taking the tray *in*. Later, although she was shocked almost into unconsciousness by his death, she noticed automatically that the cup that had dropped on the floor was an empty cup and there was no stain of coffee left by it."

Hester cried out:

"But Kirsten couldn't have stabbed her! Tina walked downstairs and out to Micky. She was quite all right."

"My dear child," said Calgary, "people who have been stabbed have walked the length of the street without even knowing what has happened to them! In the state of shock Tina was in she would hardly have felt anything. A pin-prick, a slight pain perhaps." He looked again at Kirsten. "And later," he said, "you slipped that knife into Micky's pocket. That was the meanest thing of all."

Kirsten's hands flew out pleadingly.

"I couldn't help it—I could not help it. . . . It was coming so near. . . . They were all beginning to find out. Philip was finding out and Tina—I think Tina must have overheard Jacko talking to me outside the kitchen that evening. They were all beginning to know. . . . I wanted to be safe. I wanted—*one can never be safe!*" Her hands dropped. "I didn't want to kill Tina. As for Philip—"

Mary Durrant rose. She came across the room slowly but with increasing purpose.

"You killed Philip?" she said. "*You* killed Philip."

Suddenly, like a tigress she sprang at the other woman. It was Gwenda, quick-witted, who sprang to her feet and caught hold of her. Calgary joined her and together they held her back.

"You—you!" cried Mary Durrant.

Kirsten Lindstrom looked at her.

"What business was it of *his?*" she asked. "Why did he have to snoop round and ask questions? *He* was never threatened. It was never a matter of life or death for *him*. It was just—an amusement." She turned and walked slowly towards the door. Without looking at them she went out.

"Stop her," cried Hester. "Oh, we must stop her."

Leo Argyle said:

"Let her go, Hester."

"But—she'll kill herself."

"I rather doubt it," said Calgary.

"She has been our faithful friend for so long," said Leo. "Faithful, devoted—and now this!"

"Do you think she'll—give herself up?" said Gwenda.

"It's far more likely," said Calgary, "that she'll go to the nearest station and take a train for London. But she won't, of course, be able to get away with it. She'll be traced and found."

"Our dear Kirsten," said Leo again. His voice shook. "So faithful, so good to us all."

Gwenda caught him by the arm and shook it.

"How can you, Leo, how can you? Think what she did to us all—what she has made us suffer!"

"I know," said Leo, "but she suffered herself, you know, as well. I think it is *her* suffering we have felt in this house."

"We might have gone on suffering for ever," said Gwenda, "as far as she was concerned! If it hadn't been for Dr. Calgary here." She turned towards him gratefully.

"So at last," said Calgary, "I have done something to help, though rather late in the day."

"Too late," said Mary, bitterly. "Too late! Oh, why didn't we know—why didn't we *guess?*" She turned accusingly on Hester. "I thought it was *you*. I always thought it was *you*."

"*He* didn't," said Hester. She looked at Calgary.

Mary Durrant said quietly:

"I wish I were dead."

"My dear child," said Leo, "how I wish I could help you."

"Nobody can help me," said Mary. "It's all Philip's own fault, wanting to stay on here, wanting to mess about with this business. Getting himself killed." She looked round at them. "None of you understand." She went out of the room.

Calgary and Hester followed her. As they went through the door, Calgary, looking back, saw Leo's arm pass round Gwenda's shoulders.

"She warned me, you know," said Hester. Her eyes were wide and scared. "She told me right at the beginning not to trust her, to be as afraid of her as I was of everyone else. . . ."

"Forget it, my dear," said Calgary. "This is the thing you have to do now. *Forget*. All of you are free now. The innocent are no longer in the shadow of guilt."

"And Tina? Will she get well? She is not going to die?"

"I don't think she will die," said Calgary. "She's in love with Micky, isn't she?"

"I suppose she might be," said Hester, in a surprised voice. "I never thought about it. They've always been brother and sister, of course. But they're not really brother and sister."

"By the way, Hester, would you have any idea what Tina meant when she said. 'The dove on the mast'?"

"Dove on the mast?" Hester frowned. "Wait a minute. It sounds terribly familiar. *The dove on the mast, as we sailed fast, Did mourn and mourn and mourn.* Is that it?"

"It might be," said Calgary.

"It's a song," said Hester. "A sort of lullaby song. Kirsten used to sing it to us. I can only remember bits of it. *'My love he stood at my right hand,'* and something something something. *'Oh, maid most dear, I am not here, I have no place, no part, No dwelling more by sea nor shore, But only in thy heart.'*"

"I see," said Calgary. "Yes, yes, I see . . ."

"Perhaps they'll get married," said Hester, "when Tina gets well, and then she can go out to Kuwait with him. Tina always wanted to be somewhere where it's warm. It's very warm in the Persian Gulf, isn't it?"

"Almost too warm, I should say," said Calgary.

"Nothing's too warm for Tina," Hester assured him.

"And you will be happy now, my dear," said Calgary, taking Hester's hands in his. He made an effort to smile. "You'll marry your young doctor and you'll settle down and you'll have no more of these wild imaginings and terrific despairs."

"Marry *Don?*" said Hester, in a surprised tone of voice. "Of course I'm not going to marry *Don.*"

"But you love him."

"No, I don't think I do, really. . . . I just thought I did. But he didn't believe in me. He didn't *know* I was innocent. He ought to have known." She looked at Calgary. *"You* knew! I think I'd like to marry you."

"But, Hester, I'm years older than you are. You can't really—"

"That is—if you want me," said Hester with sudden doubt.

"Oh, I want you!" said Arthur Calgary.